Published by

JAMES THORNTON, OXFORD.

———————

London ... ... {SIMPKIN, MARSHALL, AND Co.
{HAMILTON, ADAMS, AND Co.

THE

SIXTEEN SATIRES

OF

JUVENAL.

A NEW TRANSLATION,

WITH AN INTRODUCTION, A RUNNING ANALYSIS,
AND BRIEF EXPLANATORY NOTES

BY

S. H. JEYES, M.A.,

Of the Inner Temple, Barrister-at-Law;
LATE LECTURER IN CLASSICS AT UNIVERSITY COLLEGE, OXFORD.

Oxford:

JAMES THORNTON, HIGH STREET.
MDCCCLXXXV.

PREFATORY NOTES.

STUDENTS of Juvenal would find their labours much diminished in bulk if they could accept the comfortable doctrine which rejects six out of the sixteen canonical satires. But were such wholesale condemnation supported on better evidence than any which has been hitherto supplied, the general judgment would be slow to ratify it. Three of the six incriminated satires happen to be just those which are most widely read and most commonly admired. The undeserved favour, which is vested in them quite securely, depends partly upon a negative (but solid) title : they are free, or comparatively free, from the grossness of thought and language which disfigures some of the better authenticated or less questioned satires, and has relegated them to an obscurity from which their intrinsic excellence can never rescue them. But the critic who does not permit his literary vision to be distorted by the moral medium will see that, edifying as they are, the Tenth, Thirteenth, and Fourteenth are separated by a long artistic interval from the earlier satires, whilst the Twelfth, Fifteenth, and Sixteenth mark the lowest point to which Juvenal sank. The red-hot eloquence and stinging wit have been replaced by frigid declamation and unpointed jocosity: the terse sententiousness has degenerated into a plethora of tedious and obvious platitudes, only valuable to the modern quotation-mongers who set off their unlovely commonplaces by polyglot patchwork.

The defects which are to be discovered throughout all the later satires in a greater or less degree are most fully exemplified in the Fourteenth : and, for the purposes of depreciatory illustration, it will be fair almost to confine to that satire these (necessarily limited) remarks, because it contains isolated lines and passages which testify to the workmanship of a master-hand, and because it abounds with minor touches which seem to indicate that the hand was none but Juvenal's own. But within the short space between lines 38 and 47 there are no less than four sentences which nobody could have become a wiser or better man for reading them :—

" Hold aloof from sin."

" We are all apt pupils in baseness and wickedness."

" Let no sound or sight of shame pass the threshold of a child's home."

" The child has a claim to deepest respect."

At lines 73 and 74 we are informed that " a young man's character and qualities very much depend upon the manner of his training." The maxims about Avarice are not less trite in sentiment, although they are more skilfully expressed.

" It is stark madness, it is plain lunacy, to live like a pauper for the sake of dying rich."

" The lust for gold increases with every piece that is added to the store."

" Whosoever would be rich would be rich quickly."

" The charge of a great fortune is a wretched thing."

Platitudes so undeniable and so dreary reveal their impotence when they are put into contrast with the direct virility

of aphorisms which may be taken almost at hazard from
the earlier satires :—

"What cares Marius for degradation if his money is
safe ? "

" When did the gulf of Avarice yawn so wide as now ? "

"Who can tolerate such meanness with such self-
indulgence ? "

Simple and pithy sentences like these are fair samples
of the phrase-making and maxim-coining fecundity which
marks Juvenal's best work, and they go some way to illustrate the familiar remark that "the poets of the Silver Age
read best in quotations." It is a judgment which does not
meet the case of Juvenal's earlier satires ; but to his later
and inferior work it is eminently applicable. But no matter
how great may be the disparity of merit between two pieces
of writing, none but the most confident (and least competent) critic would say of any one poem, "This is genuine
because it is good," and of any other, "That is not authentic
because it is not good enough." The history of art shows
too many examples of unequal bits of work being done by
the same hand for any but a neophyte to be deluded by
such a random judgment. The authenticity of Juvenal's
later satires would never have been called into question, at
least it would not have been seriously debated, if the
"Chorizontes" had not better evidence to rely upon : a
radical difference in method, not only disparity in execution.
Mere slovenliness of language, mere decay of humour, and
mere poverty of thought might be attributed to the failing
powers and increasing indolence which sometimes, though
seldom, accompany a poet's advancing years. But the distinction between the early and late satires is not one that
could be accounted for by mental sloth or decrepitude. It

is a distinction which is almost the reverse of what we should
have expected to discover. If we might imagine ourselves
entitled to almost invert the order of the satires and to say
that the fragmentary Sixteenth was a "first attempt" which
was very properly considered unworthy of being finished; to
point out that the Thirteenth and Fourteenth showed the
crude and sermonizing efforts of a strong young spirit towards reforming a world of which it had not yet gained
much knowledge, whilst they gave rich promise of the wit
and eloquence which were to be matured in after life; in the
Twelfth and Fifteenth to trace the first clumsy movements
of a saturnine humour which had not yet learned to seem
spontaneous; and in the Tenth and Eleventh to see the
natural outcome of that period of transition and development which intervened between the straggling exuberance
of inexperienced youth and the solid harvest of a full life
absorbing the very essence of its own environment—if we
started such a theory, we should put ourselves in accord
with all the antecedent probabilities and violate nothing
but the facts.

The later satires (all but a few lines and passages in each)
might have been written by any clever man of letters, at any
time, in any place. The lessons which they enforce and the
illustrations which they present might with equal fitness have
been applied to, and drawn from, modern London, Vienna,
or New York, and ancient Rome or Babylon. Commendation of virtue and chastisement of vice are universally appropriate and universally inappropriate, like ready-made clothing
which fits anybody and suits nobody. It is not too much to
say that the test which we apply to literary reputations in
general must be reversed in the case of a satirist. If we are
considering the claims of a great imaginative poet, the ques-

tion which we naturally and rightly ask ourselves is, "Will his fame last? Will his writings possess the same interest for future ages as they claim from a contemporary generation?" If we cannot believe that his posthumous honours will be at least equal to those which he is now enjoying, we refuse to call him a great poet. But the satirist is nothing if he is not the creature of his own time and place. That part of his work which endures after he and the men and women about him have passed away may have merits of its own, but it is not satire. The marvellous picture of the nestling swallow being fed by its loving, famished mother, drawn by Juvenal in a few simple strokes, and remaining to baffle translators and defy imitation, will last so long as men can feel for what is beautiful in nature and glorious in art: still it is not satire. The Cannibal, hurrying up for the division of the raw corpse only to find that the last steak has been given away, but scraping his fingers along the ground and enjoying the twang of human blood with horrible gusto, presents a figure of monumental grotesqueness; but, once again, this is not satire. That we find most completely typified in the early writings, which really seem to "palpitate with actuality"—sometimes a disagreeable actuality—which reaches its highest point in Lauronia's scornful exposure of the smug puritans of Rome whose decorous profession and odious practice made virtue to stink in the nostrils of men. The dreaded informer, the ruined gambler, the horsey spendthrift, the too versatile Greek adventurer, the gluttonous priest of Cybele, effeminate ascetics, low-born upstarts from the East, and petted slave-boys: the high pressure of life in the Capital, lodging-house hardships, street ruffianism, the insane luxury and insane cruelty of Domitian's court, cringing flattery on one side and besotted credulity on the other, the mean arts of dependants and the great man's heartlessness and snobbishness, the omnipotence of money, and the diverse developments of women's depravity : the poetaster patron of poetry with his tricks and subterfuges, the pushing lawyer and his pretentious expenditure, the teacher and his maltreatment by rebellious pupils and stingy parents, the degenerate noble and degraded magistrate, the oppressed provincial—these are but a few of the many characters and scenes photographed from life which cram the early satires with allusion and information.   Every line of them, and sometimes every word, is charged with a concentrated venom of personality, full of meaning when the sting was delivered, but dull and tedious to the modern reader unacquainted with the facts of Roman society, who turns for relief to the easier generalities of the later satires which he can understand without knowledge and remember without effort : *obiter leget vel dormiet.*

From the Fourteenth, which is longer than any except the Sixth and Tenth Satires, we should have expected to pick up a good many pieces of direct and indirect information about its ostensible subject, the home-life of Rome. But it proves to be almost bare of statement and allusion. The dissipated vigils of the parasite, the use of the cupping-glass for disorders of the brain, the licence extended to house-dogs, the rich man's craze for bricks-and-mortar (out-matched by a eunuch's offensive extravagance), the practices of Jewish proselytes, the daintiness of a " Bridge beggar," the land-grabber's high-handed injustice, the means of promotion in the army, the prohibition of stinking trades on the city side of the Tiber, a sacrilegious theft, and the custom of " cornering " such articles of common use as wheat and pepper—these are the scanty and (most of them) trivial statements which bear upon domestic and social Rome, and they occupy less than fifty out of more than three hundred lines. All the rest of the satire might have been composed by a clever *littérateur* whose view of life had been bounded by the four walls of his own chamber. The tone is throughout academical, nowhere actual. *Pluteum cædit, demorsos sapit ungues.* This is the strongest of the internal grounds of evidence which makes some critics reluctant to believe that Juvenal was the author of this and the other late satires.

The general impression which is left by a reading of the Tenth, Thirteenth, and Fourteenth Satires is strongly adverse to their authenticity. We seem to be drinking thin Veientan when we had expected a more potent vintage—*Albani veteris pretiosa senectus.* But a different verdict will probably be given by any one who has the patience to examine these poems at greater length and with more minuteness. He will detect many subtle but unmistakable traces of Juvenal's hand; points of resemblance too exact to be anything but proofs of identity, and too delicate to be the forgeries of any but the most consummate imitator. But the forger, if there was a forger in this case, must have been (for all his occasional indications of poetical genius) no better than a bungler in his fraudulent art; else he would not have so defiantly abandoned Juvenal's early style, and challenged an inquiry which was not certain to end in his favour.

At XIV. 252, Juvenal has been describing the danger of being poisoned which is incurred by the old man who keeps his son too long out of his inheritance :—

" Away with you to the apothecary, old sir ; buy the Mithradates Antidote if you would pluck next autumn's figs

·or pick next spring's roses.   We want some specific to be
taken before each meal by kings and—fathers." [1]

The allusions to the well-known doctor Archigenes and
the antidote prepared by Mithradates III. are very much in
Juvenal's style. These, however, are obvious and superficial
resemblances which might have suggested themselves to the
least artistic imitator, and they afford none but the smallest
presumption of authenticity.   The same remark may be
applied with less confidence to the powerful and truly satirical conjunction of *pater* and *rex*, that juxtaposition of
seemingly unconnected ideas which is of the essence of
wit and is more humorously (because less bitterly) exemplified in II. 104–105, where Otho's foppishness is derided :—

" We expect the first commander of the day to shed his
rival's blood and to preserve his own—complexion ! " [2]

And again at III. 237–238, about the street noises "which
would awaken a sea-calf or—a Drusus ! " [3]

The two undoubted passages and the doubtful one are
each in the best and most characteristic style of Juvenal's
wit ; but (on merely internal evidence) any one of them
might be considered spurious.   It is in the few words about
"the figs and roses" that we find the very impress of our
poet's fingers ; we can testify to them as confidently as if we
had looked over his shoulder while the verses were being
written.   His fantastic genius took a special pleasure in

---

[1] Ocius Archigenen quære atque eme quod Mithradates
  Composuit, si vis aliam decerpere ficum
  Atque alias tractare rosas.   Medicamen habendum est
  Sorbere ante cibum quod debeat et pater et rex.

[2] Nimirum summi ducis est occidere Galbam
  Et curare cutem.

[3] Stantis convicia mandræ,
  Eripient somnum Druso vitulisque marinis.

lighting up a horrid or grotesque passage with some such pretty or innocent thought. He rests for a moment from describing the wholesale domestic poisoning which was the wickedest aspect of Roman life so that he may tell us how the old father may prolong life, " just to pluck the roses of another spring, just to pluck another autumn's figs." Partly, no doubt, Juvenal wished to intensify the darkness of the scene by this transitory illumination, even as the blackness of night within a curtained chamber is best realized after the eyes have rested for a moment upon some glittering jewel. Perhaps, too, there is something of mere waywardness in this introduction of prettiness amongst ugly things—the gratuitous delight in playing tricks with the reader's feelings, the coquetry of humour which loves to puzzle matter-of-fact minds, and, doubling like a hare, to leave its less agile pursuers running in the wrong direction. Even when Juvenal is most in earnest, he is fond (if the expression may be pardoned) of holding his tongue in his cheek, just as he uses ridicule at other times only to disguise the more serious emotion which he does not always care to avow. Open and even turgid as much of his declamation is, none of the great satirists (Rabelais alone excepted) has shrunk more sensitively from wearing his heart upon his sleeve. Similar examples of Juvenal's curiously Hogarthian pleasure in contrasting beauty with hideousness may be found in the graphic words from the Tenth Satire, where, in describing the impotent old glutton's struggles with his food, he suddenly arrests the nasty realism to introduce his tender picture of the mother swallow feeding her young brood, and brings, as it were, a puff of fresh outside air into the sickening vapours of an invalid's room. Even a better illustration, because it is less intrinsically

beautiful, is to be found at III. 199–202, where he has been
dilating upon the alarms of fire which add to the miseries of
a lodging-house life. He consoles the occupier of the
garret with the sarcastic reflection that "he will not know of
his danger—until it is too late, and that he will be burnt
last because he is living next to the tiles, nearest to the
rain, and—amongst the gentle nesting doves!"

Beside the subtler indications of authenticity which have
been illustrated, there are many other confirmatory points of
resemblance, fewest in the Fourteenth but more numerous
in the Tenth and Thirteenth Satires, which will present
themselves to any careful reader. In spite of Juvenal's
openly expressed contempt for ancient mythology and history, there is no tendency in his writing more distinctive
than his allusiveness. The young nobleman who drives his
own horses is called Automedon, after the charioteer of
Achilles: Jehu, as we might put it.   "The next-door
neighbour," whose house takes fire, is "Ucalegon," by a remi-
niscence from the Æneid; Domitian is "Agamemnon," king
of men; and the baby son is "a hopeful Æneas." Nor are
we surprised to find Rutilus, the domestic bully, called
"the Antiphates and Polyphemus of his terrified household," much as we might say that a thrice-made widower
was a modern Bluebeard.   Many of Juvenal's thoughts
and some of his expressions would not be fully intelligible
to any one who had not the Æneid at his fingers' ends, like
the schoolmaster who is described in the Seventh Satire as
being expected to "tell you off-hand the name of the nurse of
Anchises, all about the stepmother of Archemorus, the exact
age of Acestes when he died, and the number of wine-jars
which he gave to the Trojans."

In the Fourteenth and other late satires there are a good

many lines which exemplify that phase of Juvenal's humour which showed itself in applying sonorous language to a mean idea : *e.g., a magna non degenerare culina,* " the son's desire will be never to tarnish the glories of his father's kitchen," and where a speculative grocer is described under his full legal title as *dominus* (*piperis cöempti*). Even more characteristic are the lines which describe the innate and incorruptible rectitude of those strong young natures " which the Maker has fashioned with special loving-kindness and —superior clay ! " The satirist had nearly allowed himself to praise something which was human, he had almost committed the oversight of tenderness, when he turns round with a jerk to mock at Man and his legendary Creator.

Here it may be remarked that running all through the sixteen satires we can trace a vein of interest in animals. The few passages in which Juvenal allows himself to be tender are (most of them) connected with his sympathy for "dumb creatures." He was not a naturalist, nor even a close observer of animals ; else he would not have adopted the marvellous legend about the Beaver, which he reproduces at XII. 35 :—

> Imitatus castora qui se
> Eunuchum ipse facit cupiens evadere damno
> Testiculi.

Nor would he have described " the crooked talons of the crane." But he seems to rejoice whenever he can escape awhile from the contemplation of human iniquity to chat about animals. In the Eighth Satire, which deals with the degradation of the Roman nobles, he devotes fifteen lines to discuss what makes " blood " in horses. At XIV. 74–85 there is a similar digression to illustrate the importance of early training to children by the different habits

which are produced in the matured birds of different kinds,
according to the nature of the food which they receive from
their parents in the nest.   At XII. 102–110 there is a
gratuitous and somewhat tedious account of the elephants
kept in the Imperial Parks ; and at the beginning of the
same satire there is a pretty picture of the young steer
doomed to the sacrificial knife, " who is already ashamed of
tugging his mother's teats, and bullies the oak-trees with his
budding horns."   X. 194–195 introduces a quasi-comic
description of " the matron-monkey scratching her withered
jowl in Tabraca's vast and leafy forest," which may be compared with the lines at V. 153–155, about the *insouciance*
of a domesticated performing-monkey dressed in a soldier's
helmet, which " gnaws a sour crab-apple whilst it is whipped
through its drill upon the back of a shaggy goat."   Theo-
retically, Juvenal admits that Man is above the beasts because he alone is endowed with " a grand intelligence, a
capacity for rising above his human self, and an aptitude
for grasping and wielding knowledge, an understanding
which has been sent down to him from its heavenly citadel
and denied to the stooping creatures whose eyes are
fixed upon earth."   But Juvenal only admits the superior
powers of Man in order that he may revile him for their
misuse ; he is glad to shame humanity by examples drawn
from animal life ; and he oversteps the narrow line which
separates rhetoric from exaggeration when he tells us that
no lion takes advantage of his greater strength to slay a
brother-lion, that the wild boar's tusks are never fatal to
one of his own kind, and that the tigers of India keep the
peace one with another.   He seems to indulge the same
tendency which was exemplified in another poet misan-
thrope, greater as a poet but not so sincere a misan-

thrope, who testified to his dog possessing those human virtues which he had failed to discover in the men about him. In the Thirteenth Satire, Juvenal strikes at the root of the (ancient) doctrine of atonement by his indignant question—" What victim's life is not worth more than the human sinner's ? "

But if an admirer of Juvenal's satires were asked what was their highest merit, he would not point to their wit (which is seldom pleasant, and never appeals to the merely risible faculty, but is always either stinging and personal, or cynical and saturnine, when it is not tedious as in Sat. XII.), he would not point to the trenchant vigour of the moral indignation (because that is often overdone), nor to the extraordinary talent for inventing aphoristic phrases which stick to the memory and have grown into household words with persons who have never read one of the satires, like the modern theatre-goer who was "surprised to find that Hamlet was so full of quotations." (*Quis tulerit Gracchos de seditione querentes ?* is a line which has been applied, and misapplied, by many a politician who was innocent of the Second Satire.) Juvenal's chief claim to literary honour is a power which he is somewhat niggardly in exercising, but which is at once so great and so rare that by itself—if he had neither wit nor eloquence, and was not, next to Horace, the most quotable of Latin poets—it would vindicate his claim to immortality. It is a power which may be imperceptible to the mental sloven, and perhaps it was not used by Juvenal himself with complete consciousness. It seems to resemble that curious faculty which is possessed by some unscientific working-men, which they cannot or will not transmit, the knack of combining chemical elements so as to produce a valuable substance from unascertained proportions. The

effects of Juvenal's peculiar power cannot be even reflected
in a translation, because they are inherent in the very words,
not in the ideas which they are used to express. The grand
or beautiful thought does not suffer greatly by the transmu-
tation of its form. That is why the prophecies of Isaiah,
or the story of Odysseus, or the idylls of Theocritus can
be translated with something like success, while Vergil's
eclogues never have been, and perhaps never will be.
Juvenal's genius was not catholic: he lacked the wide sympathy and moral enthusiasm which alone can justify the
poet in addressing posterity or speaking to an international
audience. Therefore he did not trouble himself to find
ideas. Ordinary sentiment and a circumscribed imagination
supplied him with the material of his poetry, and he worked
with words. It is in the picking and placing of a few simple
words that he reaches the highest note within his literary
compass. Quite suddenly he will interrupt the even course
of a style which is not seldom pedestrian, and show us what
he can do when he likes to call upon the power within him.
In a moment we are presented not with a bare outline or
vague sketch, but with a picture complete in its details
while it is full of infinite suggestiveness. This graphic
faculty is not the same thing as word-painting, which is
conscious in its method and elaborate in its effects. But
whenever Juvenal becomes either conscious or elaborate, he
spoils his work by diluting it or overloading it. He can
make vigorous spurts, but he is deficient in "staying
power." This may be illustrated from Sat. III. 265–267,
where a few bold strokes produce a vivid scene—the dis-
embodied Spirit shivering on the bank of Styx, cowering
with a neophyte's nervousness before the grim ferryman,
and despairing of his passage over the murky stream :—

Jam sedet in ripa tætrumque novicius horret
Porthmea nec sperat cenosi gurgitis alnum :

But the passage is spoilt by the weak and worse than useless line which is appended :—

Infelix nec habet quem porrigat ore trientem.

The Second Satire, which is the most finished and forcible of Juvenal's writings, presents us with another instance of his over-refinement of a good point. His denunciation of the effeminate apparel affected by foppish men is brought to the rhetorical climax :—"Would you not protest aloud if you saw such garments worn upon the Seat of Judgment?" But he is so pleased with what he has written that he insists upon it and makes it tedious:—*Quæro an deceant multicia testem.* It is still stranger that he should have allowed himself to fritter away the force of his finest comic climax :—at VIII. 211–223 he is comparing the guiltiness of Nero and Orestes, both of them sons who plotted murder against their own mothers: but he says that Orestes "never stained his hand with the blood of wife and sister, never sang upon the stage, never wrote the Tale of Troy Town!" But the joke loses all its pungent bitterness when it is explained by the matter-of-fact lines which follow it :—

Quid enim Verginius armis
Debuit ulcisci magis aut cum Vindice Galba
Quod Nero tam sæva crudaque tyrannide fecit?

These and other examples (which may be collected from the earlier and later satires alike) show that Juvenal was deficient in the finer sense which should have told him when he had said enough. His thorough knowledge and constant use of classical models had not taught him to appreciate that sense of proportion which is the richest legacy that the world has received from Greek literature. Failing as Juvenal fails in one of the most important elements of literary taste, it is the more surprising that his finest effects were produced with subdued colours and simple drawing, as in the picture of the homesick slave-boy at XI. 153 and 154, "sighing for the mother whom he has not seen for a dreary while, and thinking wistfully of his cottage home and the kids his playmates;" or in the more ambitious imagination which redeems the horrors of the Ninth Satire :—"Even as we quaff the wines and are calling for roses, perfumes, and sweethearts, Age is creeping on us though we see Him not."

To recall none but the most vivid of Juvenal's pictures would be to extend these remarks beyond their proper limit. The force with which he could wield an abstract idea, or introduce a supernatural terror, may be seen at XV. 48–51, where he imagines Famine and Malice to be glowering at the grotesque rejoicings of dusky revellers, and at XIII. 220-223, where the sleeping sinner is said to be "bathed in a cold sweat of terror on beholding a ghostly and gigantic form, the vision of him whom he has wronged, which terrifies the coward and forces him to make confession." Mere descriptive power, appealing only to the mental vision and not to the moral feelings, is seen at XI. 88 and 89, where the farmer statesman is said to "honour a family gathering by doing a short day's work, shouldering his spade, and trudging home from the mountain-farm which he has brought to order," [1] and in the still more graphic and even briefer clause at I. 100, which puts before our very eyes the ruined gamester who "stakes the shirt from his

---

[1] Ad has epulas solito maturius ibat
Erectum domito referens a monte ligonem.

slave's back, loses it, and leaves him to shiver,"[1] and at IX. 130, in the description of the "Lord Fannys" of his own time, "who dare not give an honest scratch to their heads."[2] Even more characteristic of Juvenal's art and genius are the humorous or contemptuous lights which he loves to throw upon human life: *e.g.*, the little woman (at VI. 508) who "can only reach a kiss by tilting herself on tip-toes,"[3] the draggled sewing-wench at II. 57, "squatted on her wooden stump,"[4] the cringing beggar at The Bridge (IV. 118) "throwing his kisses after the disappearing carriage,"[5] the drunken gossip (IX. 112–113) "marking down his victim and drenching his ears with tippler's talk,"[6] and the frothy advocate (VII. 105–111) "talking big of his earnings, especially when a dun is there to hear him, or when he has been nudged by a worse-worrying client, come with the huge ledger to prosecute a disputed claim—puffing out his lungs like bellows for the stupendous lies, and covering his front with slobber."[7]

These examples of graphic power have been selected from the satires of unquestioned authenticity. It remains to be seen whether the later writings can supply instances of an equal

---

[1] Horrenti tunicam non reddere servo.
[2] Qui digito scalpunt uno caput.
[3] Levis erecta consurgit ad oscula planta.
[4] Horrida . . . residens in codice pellex.
[5] Blanda . . . devexæ jactaret basia rhedæ.
[6] Qui te per compita quærat
Nolentem et miseram vinosus inebriet aurem.
[7] Ipsi magna sonant, sed tunc cum creditor audit
Præcipue vel si tetigit latus acrior illo
Qui venit ad dubium grandi cum codice nomen.
Tunc immensa cavi spirant mendacia folles
Conspuiturque sinus.

or similar combination of vividness with terseness, such that
we could feel some degree of confidence in assigning them
to Juvenal's hand.   It must be admitted that the few such
lines which can be gleaned from the Fourteenth Satire do
not come within a long artistic distance of the passages
which have been quoted.   Equality is out of the question,
but there seems to be a resemblance strong enough to
discredit, if not to disprove, the theory of imitation.   Perhaps
the most Juvenalian line is 272—where the rope-walker
is described as "earning victuals by risking his life every
time he sets his heel down." [1]   Other passages of the same
kind are found at lines 46, 85, 148–149, 165–171, and
296–297—the dissipated parasite "singing his songs and
keeping it up to morning," [2] the eaglet in the eyrie "taking
its first meal after the shell has been cracked," [3] the dis-
appearance of a growing crop inside the stomachs of a
famished herd, "clean gone as if the reapers had been at
work," [4] the scene of rustic home-life, "the master of the
household and his cottage company, the good woman lying
in child-bed, and four romping lads (one of them a slave-
boy, and three young masters), while great pots of porridge
are steaming at the hearth, a late and special dinner for the
big brothers on their way home from trench or furrow," [5]

---

[1] Hic tamen ancipiti figens vestigia planta
   Victum illa mercede parat.
[2] Cantus pernoctantis parasiti.
[3] Quam primum rupto praedam gustaverat ovo.
[4] Prius . . . quam tota novalia saevos
   In ventres abeant ut credas falcibus actum.
[5] Patrem ipsum turbamque casae qua feta jacebat
   Uxor et infantes tudebant quattuor, unus
   Vernula, tres domini : sed magnis fratribus horum
   A scrobe vel sulco redeuntibus altera coena
   Amplior et grandes fumabant pultibus ollae.

and the shipwrecked merchant struggling one-handed against the overwhelming waves, and "gripping his purse between left hand and teeth." [1]

Another characteristic of Juvenal's early style which is reproduced in the later satires is the unexpected (and sometimes gratuitous) introduction of an unpleasant or downright disgusting thought ; as at XIV. 64 and 65, "Stercore fœda canino Atria," and (more strongly) at XIV. 30, " Dat eisdem ferre cinædis," where the last word arms the tail of the sentence with a venomous sting. More justifiable and more innocently satirical effects are seen at XIV. 99 and 204–205, one passage ridiculing the extravagance of religious proselytes, and the other very happily recalling a parsimonious emperor's famous witticism.

Such are some of the points of internal evidence which should make the critic hesitate, and the translator refuse, to acquiesce in the strong presumptions which may be brought against the authenticity of Satires X., XII., XIII., XIV., XV., and XVI. The preceding remarks have been almost confined to the case of Sat. XIV., partly because they must have been extended far beyond their proposed scope if they had been applied in any detail to the other five satires, but chiefly because the suspicion which hangs over all is best justified against the Fourteenth, which is weaker than any except the fragmentary Sixteenth, while it is the most cumbrous and pretentious of them all. But even if the ground for scepticism were stronger than it is, the translator would have no right to arrogate that liberty of judgment which is allowed to editors and commentators. It is for him to take the text as a canonical whole and to do his best with it as it

---

[1] Cadet fractis trabibus fluctuque premetur
Obrutus et zonam læva morsuque tenebit.

stands. That is a duty especially incumbent upon him when his version is designed to meet the actual needs of practical students. This consideration has finally determined the retention not only of the whole sixteen satires, but also of all the passages in each which have been regarded as inter- polations even by tolerant critics and actually elided from some editor's texts. The only line omitted in this trans- lation is the impossible one at VII. 15, together with certain short passages which have been (for a different reason) either passed over or modified. At a few places the connection of ideas has been developed by a very brief but seemingly indispensable insertion of words which are not to be found in the original Latin : *e.g.*, before the three (almost universally rejected) lines which follow XIV. 240. The short interposition, most reluctantly made, seems to be a justifiable expansion of the scepticism as to Greek legends which Juvenal had expressed in the words of the preceding line, *Si Græcia vera.* Had no such device been adopted, the chasm between the ideas, wide enough in the Latin, would have been in the English, not reproduced in its original measurement, but inevitably broadened—so that the mental leap would not have remained difficult, but have been rendered impossible.

The special object which the present translator has tried to keep in view has not been to court failure by seeking to produce an English version which would "read like the Latin." That would be in prose impossible, because many of Juvenal's best and truest effects were gained by his mastery of the Hexameter in its varied developments ; now pedestrian and satirical, as in the *Sermones* of Horace, now epically simple or simply poetical like the verses of Juvenal's favourite Statius or his master Vergil and sometimes mock heroic. An experiment in blank verse might be worth attempting by any one who possessed the requisite power of varying that most difficult of metres. But rhyming heroics are put out of the question by the number of unmanageable proper names which cram the best parts of Juvenal's work. The success which was achieved by Dryden, Gifford, and the other poetical translators is greatest in those satires and parts of satires which are least meritorious, and it leads to a' very wrong estimate of their poet's style and powers. The consideration which was finally decisive against a metrical version was that it would necessitate so many and so wide departures from the original syntax as to render the translation all but useless to students who might wish to read Juvenal for the purposes of an examination. Wherever the Latin could present a difficulty of construction to a moderate scholar, the English has been made scrupulously literal; but in other places a greater latitude has been exercised. And wherever the Latin seems to offer a choice of alternative versions, one or the other has been taken unreservedly, without resort to those "hedging" expedients by which some translators seek to "maintain the original ambiguity." We may not be certain which of two or more things was intended by our author; but that must be imputed to our own want of knowledge or imperfect criticism. In Juvenal there is nothing to justify that exasperating subtlety of interpretation which delights in discerning a double sense; a Jesuitical self-deception (or mere watery vagueness) which was caricatured by the young curate who apologised for his unmeaning delivery of the Prayers by saying that he had no right to put his private interpretation upon what the Church had left open for everybody to take as he chose. There are some, but very few, cases of *equivoque* (*e.g.*, at XVI. 21, and VI.

338, and more doubtful cases elsewhere) ; but at every other passage which makes the translator halt or hesitate there is either a corruption of the text or an obscurity which owes its origin to our own fault or misfortune. Juvenal's down-right style is alien from anything like verbal duplicity.

The present translator has not aimed at giving happy renderings,[1] because he considers that such work has already been over-done, and is more likely, when it is well done, to impair than to advance the educational value of classical authors. The student gains little or nothing by adopting, much by discovering for himself, what is at once the truest and tersest English for a Latin phrase. At a time when the value of classical training is being denied or depreciated, it may not be out of place to state what, perhaps, looks like a paradox—that the quickest and most effective manner of realizing the resources of our own language is the practical contrast which is afforded by the task of translating passages from a Latin author. This statement is best tested, and most fully confirmed, by comparing the English work, which is done in an examination by the boys on the Classical Side

---

[1] Such verbal felicities as may be discovered in this version are due to the valuable assistance which has been received from Mr. F. Storr (of the Merchant Taylors' School), Mr. F. T. Richards, Fellow of Trinity College, Oxford, and Mr. E. C. Hamley, who have revised the proofs, as well as from Mr. R. W. Raper, Fellow of Trinity College, Oxford, who lent the whole of his MS. notes and translation. It may be added that free use has been made of most English and foreign editions and versions, and that many ideas thus suggested have been silently incorporated. The very short notes on the right-hand side of each page were not intended to supersede the use of commentaries and books of reference, but only to give a provisional and temporary explanation of names and allusions, so that the reader's mind should travel easily along the context and grasp the general sense at once.

of a great school, with the slip-shod writing on a Modern Side which has been trained in French and German. Or a more personal illustration is supplied by the language in which Mr. Herbert Spencer once criticized Mr. Matthew Arnold's literary style.

The object of this version has been to grapple with the greatest difficulty which Juvenal presents to the modern reader : that abrupt shifting from one thought to another which is widely different and seemingly unconnected, and that habit of parenthetical observation which has made many of the lines look like interpolations. These tendencies are best illustrated when Ribbeck's bold and (from his own point of view) successful re-arrangement of the Sixth Satire is put alongside the accepted text. Any one who wished to analyze and tabulate the contents of these 661 lines would be glad if Juvenal had worked by this orderly critic's method. But the original disorder is vindicated, and the logical consecutiveness of its revision stands condemned by the only good critical test. Which of the two is the better to read at one sitting? Ribbeck's Sixth Satire has wearied the mind by its transparent artificiality long before the end has been reached. The methodical treatment which it professes calls attention to an incompleteness that is concealed by Juvenal's sudden departures and capricious returns. Artistic disorder, the perfection of arrangement, keeps the attention unabated and the interest ever fresh. It is like turning at pleasure from one article to another in some volume of an encyclopædia just as interest or chance directs the mind or fingers, instead of working laboriously through the A's or B's. But some of the suggested displacements of short passages are so happy in themselves that it is hard to reject them, and two of them have been adopted.   More would have been incorporated, but the translator must be vigilant against the temptation of making his way easy by departing from the appointed track.   It is his duty to follow the hounds, not to take a line of his own.

In dealing with Juvenal it must be remembered that the transitions and digressions, which seem to us very like incoherencies of thought, were not designed for the student in his chamber, but for a reciter's audience.   Recitation was practised and studied as an art; the skilful modulation of a trained voice could make passages seem natural and appropriate which puzzle the mind or irritate the taste when they come to us through a strange language without that convincing apology and lucid commentary which the *vox viva* supplies.   Elocution might be exercised with legitimate effect in giving life and meaning to the passage at III. 186–189, which the written translation cannot redeem from obscurity and tameness.   Other applications of the art would be found in marking the transitions (as in Sat. IX.) from dialogue to apostrophe, and perhaps in supporting the (apparently novel) view which has been adopted in this translation as to the dialogues (in Sat. X.) over the Fall of Sejanus.   The reference of *Victus Ajax* to Tiberius as an unsuccessful litigant seems at first sight to be impossible, because we have already heard that he had carried his wish. But those who are familiar with Juvenal's zig-zag style of narration will find it easy to imagine that we have here not a single conversation between the same interlocutors resumed after the author's interruption, but two distinct conversations between different pairs of speakers, and that the comments which should come first in order of time have been put last in order of narration.   This seems to be one of those passages which puzzle the lonely reader, but which could be made clear enough by a Roman (or Greek) Brandram. We may apply to Juvenal's satires what he declares may not be said of Homer's and Vergil's epics : "The reciter's tones can make or mar them." [1]

A few words, not apologetic, may be ventured with reference to a departure from the precedent which has been set in some quarters of omitting, upon grounds of morality, three of the sixteen satires. That course would have been very properly adopted in a book which was designed for wide circulation and popular reading, or, *virginibus puerisque,* "intended for the use of schools." But this, like other "cribs," should be kept out of a young learner's hands; and it is hoped that the mature student will not debar himself from a proper understanding of Juvenal by not reading the many grand passages in the Sixth or the Second Satire. The translator did not see how he could consistently omit the satires which are most objected to without also eliminating the equally objectionable passages which may be found in other satires, and he was not conscious of the power to bowdlerize a satirist. Nor did he see the utility of doing so in view of the fact that the Sixth Satire is a very mine of information, both by direct statement and indirect allusion, for those who desire to learn about the daily life of ancient Rome, and that the Second is the most vigorous and most sustained of all the satires in its eloquent scorn and indignation. The coarse or disgusting ideas of the Latin have been allowed to retain their position in the English, but it has been necessary to modify the language in which they were expressed, and to altogether reform a few short passages by omitting them. If there were no other justification for this licence, one that is good enough would be found in the fact

[1] XI. 182.

that the direct and almost scientific exactitude of some of
Juvenal's words and phrases could not be met with English
equivalents except by resorting to the vocabularies of the
blackguard or the physiologist. There is one plea which
can be urged in defence of Juvenal's terrible grossness, in-
sufficient before the tribunal of literary taste even when
due allowance has been made for the custom of his age and
country, but strong enough to absolve him from moral condemnation. There is not a line or word which could gratify
an evil or corrupt a pure imagination. Every passage which
deals with sexual matters holds vice up to scorn or detesta-
tion or ridicule ; nor is there any of that prurient purity
which so often revels in depicting the sins which it repro-
bates, exemplified in Byron's " Waltz," or in a female
writer's reference to "the vices which are shut up in the
pages of Suetonius and Livy." Perhaps it would be easy to
be over-delicate at a time when the London University in
its wisdom has selected the satire of Sir David Lyndsay as
a special subject for the examination of young girls. But what
is most offensive in Juvenal, because it is most alien to the
stricter view of morality which at present prevails in this
country, is the tone of *persiflage* (as at VI. 34–38) which
Juvenal adopts towards one of the lowest forms of human
depravity. It is curious that a similar, though far less
serious, charge should have been levelled against a modern
English writer, who, because he was more hopeful and more
charitable than Juvenal, was animated with a far stronger
desire to leave his generation better than he found it. It is
said that Charles Dickens did something to encourage our
national vice by the playful humour with which he touched
upon drunkenness. Those who take up the unhistorical
standpoint of an absolute morality—whatever that is—may

look with unsympathetic loathing upon the picture of Mr. Pickwick in the Pound, just as they are more naturally revolted by the vice which Juvenal lays at the door of Ursidius without reading him one of those edifying lectures which some people think cannot ever be unseasonable. Whether we disapprove of Juvenal's attitude in this respect, or whether we think that he was using the most effective weapon at his command by treating a painful subject with light raillery, we cannot strike out one scintilla of indulgence to the gratuitous defamers who declare, on such grounds as this, that Juvenal simulated a literary indignation against vices which he practised himself, *Improbior saturam scribente cinædo.*

The lecturer on first principles who is instructing an audience of Mutual Improvement young men in the "Origin and Development of Society and Government," and has little more than an outside acquaintance with the title of Gibbon's great work, is apt to illustrate his text by what he calls the premature decline of the Roman Empire, which, after all that has been said about it, was that one amongst human institutions which has been the most durable and most beneficent in its results, and which best exhibited its tenacious vitality by its power of progressive self-adaptation to political circumstances. In a similar spirit, the modern Pharisee, who contrasts the conscious virtues of our own age and country with the benighted wickedness of past generations and foreign lands, dwells with an unctuous horror on the depravities of pagan Rome. Nor is there any authority which he lays under heavier contribution than Juvenal's satires. Martial is pressed into occasional service, so are the "sordid fictions of Petronius and Apuleius;"[4] but even a moralist feels that it would not be quite fair to judge of an age

---

[1] Archdeacon Farrar in the "Early Days of Christianity."

by the tales which are written to amuse its leisure. Tacitus
is quoted, but he is not sensational enough; and it requires
a somewhat robust conscience to pass off Suetonius as a
veracious historian. Thus the heavy work of approver falls
upon Juvenal.

But is Juvenal a credible witness?' That is not a question
which can be met with a simple answer. It may be granted,
to begin with, that he was not a libeller. It seems most
likely that each specific charge which he has fixed upon any
particular man was not merely founded upon fact but the
conscientious statement of an actual crime. Even to point
a moral or adorn a tale, Juvenal's proud and lofty spirit could
not have condescended to indulge in slanderous fictions.
Nor do we find in his writings any traces of that cynical
credulity in believing evil which goes some way to mar the
value of the records which Tacitus left behind him. We
shall not be led far astray if we place the most implicit
reliance upon Juvenal's good faith and good judgment.
But we must claim the same liberty in dealing with him as
with any other honest witness. We must accept his particular statements without any kind of reserve, but we can
attach no weight to his general impressions greater than
what is warranted by his capacity for forming them. We
need not concern ourselves to whitewash his Marius or
Varillus, his Virro or Crispinus; and we may assent, but
with more caution, to his views of Nero and Domitianus;
but we should be deluded indeed if we thought that the
selected incidents which are represented in his gallery of
pictures made a complete and truthful panorama of Roman
life. As well go to Cruikshank's famous painting for information about drunkenness in England as take Juvenal's
Sixth Satire for a record of female life at Rome. It is the

stalest of truisms to assert that no society can endure for long which is not radically moral. Its permanence in the present is the best vindication of its character in the past. If the present generation of Englishmen were the sons and grandsons of a generation of sots, we should be visited in mind and body with the sins of them who went before us. Roman society must have fallen to pieces centuries before the historical date if the overwhelming majority of its women had not been stainless wives and loving mothers. Up to the present time the position of woman has never been more independent, nor her character more elevated, nor her good influence stronger than it was at Rome about the period when Juvenal wrote his elaborated indictments of the whole sex. Most of the counsel who have had large practice in our own Divorce Court, if they liked to expose such evil garbage, could publish revelations from their own experience which would make some of Juvenal's wicked women seem innocent by contrast. The various developments of vice in all its forms which could be illustrated from modern criminal (and civil) proceedings would make the moralist hesitate before he pointed the finger of scorn at " pagan Rome." It is not unfair to press this point against Juvenal, because he says (at XIII. 159, 160) that the student of human nature need only spend a few days in the chief criminal court at Rome. From such a lecture-room it is no wonder that he should bring away a partial and distorted view of the world about him.

Contrast the street ruffianism of Sat. III. with the outrages upon the Thames Embankment ; the domestic poisoning of Roman fathers with the crimes of Schenk at Vienna, or with the senseless outrages of Irish dynamitards ; the breach of trust in Sat. XIII. with the cases which come

before our Vice-Chancellors ; the sensational rites and abject
Oriental superstitions of Imperial Rome with the Happy
Elizas and spiritualistic impostors of the present day; the
brandings, tortures, and prisons of a Roman slave-holder
with the unforgotten horrors of West Indian plantations;
the licentious dancing of Gaditanian girls with what may be
seen at Paris, or with the exhibitions which English gentle-
men patronize in India ; the coarseness of a Roman lady
athlete with the "Prize Fight between Women," which took
place not very long ago ; the black-mailing husband of
Sat. I. with some claimers of damages in "*crim. con.*"; the
petty punters of Rome with the gamblers of St. James's ;
the loafing populace of the Capital and their miserable
habitations with our own " dangerous classes " and London
"rookeries." The odious parallels might be multiplied at
pleasure ; but enough has already been said to show, not
that modern life is bad, nor that modern is no better than
ancient life, but that a country or an age is not to be judged
by the worst incidents which can be selected from its social
history. Granted that in the severity of its slave system
and in a certain form of vice Rome had two blots upon its
civilization which do not stain our own record, it must be
remembered that she was comparatively free from drunkenness and commercial dishonesty.

There is one special reason why we must not take Rome
at Juvenal's valuation. He seems to have no sense of proportion between the evils which he describes; so that " his
invective wants finish." He comes down with the same
heavy hand upon mere affectations or fooleries as upon
downright wickedness. Using Greek phrases is made out
to be as bad as practising Greek vices ; and it is not quite
in jest when he says that Nero's worst crime was his perpe-

tration of a poem. Sometimes he condemns things which seem to us innocent enough, such as over-indulgence in athletics, or a refinement in iced drinks. Curiously enough, his bitter censure of a young nobleman's taste for driving may be paralleled by the strictures which were passed on the Prince Regent for " driving his own curricle in the Park." But Juvenal was not a sportsman, nor was he quite a gentleman; else he would have seen nothing derogatory in a young nobleman looking after his horses for himself when he had brought them to the stables. Again, when he describes the impudence of petted slaves and the importance of confidential servants, he seems blind to the fact that the severity of Roman slavery was greatly mitigated by the prospects, which lay open to every clever or faithful slave, of making a career for himself and winning his way to freedom. If Juvenal wishes to condemn a master or mistress for cruelty to dependants, he is ready enough to assert the innate equality of all men, the rights of common flesh and blood; but he forgets his humanitarianism except when it is employed to shame the privileged objects of his satire. So with the Greek adventurers who supplanted Roman retainers in the favour of their patrons, he dwells only upon the vile arts which some of them used, and says little of the sterling ability which must have been the chief source of their success. Poetically and rhetorically, he is justified in only drawing attention to that aspect of every question which supports his case; but it is just because he is both a poet and rhetorician that we must discount his views and sift his statements.

We have few details of his life, and those which have been recorded are not trustworthy. Our knowledge of the man must be derived from the portrait of himself reflected in his writing, and the main features are clearly enough presented and preserved. That his life was not successful, and that he was conscious of its failure, is pretty certain. The fact and his knowledge of it are sufficient to account for the disparaging view which he took of man and man's work ; and it is all the more creditable to him that they did not make him uncharitable to individuals. There are many passages, the most pleasant but not the most powerful in his writings, where we see that he felt a hearty sympathy with virtue and virtuous men. He is never tempted to fall into the easy cynicism of ascribing low motives to good actions ; and sometimes he volunteers a kindly apology for the errors of weak-kneed but well-intentioned men like the Crispus of Sat. IV. His bitterness against individuals is only directed against those who deserved his wrath or scorn. But he lays no such restraint upon his feelings against whole classes. Men and women, young and old, rich and poor, nobles and populace, philosopher and ignoramus, slave and free, Romans and provincials, the dwellers in the Capital and the inhabitants of country towns, soldiers and civilians, masters and pupils, the poet and his patron, the dinner-giver and the dinner-beggar—they are all "bad in a lump." The story of a wife's iniquities might lead us to sympathize with her injured husband, but we soon find out that the men are as bad in their own way. The oppressive tyranny of the worst emperors and the vileness of their upstart favourites might have made us regret the degradation of the nobles from their political importance, were we not told that their position had been forfeited because they had proved unworthy to hold it. The corruption of the rising generation would call for pity to the fathers whose hopes were being deceived, if the guiltiness of their sons were not attributed to the evil example set in their own homes. The ostentatious folly of rich men, in contrast with the abject poverty of the masses, would stir our indignation, did we not see that money was better wasted in luxury than given to the mean dependants whose only object in life was to be supported on charity. How could we feel compassion for the wrongs inflicted by the Roman extortioner upon the natives of the provinces if these were such wretches as the Egyptians, Syrians, Jews, and Greeks who figure in Juvenal's satires? The pessimism which is scattered freely throughout the satires is finally formulated in the Fifteenth; even the physical powers of man have decayed: "Humanity began to dwindle even before Homer passed away; the sons of earth are nowadays weak as well as wicked beings, so that any god who has deigned a glance looks on them with laughter as well as loathing." The only kindly part of himself which Juvenal has chosen to reveal is his ardent sympathy with righteousness. Himself cold and bitter, proud and upright, without, indulgence for the shortcomings of his fellows, and perhaps without capacity for understanding the pleasures and temptations of lower natures, alone in a crowded city, averse from woman's love, and something of a failure, mocking popular legends yet not an atheist, and therefore not supported either by the believer's calm certitude or the iconoclast's enthusiasm, declaring war against all sins and shams and follies, *hostis humani generis*, he left a picture of the world about him, which he believed to be true and complete, but which we know to be misleading, because it is incomplete—perhaps as incomplete as what he tells us about the manufactures at Rome, amongst which he only deigns to notice the stinking trades. which might not be conducted on the city side of the Tiber.

4

SATIRE I.

THE NEED OF A NEW SATIRIST.

1–18. Wearied by the recitations of Poetasters, Juvenal is driven into authorship in sheer self-defence.

SHALL I be the victim always and never take revenge, though Cordus has worried me time upon time with the Tale of Theseus and his own cracked voice? What, shall there be no penalty for this man inflicting on me his Comedies and that man his Couplets? No penalty for the monster Telephus, though he wasted all my day? or for Orestes, who first crammed the margin to the end of the roll, then covered its very back, and over-lapped after all? Not a man knows the rooms in his own house better than I know the "Grove of Mars" and "the Fire-god's Dome, that lies hard by the Wind-king's rocky home." The state of business amongst the clouds, the names of the ghosts being tortured by Judge Aeacus, the place whence another Worthy decamps with the golden sheep-skin, and the size of the ash-trees which "Sir Heavy-hoof" is hurling—it is all being shouted and shouted again by the planes and the marbles and the pillars in Fronto's garden until they are split and cracked under the unresting rant. From poet big or little you may count upon the same old tales. Well, my hand dodged the dominie's stick as well as theirs,

Obscure poet.

Stock heroes of tragedy.

Jason.

Centaur.

He is familiar with poetical commonplaces as he has enjoyed "a liberal education."

and like them I gave Sulla the advice to abdicate and sleep the sleep of peace. When one jostles bards at every corner, saving the pre-destined paper is but good pity wasted.

19–50. *He is determined to choose satire by the preposterous wickedness of his age.*

Feminine men and masculine women.

Upstarts.

Why it is my special wish to compete upon the course over which Aurunca's mighty son steered his team, I will explain, if you have time and patience and reason.   When flabby Impotence takes him a wife, when a gentle dame pins the boar and bares her teat to wield the spears, when the barber who once scraped my rustling young stubble can now match his single fortune against the combined riches of the Order, when a consignment from the rabble of the Nile, a Crispinus born and bred in the impudence of Canopus, fidgets with the cloak of Tyrian purple drooping from his shoulder, fans the light summer rings upon his sweating fingers, and cannot support the load of a heavier gem —*not* to write satire is what comes hard.   Who so tolerant of Rome's wickedness (or so callous) as to contain himself when the pleader Matho passes in the brand-new litter which his own carcase fills ? Next to him comes one who played informer against his own protector ; soon to rend the scraps which remain from the mangled Order : and grown so mighty that the court Mountebank dreads him, and the Pet Abortion caresses and bribes him, whilst our leading actor, in fear and trembling, lends him his leading lady's

Vile fortune hunters.

favours.   Meantime you are ousted from your inheritance by men who win their places in wills by the works of darkness, and climb to bliss by

As a rhetorical theme at school.

Lucilius, the father of Roman satire.

Amazon-like

The Patricians.

In Egypt.

Massa. Carus.

Latinus and Thymele.

what is nowadays the shortest road, a rich hag's lechery. Proculeius takes his twelfth, and Gillo takes the rest—each his portion measured by his parts. Ay, let him take it, the price of his life-blood : and may he blench at the loss like one who has trodden bare-foot on a viper, or like an orator whose turn is coming at Lugdunum's Fancy Festival. Why tell you how the fire parches my innermost soul when our People is hustled by the flunkey troup of yonder wretch who lives on the ward whom he drove to shame ? Another is a condemned criminal, but his sentence was a sham. What cares he for degradation when the plunder is safe ? Banished Marius feasts in the morning-time and revels in the wrath of Heaven, whilst his spoiled province wins and weeps.

Am I to think that such wickedness does not demand the midnight oil of a Horace ?—should I not deal with it myself ? Why, who would sooner tell of the labours of Hercules or of Diomed? or the Labyrinth and its Bellower? the inventive Aëronaut and the Boy who tumbled into Ocean ? These are times when a consenting cuckold takes adulterous gold, the legacy which Law refuses to the partner of his shame! He has learnt to stare at the ceiling and to snore over his cups through a wide-awake nose! Another thinks he has a righteous claim to command a cohort, after wasting his wealth upon horseflesh and parting from the estate of his ancestors, whilst he skims the Flaminian Road on spinning wheels, for all the world like a boy Automedon, holding the

Prosperous criminals.

51–80.
The realities of Roman life are a better sub-ject for a poet than ancient myths.

Complais-ance of hus-bands.

Horsiness.

Curious pen-alties for failure were instituted by the eccentric Caligula.

Marius Priscus paid an inade-quate fine in 100 A.D. for extortions in Africa.

Minotaur, Dædalus and Icarus.

Women could not take any legacy be-yond 100,000 asses, by Lex Voconia.

The chario-teer of Achilles.

Flaunting crime.

reins himself to show off his skill to the girl-boy at his side. Does it not do your heart good to stop at a crossing and cover your broad tablet with notes when there must be six men's shoulders to support the hardly veiled chair, where, open to the right and left, you may see the Lounger, the would-be latter-day Mæcenas, the witness to forged wills, who has grown rich and grand on scraps of parchment and a damped signet-ring. You may meet a great lady who, before she gives the generous grape when her lord is athirst, mixes it with the poison of toads, and, improving on Lucusta, has shown her artless kins-women how to defy scandal and the eyes of Rome by attending the livid corpse's funeral. Would you be great? then be bold and risk confinement in an islet or a dungeon. Virtue wins lip-honour—and shivers in the streets. The wages of sin are parks, palaces, fine tables, old silver, and goblets with embossed grotesques. Who can sleep in peace when a son's bride turns whore for his father's gold, when betrothed girls are soiled, and ungrown lads debauch our wives? If mother-wit stints me, Passion prompts the lines—such as they are, such as I or friend Cluvienus writes.

The accomplice in forgery.

Domestic poisoning.

The real Mæcenas was a man of rank and culture.

A famous poisoner in Nero's time.

80-86.
Human life is the Satirist's theme.

Man is my subject, beginning from the Flood that was swollen by the clouds of heaven, from the day when Deucalion scaled the mountain in his ark and craved answer from God, when the stones of the ground slowly softened with the warmth of life, and Pyrrha showed our sex the charms of naked girlhood : all the doings of men, their wishes and fears, their angers, their pleasures and joys, their

Wife of Deucalion.

comings and goings, make up the medley of my book.

86–146.
But the richest material was to be found in Juvenal's contemporaries. The evils of gambling, and of avarice.

When was there a richer crop of wickedness than now? when did the gulf of avarice yawn wider? when did gambling wear a bolder front? The player does not take his "petty cash" to the hazard of the table, but stakes his strong-box on the game. What fighting you will see upon that battle-ground where the cashier is weapon-bearer! Is it madness? is it not worse than madness to lose ten times ten thousand sesterces and to cheat your shivering slave of the shirt from his back? In the times of old who ever reared a multitude of mansions, or ate through seven courses by himself? Nowadays

The abuse of charity and the break-up of the old kindly relation between patron and client.

we put our basket of scanted doles at the doorway's very edge for the toga'd crowd to grab. Yet the giver first inspects the faces in a fever of fear lest you are an impostor coming or claiming alms under a false name. You must be "passed" before you will receive: all must answer their names to the clerk, even those who boast the blood of Troy, for even they hustle us at his door.

The nobles as descendants of Æneas and his companions.

"Serve the Praetor, and serve the Tribune next."

The worship of wealth results in the insolence of upstarts and the humiliation of worthy men, even highborn or holding high office.

No, a freedman is before them. "I am the first comer," says he. "Why fear or hesitate to keep my place? What if I *was* born upon the Euphrates? why deny it, when the womanish gaps in my ears would bewray me? Still, my five shops are earning me the fortune of a Knight. What does the Senator's broad stripe of purple give as good if a Corvinus must tend sheep for hire in the pastures

For earrings.

A noble name.

of Laurentum? My possessions are more than those of a Pallas or Licinus."

Favourite freedmen at Court.

Then let a Tribune wait his turn, let wealth win : the Holy Office must give way to one who entered the city not long ago with the chalk of slavery on his ankles, since it is to Wealth we pay our holiest honour, although the cruel god Money is not yet housed in a temple, neither have we yet built altars unto Cash, even as we worship Peace and Honesty, Victory and Virtue, or Concord (beneath whose mystic roof men hear a sound as of twittering birds when they bow before—the nests !). But when the bearer of high office reckons at the year's end how much the Charity brings him in and what it adds to his accounts, what must retainers do who depend upon it for their clothing and shoe-leather, for the bread of their mouths and the fuel of their hearths? There is a crush of litters to beg the hundred pieces, and the husband takes an ailing or pregnant wife along with him and drags her through the round.

The customary dole.

A dirty trick.

Another claims for his, though she is not there. Grown crafty in the old dodge, he points to the closed curtains of an empty chair. "Here is my wife Galla," says he. "Let us go at once : you are keeping her. Galla, put your head out. Ah, do not disturb her, you will find her asleep."

Read *quiescet.*

A dependant's duties.

Every day is graced with its own pretty rubric of duties. First comes the alms-begging : then the Forum, with its temple of Apollo "learned in the law" and its statues of our heroes, amongst whom some Egyptian or Arabian Nobody has ventured to set up his own record, a creature against whose image you have a right to do more than commit a nuisance. Old and worn dependants turn away from the great man's porch and abandon their hopes, though what dies hardest in man's heart is the chance of dinner. No, the poor wretches must pay for their cabbage and their firing. Meantime their lord and master will swallow the richest prizes of forest and sea, and will loll by himself amongst empty couches. For though men like him have a multitude of huge, antique, round tables, they use but one to devour a fortune. Some day diners-out will be an extinct species; yet who could endure such shabbiness with such self-indulgence? Imagine the man's gullet who has a boar served whole for himself, though it is a beast created for good fellowship. But the punishment is at hand, when you strip the clothes from your bloated body and carry an undigested peacock to the Baths. This is why we hear of sudden deaths and of old men leaving no wills. The news is talked of at every dinner-table, not regretted; and the funeral moves out only to meet the applause of embittered friends.

There will be nothing for an after-age to add to our wickedness; and our sons can but copy our own lusts and crimes. Every sin is halted over a brink. Up with your sails, my Muse, and spread all canvas.

Here perhaps one may say to me, " Whence the "genius to match the theme? Whence the spirit to "write down every dictate of the impassioned heart,

[margin notes]

Selfishness and luxury.

Presumably for hospitality.

146–170. Vice has reached its acme.

Remonstrance of a friend who points out the danger of attacking real men.

"the frankness of days gone by—That, the name of
"which I dare not whisper? Do you ask what
"matters it whether a Mucius give or withhold his
"pardon? Then attack your Tigellinus, and you will
"soon make a light at the stake where men stand to
"blaze and smoke with impaled necks, and where
"your pitch draws a broad furrow in the sand around
"you.   No, let the man who gave aconite to three
"uncles be borne aloft on swaying down, and survey
"us from his height.   When you meet him, lay the
"finger of silence to your lips. It will be slander if
"you say so much as 'That is he.' You need not fear
"to set Æneas and 'the bold Rutulian' fighting ;
"none will take offence at the Smiting of Achilles or
"the Search for long-lost Hylas who followed the
"fate of his pitcher.   But so often as a hot Lucilius
"has drawn his sword and set his teeth, a flush rises
"on the hearer's face—his soul is frozen under accu-
"sation whilst the clammy sweat of unspoken sin
"lies on his heart.   Hence comes ' the weeping
"' and gnashing of teeth.' Think of it with yourself
"before you sound the battle-note.   When the
"helmet has been donned, it is too late to repent."

Well, I shall try what licence will be given me
against them whose ashes are covered by the
Flaminian and Latin Roads.

Side notes:

Viz.,Liberty.

Attacked by Lucilius.

Read *deducis.*

It is safer for the poet to keep to the old mythical subjects.

Turnus.

170–171. Juvenal's answer.

SATIRE II.

HYPOCRISY AND VICE.

1–63.
The austere
exterior of
sham philo-
sophers
conceals the
most shame-
ful vices.

Their igno-
rance.

IT makes me long to escape far away beyond Sarmatia and the ice-bound seas when puritans by profession, but debauchees in practice, set themselves up for moralists. (To begin with, they are dunces, though you will find every corner in their houses crammed with a clay Chrysippus. Indeed, they award the honours of learning to any one who has paid for a good image of Aristotle or Pittacus and charges his shelves with the keeping of genuine Cleanthes busts.)

As the
founder of
Stoicism.

Their
hypocrisy.

Put not your trust in faces. There is prim lewdness walking every street in Rome; and the voice which rebukes sin belongs to the most notorious evil-liver amongst philosophising sodomites. True that a manly spirit is betokened by his hairy body and the stiff growth upon his arms—but ask the grinning surgeon where and why he used the knife !

Their
affectation.

They are
worse than
open sinners.

Our hypocrites are men of few words; their spirit moves them *not* to speak, and they wear their hair cropt shorter than eyebrows. Compared with them, Peribomius is a true and honest man; the blame of his life is with Destiny, whilst his

It was
"fast" to
wear the
hair long.

face and gait confess the curse which lies upon him. The frankness of men like him stirs pity, and the very devil within them disarms our loathing. Not so with the worse wretches who attack sin with " brave words," or the praters about virtue who do the deeds of darkness.

" Is it for me," cries disgraced Varillus, " to respect a Sextus taken in the act? How am I worse than he? "

They are the wrong persons to denounce vice. Let them who are without blemish scoff at bandy legs and Ethiopian skins. Who will endure a Gracchus declaiming against agitators? Who would not cry for heaven and earth, for sky and sea, to change places if a Verres were disgusted with robbers or a Milo with murderers? if a Clodius complained against adultery, or a Catiline against treason? if Sulla's three pupils in proscription found fault with his Lists? So it was when one who still reeked with the pollution of a truly classical lust sought to revive laws (which were hard on all men and formidable even to Mars and Venus) at the very time when his too prolific Julia was working her malpractices and spawning abortions in the likeness of their uncle. Has not Infamy a good and proper right to despise sham censors and to bite the hand which strikes it?

Antonius, Octavianus, and Lepidus.

Domitian enforced the laws about adultery.

Julia Sabina was his cousin and debauched by him.

The protest of a harlot. Lauronia could no longer endure one of these martinets with his cant appeal—" what had become of the Julian law? was it dormant?" She answers with a smile :

About adultery.

" It is a fortunate generation which pits you " against wickedness. It is time, indeed, for

" Rome to regain her modesty when another Cato
" has dropt from the skies. All the same, tell
" me where you buy the balsam which perfumes
" that manly throat.   Do not be ashamed to point
" out your purveyor.   But if Law and Justice are to
" be whipt up, the Scantinian Act must first answer   Against male vice.
" to the call.   First look to the men and examine
" them: they are worse criminals, but they are safe   Men are worse than women.
" in their numbers and lock their shields in phalanx.
" There is a marvellous sympathy amongst you
" un-manned men. You will find nothing amongst
" us to match your loathsomeness. Tedia and
" Flora cannot be set against your Hispo, either in
" their vice or in its penalties.   When do we turn
" pleaders or doctors in civil law, or raise an up-   The rights of women.
" roar in your forum ?   A few of us are wrestlers,
" and a few devour the training-rations.   But you
" have become spinners of wool and carry your   Effeminate affectations of men.
" completed quota in work-baskets.   More in-
" dustrious than Penelope and more delicate than
" Arachne, you ply the spindles with their belly-
" fuls of thread, like the draggled wench squatting
" on her lump of wood.   It is no secret why   Effeminate vices.
" Hister's will contained none but his freedman's
" name ; nor why in his lifetime he was so gener-
" ous to his bride. She who makes room for a rival
" in her bed will become a wealthy woman.   Girls   The effect on married life.
" should become wives—and hold their tongues
" afterwards ! Keeping secrets brings in gifts of
" jewels.   Nevertheless, it is on us women that the
" harsh verdict is passed : crows are pardoned, but
" the pigeons are found guilty."

The plain truth of her declamation scattered the Stoic-puritans in confusion. Wherein had Lauronia spoken amiss?

65–81. Effeminacy in dress, as exemplified in a man of noble family and high position.

But what must we look for from others, Creticus, when you wear gauzes to denounce a Procula or Pollita while the people are staring in amazement at your garments? Granted that Fabulla is an adulteress; and, if you will, let sentence be passed upon Carfinia. Still the condemned woman herself will not put on such a dress as yours. Do you say that July is sultry and you are in a sweat? Then strip to plead. (Stark lunacy would be less disgrace.) What a dress to be found wearing while you proposed laws and measures, when your countrymen returned in the full flush of victory with their wounds yet unhealed, or by the hardy peasants from their ploughs upon the hills. What an outcry you would make if you saw such clothes upon the body of a judge! Tell me, would the gauze sit well even upon a witness? But the proud and independent Creticus, the free master of his own soul, is naked and not ashamed.

Profligate women.

As in the good old times.

As a Stoic.

His example will make the fashion.

The plague has spread by contagion, and will spread further, just as the whole herd is laid low on its feeding-grounds through a single scabby or scurvy pig, or as the blight passes on by contact from one grape to the next.

82–89. The affectation will develope into downright wickedness.

One day you will venture upon things more shameful than your dress. Infamy is never born full-grown. Little by little you will be drawn towards them who privily deck their heads with long ribands and hang chains over all their necks,

The notorious rites of Bona Dea were (properly) confined to women.

and honour the "Good Goddess" with a young sow's belly and big bowls of wine; whilst a blasphemous perversion drives women away and forbids them to set foot on the threshold.

89–114. *The unnatural perversion of sensational religion.*

The shrine of the "Good Goddess" is reserved for men. "Away with the unclean sex!" they cry; "we want no women-minstrels here, nor their grunting horns." (Not worse were the orgies kept privily at Athens to the light of torches by the Ministers who sickened their acclimatised Cotytto.) *Introduced from Thrace.*

Preparation for the orgies by the male masqueraders.

One man slants the tiring-pin and lengthens out his eyebrows with moistened soot and turns up his quivering eyes to daub them. Another drinks from a bestiality-in-glass and stuffs his masses of hair into a net of golden twine, and dresses himself in patterns of azure lozenges or fine green stuffs, whilst even the tiring-man swears by the Juno of his master-mistress. *Especially the goddess of women.*

Men using mirrors like the Emperor Otho.

A third holds up a mirror (the very one, no doubt, which was borne by the unsexed Otho — "spoil taken from Auruncan *Vergil.* Actor's corse"—wherein he would survey his fighting toilet just as he was giving the word for all standards to advance. It is a thing to be noted in modern records and the history of our own times that the kit for civil war includes a mirror. We expect the first general of his day to shed Galba's blood and preserve—his own complexion; the first citizen to claim the palace spoil upon the *69 B.C.* Bedriacum's field, and—to plaster his face with a mould of dough; though it was not so done by the quiver-wearing Queen Semiramis when Assyria ruled the world, nor by Cleopatra when she fled in desolation on her Actian galley).

The coarse vice.

At such a scene there is neither nicety of language nor the decencies of table; there is all Cybele's filthy licence—all the licence of falsetto voices : the president and priest is a frantic old man with white hair, a rare and memorable prodigy of guzzling, worth a professorship in his art.

115–142. The practices of effeminate men.

What are they waiting for? Long ago it was time for them to carve their bodies to the Phrygian fashion. Gracchus has brought the fortune of a knight as his dowry for one who blows "the wreathed horn" (or maybe it was straight): the

Mock marriages.

documents have been signed and the blessing pronounced ; the huge supper party is seated, and the bride has leant upon his husband's bosom. Nobles of Rome ! which do we want—the Censor or the Prophet? (You are reckless, yet no doubt you would be shocked and think the omen more perplexing if a woman gave birth to a calf, or a cow to a lamb.)

To explain such a monstrosity.

Even priests do not refrain,

A priest who has supported the sacred weights depending from the mystical thongs and has sweated under the shields of Mars, is wearing womanish

Salii, priests of Mars carried Ancilia in procession.

Juvenal's appeal to Heaven.

ribands, long robes, and veils. Father of Rome ! whence came such wickedness upon the peasants of Latium ? Whence this itching plague which has stung the children of the God of Battles ? Behold ! a man of high lineage and wealth is being married to another man : yet thou shakest not thy helmet, smitest not the ground with thy spear, neither complainest to thy Father on high ! Then away with thee and depart from the estate, which thou neglectest, in the Field of Valour.

The Campus Martius.

"I have a task of courtesy to perform," says somebody, "at early dawn to-morrow in the Valley of Quirinus."

"What is the occasion ? "

"Need I tell you ? A friend of mine takes a husband to himself; but it is to be a select party."

134–142.
They are restrained, not by moral, but by physical, checks.

If we only live to see it, such things must and will be done without concealment, and will claim a place in the Public Register. Meantime our "brides" live in fearful torture because they cannot have a family and make sure of their husbands by the bond of children. It is well indeed that Nature will not grant power over the body to the desires of their minds. They die barren, nor can bloated Lyde help them with her box of drugs, nor can they help themselves by stretching out their palms for the nimble Lupercus to strike.

As a fertilizer.

143–148.
The worse infamy remains that a noble and a priest fights in the arena like a common gladiator.

Even this prodigy was outdone when a Gracchus, stript to his tunic and wielding the gladiator's three-pronged spear, ran for his life across the mid arena, though he was of a purer strain than Capitolinus, Marcellus, or Catulus; purer than the lines of Paulus or Fabius—or all the nobles who sat along the tier which faced the ring-wall; of purer

As a retiarius armed only with a net and a three-pronged spear.

149–158.
What the old Romans would feel about modern life, *if* their spirits had consciousness.

strain (you may add) than the President ·who bade him throw the net.

Perhaps Domitian.

The life after death, the infernal kingdom, the pool of Styx with its punting-pole and dusky frogs, and the passage of so many thousand beings on a single boat, are myths which even boys disbelieve unless they are too young to pay their coppers at the baths. But if you can imagine them to be true stories, Gracchus, what does Curius think about you? or the two Scipios? or Fabricius and Camillus? What is thought by the heroes of Cremera, or the warriors who were lost at Cannæ, or the gallant .hearts of all our wars, when such a ghost as yours comes to join them? They would ask to be purified from the taint, if they could get sulphur and pine-wood torches and water for the laurel-spray. The Fabii.

For the lustration.

159–170.
The military successes of Rome are more than balanced by moral decadence.

Such are the depths into which our unhappy generation is being dragged. It is true that we have advanced our arms beyond the shores of Juverna, the newly-conquered Orcades, and the Britains who live contented in the region of shortest night. But there are things being done in the city of the Victor People which are not done among the vanquished nations; still scandal says that one amongst them, a young Armenian, Zalates, more womanish than the rest, listened to a liquorish Tribune's corruptions. Ireland.

Our example is beginning to take effect on the hitherto un-sophisticated peoples.

Behold the workings of national intercourse (for he had come as our hostage!). As is their childhood here, so will their manhood afterwards be: for if their sojourn is prolonged to give them more of Rome, they will do what Romans do: they will say good-bye to their trousers and hunting-knives, their whips and bridles. This is how Artaxata can reproduce the morals of our rising generation. Capital of Armenia.

SATIRE III.

TOWN AND COUNTRY LIFE.

1–9.
Disgusted by
the wicked-
ness of
Rome,
Umbricius, a
friend of
Juvenal,
emigrates to
a country
town.

TROUBLED as I am by an old friend's departure, still I commend him because he intends to make his home at Cumæ the Deserted, and to give the Sibyl one denizen at least. It is Baiæ's gate, and a sweet nook for a pleasant coast retreat. Myself, I count even barren Prochyta better than Subura's slums. What spot has ever been seen so wretched and so lonely that it were not yet worse to live in dread of fires, ever tumbling roofs, all the perils of this cruel Rome, and—poets ranting in the dog-days!

The oracle of
the Sibyl
was at the
old Greek
foundation
of Cumæ.

10–20.
Even the
simple
beauties of
Nature, with
their old
historical
associations,
have become
sophisticated
by false art,
or degraded
for purposes
of revenue.

Meantime, whilst my friend's whole household was being packed upon a single cart, he halted at the old archway of the dribbling Capene gate; we go down into "the Vale of Egeria" and the manu-factured grotto. Ah! how much better could we commune with the water-sprite if the stream were bounded by its green fringe of grass, and if no marble did violence to the simple tufa-stone. Here it was that Numa kept tryst with his quean at night. Now the grove and chapel of the Holy Well are leased to Jew tramps—their worldly wealth a basket and a bunch of hay. Not a tree,

Ribbeck's
arrange-
ment.

Under an
aqueduct.

Read
præsentius.

The deity
who was
said to have
advised the
old king
Numa.

but must bring in its quota to the public chest, and so the Camenæ are evicted for the wood to become one mass of beggary.

Roman deities partly corresponding to the Greek Muses.

21–57.
The rest of the satire is occupied with the speech of Umbricius.

Here it was then that Umbricius began: "Since "there is no room for honesty at Rome, no reward "for industry, since my substance is to-day smaller "than it was yesterday, and the Less will to-morrow "lose something of its Little, it is my purpose to "depart thither where Dædalus doffed his fainting "wings, whilst grey hairs are yet novelties and my "old age is fresh and upright, whilst some thread "is left for the Spinster-Goddess to unreel, and I "can support me upon my own feet without a staff "to prop my hand. Let me away from the home "of my fathers, and let Artorius and Catulus live "amongst you; let them stay behind who swear black "is white, who find it easy to become jerry-builders, "water-scavengers, dock and sewage farmers, or "undertakers, or to traffic in human flesh under "the sanction of the Spear. Men who began as "trumpet-blowers and strollers reappearing at every "country show (their puffed cheeks known from "town to town), are now providers of pageants; at "the signal of the vulgar thumb they shed blood "for the people's holiday. Then they go away and "farm retiring-places!—what should stop them? "They are of that stuff which Fortune loves to "raise from lowliness to the highest pinnacles of "success—when she wants a joke.

I.e., Cumæ.

Lachesis, one of the Fates.

None but vile trades thrive at Rome.

Set up at auctions.

How up-starts gain popularity.

"What is there for me to do at Rome? Liar I "cannot be; and if a book is bad, praising it and "begging for a reading is beyond me. I was never

The arts of adventurers.

Literary sycophants.

Sham
diviners.
Go-be-
tweens.
Agents of
extortion.

"taught the movements of the planets; I will not
"and cannot promise the death of a father, I am not
"curious in the bowels of frogs. The offerings, the
"messages of unlawful love, others must carry. In
"robbery I will be no man's accomplice, and that
"is why no governor takes me in his suite. I am
"but like a useless trunk with a palsied hand. Who
"is taken into favour nowadays if he be not an
"accomplice, with his soul fevered by a secret sin
"which can never be confessed? The confidence
"which is not guilty earns you no gratitude, and will
"bring you no profit. Verres only makes a friend
"of the man who can turn upon Verres at a mo-
"ment's notice. Yet put not such value on all the
"precious yellow dust which rolls down to the sea
"between the banks of turbid Tagus, as for its sake
"to abandon the sleep of peace and to take pre-
"sents which cannot be kept, only to live in sullen-
"ness and become a daily terror to the great man
"*your friend.*

The power
and profit
are too
dearly pur-
chased at
the cost of a
guilty
conscience.

The extor-
tionate
governor of
Sicily im-
peached by
Cicero.

58–125.
The inunda-
tion of Rome
by low
Greeks.

"What the people are whom our Dives loves,
"and whom I am especially running away from, I
"will make haste to tell you; and the shame of it
"shall not stop me. What I cannot endure, my
"countrymen, is Rome turned Greek! Yet how
"little of the town scum is genuine Greek!
"It was not yesterday that Orontes first ran
"into Tiber and brought its Syrian words and
"ways, its flute-players and twisted harps, its
"cymbals and the harlots who are set out on
"commission at the Circus. Thither away all of
"you who take your delight in foreign wenches and

Roman
affectation
of Greek
fashions and
vices.

Dinner shoes
Athletic prizes.
Greased.

" gaudy turbans.   Romulus, behold !   Your honest
" yeoman puts on τρεχέδειπνα, and wears νικητήρια
" upon his κήρωμα'd neck.   Here is one who has
" come from Sicyon's hill, another from Amydon,
" others from Andros, Samos, Tralles or Alabandæ
" —all making for the Esquiline and the hill which
" bears the Osier's name, to regulate the life (and
" one day to become the masters) of great houses.

Viminal.

Greek sup-
pleness and
versatility. *

" Their wits are nimble, their impudence damn-
" able, their language prompt and more gushing
" than Isæus.   Tell me what you think is yonder
" man's trade.   He is anything and everything
" you please, all in one.   Grammar, rhetoric, geo-
" metry, painting, or wrestling, prophesying, rope-
" dancing, medicine, and magic — he is master
" of them all.   Give the word, and your hungry
" Greekling will climb the clouds.   In fact the
" man who did put wings on was no Moor, nor
" Sarmatian, nor Thracian, but one born in the
" heart of Athens.   Should I not flee away when such
" men are wearing purple raiment ?   Shall one of
" them sign his name before mine ?   Shall a man
" loll in the place of honour who came to Rome
" with the same wind which brought the plums and
" figs ?   Is it quite nothing that my childhood
" quaffed the air of Aventine and was fed on true
" Sabine fruit ?

Rhetorician
who came to
Rome about
100 A.D.

Their
flattery.

" Look again, how the roguish flattery of the tribe
" praises the vulgar man's language and the ugly
" man's beauty ; they compare the long neck of
" lankiness to the throat of the Hercules holding
" Antæus high in air : they admire the piping voice

"which is no better than the shrill note of him who Viz., the barndoor cock.
"claims conjugal rights by pecking his hen ! It is
"true that we, like them, have leave to flatter, but
"they can also dupe a patron.

Their in-famous skill as actors.
 "Perhaps our comedian is still more clever
"when he acts Anonyma, or the Jealous Wife, or
"the Dorian Girl (in the national undress). It
"is a real woman that seems to speak the words,
"not a masked man. In that faultless contour
"you would say there was not a line too much,
"nor a line wanting. Yet in their own country
"not one of them will pass for wonderful; not
"Antiochus, Stratocles, Demetrius, or the girlish .
"Hæmus. It is a nation of play-actors. Do you
"laugh? then a louder guffaw shakes his sides.
"If he sees a friend in tears, he weeps too, although
"he feels no sorrow. If you call for a spark of
"fire in winter time, he wraps himself in a rug;
"or if you say that you are warm, why he is in a
"sweat. No, it is no match between us : the odds
"are with the man who can put on a borrowed
"face at any hour of the night or day, and throw
"up his hands in admiration when his friend has
"done the simplest things in life. Three lines omitted.

Lust the instrument of their ambition.
 "There is nothing sacred to him, nothing safe
"from his filthiness : not the mother of the house-
"hold nor her maiden daughter, not the promised
"husband still unwhiskered nor the yet untainted
"lad; or, in default of them, he debauches the
"old grandam. Somehow he will make himself
"master of the family secrets and use them in terror-
"ism. And since we have begun upon the Greeks,

Practical worthlessness of Greek moral philosophy.

How Greeks supplant the Roman retainer in the favour of his patron.

126–146. Hardships of the poor retainer.

He must enter into competition with high officers of State and rich upstarts.

The poor man is not believed on oath.

" let us pass to the doings in the Schools and learn " the wickedness which a long robe covers. The " informer against Barea, the shedder of his " friend's blood, the reverend betrayer of his own " disciple, was a Stoic, the offspring of that river- " side where the Gorgon-horse shed a wing-feather. P. Egnatius in Nero's time. Cydnus in Cilicia.

" There is no place for a Roman where some " Πρωτογένης or Δίφιλος or Ἕρμαρχος plays the lord. " The self-seeking Greek will not share a friend, " but keeps him to himself. After he has poured " into the credulous ear a drop of the national venom " distilled in his personal vileness, I am turned from " the doorway, and all my long term of slavery is " so much wasted time. Retainers are cheap at " Rome.

" What indeed does 'service' mean? Let me " not blink facts. What gives the poor man a " claim? He must be dressed before it is light " and make his rush. But already the prætor is " bustling his lictor and bidding him run fast lest " another prætor be before him in paying his " respects to Albina or Modia—the heirless old " ladies have been too long awake. Rich women without natural heirs.

" The son of free-born citizens must give the " wall to an enriched slave. It is yonder upstart " who pays Calvina or Catiena for exercising his " puffiness as much as a tribune earns by a year's " service in the legion; but if your taste is capti- " vated by a smart harlot's face, you stop and hesi- " tate to bid your Fancy alight from her high litter. Leaders of the *demi-monde.*

" You may produce a witness spotless as the man " held worthy to give a home to Ida's goddess; P. Corn. Scipio Nasica. Cybele.

"or let a Numa come forward, or one like him who
"rescued terrified Minerva from her burning temple
"—the first question will be, 'What *has* he?' The
"last will be, 'What *is* he?' How many slaves does
"he keep? how much land does he hold? what
"is the number and the size of the side-dishes at
"his dinners? The measure of a man's *credit* is the
"money which he guards in his strong-box? Swear
"if you will by all the gods of Samothrace and
"Rome; a poor man is supposed to make light
"of thunderbolts and Heaven, and Heaven is sup-
"posed to forgive his fault.

"Nor is this all. Every wag takes the same
"butt for his wit — Poverty, with its torn and
"ragged cloak, its soiled toga, and the split leather
"of its gaping boot, or the coarse new thread which
"shows more than one scar left where the wound
"was patched. None of wretched Poverty's pri-
"vations are harder to bear than the scorn which
"it throws upon a human being. 'Away with
"him!' they cry. 'How indecent! let him get up
"from the cushioned chairs reserved for Knights,
"if his fortune does not satisfy the law. Let the
"pander's lads keep their places, born though they
"are in any stews you please. Let the smug
"auctioneer's son clap his hands in the company
"of the gladiator or the trainer's hopeful offspring.'
"That, no doubt, is what Otho *meant* (poor man!)
"when he marked out the places.

"What father has ever accepted a suitor whose
"fortune was too small to match the daughter's
"finery? When does a will contain a poor heir's

Margin notes:

L. Cæcilius Metellus.

147–189. Poverty has become ridiculous.

Its dishonour in public places.

By the old law of Roscius Otho passed 67 B.C.

No career for poverty.

"name? when is he taken into an Ædile's office?
" Long ago the needy sons of Rome ought to have
" formed in companies and marched away.   Every-
" where it is hard for men to rise whose merits are
" weighted by cramping want, but the struggle is

Contrast of
Roman
ostentatious-
ness with the
simple life in
the country.

" fiercer at Rome.   A wretched garret costs a
" fortune; so do voracious slaves and your own
" humble dinner.   Here it is disgraceful to eat a
" meal from crockery, though a sudden change to
" Marsian or Sabine fare makes it no shame at all.
" There it is enough to wear a coarse green cape.
" And (to tell the truth) throughout the greater
" part of Italy nobody wears his toga before he is
" dressed for burial.   Whensoever the high gran-
" deur of a Feast is honoured in the turf-built
" theatre, and the stock farce returns to the boards
" and makes the country babe at his mother's
" breast shrink from the ghastly grinning mask,
" you will find no difference of garb, but senators
" in the stalls and the populace behind them
" dressed alike.   A clean white vest is the robe
" of high office which satisfies a country ædile's
" dignity.   Here the display of dress goes beyond
" our means; and we borrow money to meet the
" wants which are not wanted.   The folly is univer-

Blackmail
levied on
poor
retainers by
the con-
fidential
slaves of rich
men.

" sal; we are all living in genteel beggary.   Need
" I go on?   Nothing here can be got for nothing.
" What is the fee you pay for leave to call now

Patrons.

" and again on Cossus? or for Veiento—not to
" open his lips to you, but to turn his eyes your
" way?   One master is shaving the first beard,

Ceremony at
entrance into
manhood.

" another dedicates the love-locks, of a petted

"slave. The house is full of cakes—for sale!
"'Take one, please' (they say). Yes (say I), and
"take this, too, to stir your bile :—we dependants
"are forced to pay tribute to smart flunkeys and to
"swell their perquisites.

190-202.
The immense height and scamped masonry of Roman houses.

"Who is, or ever was, afraid of tumbling houses
"at cool Præneste or at Volsinii (couched between
"its wooded hills), or at simple Gabii or on sloping
"Tibur's eminence? The city we live in here is
"propt on crazy rods—not much more masonry than
"propping. That is how the agent blocks a tum-
"bling mass and patches up an old yawning crack.
"With a ruin overhead he bids you sleep in peace.
"Better to live where there are no fires or alarms
"by night. Hark! your neighbour cries out for
"water. See! he is shifting his belongings. See!

The fire.

"your 'second-floor' is smoking! But you are in
"happy ignorance ; if the alarm begins below stairs,
"the lodger, who has nothing but the tiles between
"himself and the rain, and lives amongst the gentle
"nesting doves, enjoys the privilege of being last
"to burn.

203-211.
The fire in a poor man's house reduces him to destitution.

"Codrus possessed one couch (too short for
"Procula), six jugs to adorn his bracket, with a ‡ His wife.
"drinking-cup to stand below and share its marble
"shed with a crouching Chiron; a basket which As pedestal.
"had seen service held some Greek manuscripts,
"where uncivilized mice gnawed the inspired
"lines. What Codrus possessed was just nothing:
"that cannot be denied. Still the unhappy man
"lost all his nothing. But the last straw to break
"his back is that, when he is naked and begging

" for a crust, nobody will help him with a meal or
" with lodging and a roof.

212–222.
How a rich man makes a profit of his loss.

" Now if the big house of Asturicius has come
" down with a crash, the matrons of Rome go
" dishevelled, the elders put on mourning, and the
" prætors adjourn their courts. At such a time we
" bewail the misfortunes of our city and curse the
" flames. While the fire is yet burning, one man
" will rush to give marble and contribute funds.
" Another brings nude Parian statues, another
" some fine bit of Euphranor or Polycletus, or the
" ancient ornaments of Asiatic gods, or books and
" shelves (with a Minerva to stand among them), or
" a bushel of silver. Indemnified far beyond his
" losses, our Sybarite is the smartest old bachelor
" in Rome, and comes to be suspected (not with-
" out reason) of having played incendiary in his
" own house.

Contemp. of Alex. Great. Contemp. of Pericles.
Read Hic Asianorum.

223–231.
Good houses with land are cheap in the country.

" If you can wrench yourself away from the
" Circus shows, an excellent house is to be got at
" Sora or Fabrateria or Frusino for the sum which
" you pay here as one year's rent of a dark hole.
" There you may have a garden and a shallow well,
" which you need no rope to work, for you just
" dip your bucket and water the young plants.
" Here you may live with your beloved hoe as the
" gardener of a fruitful plot which would find you
" entertainment for a hundred Vegetarians. Some-
" thing it is, no matter where or in what corner, to
" have gained the real estate in one lizard's run.

Towns in Latium.

Disciples of Pythagoras.

232–238.
Miseries of the lodger's life.
(Side hit at gluttony.)

" Many a sick man dies here for want of rest
" (the first illness, it is true, was caused by food

"undigested and clogging a feverish stomach).
"But lodging-houses do not allow of slumber; and
"it costs much money to have a sleeping-place at
"Rome.   That is the root of the mischief.   The
"traffic of carts at the crowded street-corners and
"the wranglings over the blocked droves will knock
"the sleep out of a sea-calf—or a Drusus !

? the Emperor Claudius.

239-248. The streets impassable for those who must walk when they go to pay their respects to their patrons.

"When the rich man has to pay his duty calls, he
"will be carried on a high litter and skim the heads
"of the retreating crowd, and he will read as he
"goes or write or doze perhaps—for a chair invites
"sleep when the windows have been closed.   All the
"same, he will arrive before me; bustle as I may,
"my steps are blocked by the human tide in front,
"and there is a long column crammed against my
"back: here an elbow, there a hard pole, is poking
"me; one knocks a beam against me, another
"knocks a cask.   My legs are caked with mud, and
"presently huge hoofs are trampling all about me,
"and the nail from a soldier's boot is left sticking
"in my toe.

249-253. The old hospitable relation between patron and client travestied by the scramble for lukewarm scraps.

"Notice the clouds of smoke rising over the
"crowded Dole.   It is a dinner-party of one
"hundred, each guest attended by his own cook-
"ing-stove !   Why a Corbulo could hardly support
"all the vessels and all the wares packed on his
"head which the unhappy slave carries with un-
"bending neck as he runs to fan the flame.

254-267. Street accidents.

"Our lately patched tunics are torn anew; the
"approaching waggon bears a long quivering fir-tree,
"and another cart brings a pine that shakes its high
"head ominously at the crowd.   Why, if the wheels

"supporting yonder Ligurian stone have collapsed
"and spilt that uprooted mountain on the living
"mass below, not an atom is left of their humanity.

Death of a
citizen and a
picture of his
home con-
trasted with
another
picture of
his soul in
Hades.

"Who could find limb or bone? Every carcase
"in the crowd is pulverized, and disappears like
"a breath.

"Meantime, in an unsuspecting household they
"are now washing the plates, blowing up the fire,
"rattling the oiled flesh-scrapers, and laying out
"the towels beside the filled unguent bottle. Such
"is the bustle and stir among the servants: yet
"even now their master is seated on the bank of
"Styx and shuddering novice-like before the grim
"Ferryman, despairing of his passage over that
"muddy channel, unhappy man! nor has he the
"copper-piece in his mouth to pay the fare.

268-314.
Dangers of
the night.

"Turn you now to the night with its own list of
"different perils. What a distance from the high
"house-tops if a pot comes down upon our skulls
"when the cracked or chipt crockery is being
"thrown out of the windows! how heavily it
"scores and damages the pavement! You might
"be called lazy and careless of life's surprises if
"you went out for dinner with your will unmade.
"Each and every window which is awake and
"opened as you pass may mean a separate death
"for you on that very night. Let it therefore
"be your hope and your constant humble prayer
"that they may be contented if the flat-pans are
"only *emptied* on your head. The drunken

Ruffianism in
the streets.

"brawler suffers tortures if he happens not to
"have thrashed his man—endures the anguish of

"Achilles lamenting his lost friend, rolling now on "his face and now on his back. Then cannot he "rest without it?   No, a brawl is some men's only "sleeping-draught.   Still, though he is full of young "skittishness and flushed with wine, your bravo "is cautious of the man who is marked Danger-"ous by his purple wraps and his long line of "attendants as well as by a blaze of light and "brazen lamps.   I am escorted home either by "the moonlight or by the short-lived gleaming of "a single candle, and have to manage and manipu-"late its wick—so he despises me!   Here you "have the prelude to our miserable fight (if you "can call it fighting when I receive, and he gives, "all the blows).   He stops before me and bids me "stop : there is nothing but to obey.   What can "you do when a lunatic who is stronger than you "are uses force ?   *Patroclus.*

"'Whence are you?' he demands; 'whose vine-"gar and beans stuff your belly? what cobbler "has been sharing with you his mess of leeks and "his lips of boiled sheep's head?   Do you not "answer me?   Speak or be kicked.   Tell me where "is your begging-stand; what *synagogue* shall I find "you at?'   *As to a Jew.*

"It makes no difference whether you would "make some answer or retire without a word. "You are battered all the same.   Then the bully "goes off in a passion and lodges a complaint "against you at the Prætor's court.   This is what "a poor man's rights are worth : after a thrashing "he may beg, and after a punching he may pray,   *No redress.*

"permission to retreat with a few teeth left in his
"head.

Robbery
with
violence.

"Nor is this all you must fear. There will be
"men to rob you after all the hushed shops have
"been everywhere secured with bolt and chain.
"Sometimes, again, the foot-pad takes you by sur-
"prise and sets to work with the knife. Whenever
"the Pomptine Fen and the Gallinarian Firs are
"protected by an armed patrol, it is the signal for
"all the rogues to run away to Rome for covert.
"Where is the furnace or the anvil which is not
"forging chains? The best part of our iron is
"spent on fetters, so that you may look out for a
"short supply of ploughshares and a scarcity of
"mattocks and hoes. Happy were our fathers'
"fathers; happy the old days when a single prison
"was enough for all Rome, in the epoch of the
"Kings or the People's Tribunes.

On coast of
Latium.
Near Cumæ.

The Mamer-
tine Gaol
built by
Ancus
Martius.
I.e., in old
republican
days.

315–322.
Farewell
words of
Umbricius.

"To these reasons I could add many others;
"but my team wants me and the sun is sinking.
"We must start. My muleteer cracks his whip
"again and beckons me. Farewell, then, and do
"not forget me. Whenever Rome restores you
"to your beloved Aquinum in the search for new
"health, remember me and take me from my
"Cumæ to the Helvian Ceres and your own Diana's
"shrine. If your muse does not disown me, I
"will come as adjutant, and boot me for your expe-
"dition to the Land of Coolness."

SATIRE IV.

THE STORY OF A TURBOT.

1–36.
Introduction
The wicked-
ness of
Crispinus
defies the
powers of
Satire.

"WHAT is this? 're-enter Crispinus.'" Yes, he must often come to play his rôle—a monstrous mass of vices unredeemed by one virtue. Feeble, save when lechery lends him vigour, our adulterer scorns the taste of game which is not poached. Who cares then how long are the colonnades through which his team is flogged, or how wide the shady groves where he is borne upon his litter, or how much acreage or what houses he has bought in the very heart of Rome! The wicked man can never be a happy man. Then what of this seducer, this profaner of holy things; with whom the sealed Vestal sinned but yesterday under her forfeit of a living tomb? We are now to speak only of his peccadilloes—yet they are gross enough to be condemned under our "moral guardian," if another did them. What would be shame in plain folks like you and me is honour in Crispinus. What can you do when your criminal's accursed filthiness defies indictment?

But his
fantastic
follies can be
described.

They cul-
minated in
his purchase
of a mullet
at a fancy
value.

He bought a mullet for 6000 sesterces! It is true there was a pound of fish for every thousand sesterces—or so say they who make big things

Read
*Redemtum
a vitiis.*
Read *Deli-
cias viduæ.*

i.e., The
Emperor.

6

bigger in the telling. It was a master-stroke, I confess, if such a present gave him first place in an heirless old man's will. Or there was a further motive if he sent the offering to the grand mistress who comes abroad in a closed cavern with its wide windows open. But do not imagine anything of the sort. He bought it for himself. There are many scenes nowadays which make The Glutton's *Apicius.* Progress seem mean and frugal. Is a price like that to be paid for a thing of scales by this Crispinus, who began life with a rough Egyptian shirt tucked above his knees ? Why you might buy the man who caught it cheaper than the fish. Such a sum is what you pay for an estate in the provinces, more than you pay in our own Apulia. What must have been the banquets guzzled by "the Sovran Lord" himself, when all this money has gone only to provide a small corner of the side-dishes at a "little dinner" to be hickuped over by the purple-clad palace jester ? Now he is the Premier Knight, although he used to exercise his big voice in selling, as part of his damaged stock, the shads his countrymen. Begin, Calliope—but you may take a seat. We want no inspiration ; these are plain facts. Tell a simple story, maidens of Pieria ; I *Muses.* deserve something for having called you maids.

37–72. The folly of Crispinus introduces the greater scandal connected with another phenomenal fish at the Court of Domitian.

    When the last bearer of the Flavian name was still torturing a fainting world, and Rome was in *Domitian* bondage to Nero the Bald, before the home of *was nearly* *bald.* Venus reared on Ancona's Dorian cliffs, an Adriatic *On coast of* *Picenum.* turbot, of monstrous girth, fell into the nets and filled them. The clinging mass was big as the

monsters which are hidden under the Mæotian
ice, before it breaks up at last under the
sun's heat and washes them into the sluggish
gulf of Pontus, languid and lumpish with the long
idleness and cold. This prodigy the master of
boat and line designs for the High Pontiff. Who
indeed would dare to expose such a creature for
sale, or to buy it, when the very coast is peopled
with Informers? Before the fisherman had put his
clothes on, active "commissioners of sea-weed"
would be suing him, who would not hesitate to declare the fish was a stray which had long been fed
in the Emperor's preserves and having escaped
thence must be restored to its former owner. If we
believe a word of what Palpurius or Armillatus says,
there is not a rarity or prize swimming in all the
high seas which is not an imperial due. So the
thing must be a present, for fear it should be quite
lost.

Deadly autumn was passing away before the
frosts, ague was hoping for its three days' respite,
and ugly winter was howling and keeping the prize
fresh; nevertheless he hurries as if the south wind
was at his back. When the waters lay below him,
where the ruins of Alba still preserve the sacred
fire of Troy and the shrine of their own Vesta,
his entrance was blocked awhile by a wondering
crowd. As it gave way, the gracious hinges opened
the folding doorway, and excluded senators see
audience given—to the fish. Ushered to the King
of Men, our Picenian speaks :
     "Accept what is too great for a subject's

Marginal notes:
Sea of Azov.
The Emperor.
The pest of "informers."
The fisherman's haste.
i.e., at the quartan stage.
Degradation of the Senators and the prevalence of adulation.
The fisherman.

kitchen. Dedicate your day to Jollity, and hasten to distend your belly's sail with good cheer; devour a turbot which had been reserved for your own epoch. *The fish himself wished to be caught.*"

What could be more palpable? Yet the hearer pricked up his ears. There is no flattery too gross for a despot in his paradise.

Read saginis.

73-128.
Description of the Court favourites.

But there was no dish to fit the fish's measure. Thereon he calls a meeting of the senators whom he hated [and whose pallid cheeks wore all the wretchedness of a great man's friends. When the Usher shouted, "Hasten, My Lord is seated," the first to clutch his cloak and bustle forward was

Pegasus.

Pegasus, the new-made Overseer of astonished Rome. For what better than overseers were the Prefects in those days? Amongst them he was the best and purest expounder of the law, although he thought that Justice wanted no sword to cope with that age of awful wickedness.

Crispus.

Next comes cheery old age in the person of Crispus, good as he was eloquent, and a gentle spirit. What better adviser could there be for the lord of the world and its peoples if it were possible under that murderous pest to denounce cruelty and give honest advice! But there is mischief in a despot's ear. A courtier's life would tremble in a scales though the talk was to be only about the rain or heat or spring showers. Therefore Crispus never stemmed the torrent, nor was he patriot enough to speak out the free thoughts of his heart or to stake his life upon the truth. This was how so many winters and fourscore summers had passed over his head : this was the armour that saved him even in that court.

Acilius Glabrio and his son.

The next who hurried up was one as old as he, Acilius, with the son whom an end awaited at his sovereign's hands, so unmerited, so cruel and untimely.　But the union of noble birth and long life we have come to reckon a miracle (that is why I should prefer to be numbered among the *Sons of Soil*).　What profit was it to him that when he stript for the chase (in Alba's circus) he could pin the bears of Africa in close combat ?　There is no man nowadays who is blinded by the policy of Nobles, no man to admire the antiquated cunning of a Brutus.　(In the Age of Beards it was easy work to cheat kings.)

Executed through Domitian's jealousy of his prowess.

The first M. Brutus.

Rubrius.

Montanus.

Crispinus.

Pompeius.

Fuscus.

Catullus.

A blind profligate.

Baseborn though he was, not a whit more cheerful was the face of Rubrius, notorious for an old offence too foul for words, but more brazen than a sodomite turned satirist.　Then came Montanus —or his belly, lagging under a load of guts ; Crispinus, reeking in the early morning with perfumes enough to disinfect two corpses ; Pompeius, who burnt with a yet more savage lust for slitting throats by little whispered words ; Fuscus, who was reserving his flesh to be carrion for Dacian vultures, and dreamed of battle in his marble mansion ; crafty Veiento with murderous Catullus, who lusted after flesh which he could not see, a creature monstrous even in these prodigious days, the blinking sycophant, the filthy parasite from the Bridge only fit to beg alms at the wheel's side in the Arician Road and throw coaxing kisses after the disappear-

Seduction of a niece of Domitian in her childhood.

ing chariots. Not one of them all was more startled by the turbot : turning to the *left* he delivered himself of his wonder, whilst the creature was lying on his *right.* Even so would he praise the fencing and thrusting of a gladiator, or the stage-traps that threw live boys up to the awning's level.

The rivalry of Catullus and Veiento in adulation.

Veiento is not to be beaten ; but prophesying (like a man distraught, under the smarting of Bellona's gad-fly) he declares :

Veiento's random augury.

" Here you see the great omen of a grand and brilliant victory : some royal prisoner will be taken, or some Arviragus will be tumbled from his British car. Look ! the creature is a foreigner. See you not his ridge of spikes set for insurrection ? " Our Fabricius told everything except the turbot's origin and age.

? a name invented on the spur of the moment.

Name of Catullus.

129-154.
Senators insulted by a mock Council of State.

" What then is your vote ? " it is asked. " Shall the fish be divided ? "

" Nay," cries Montanus, " out upon the shame ! Let a lordly dish be built, with a low wall to bound the wide circumference. We want the miraculous aid of a great Prometheus. Haste you to make ready the wheel and clay ; and from this day forward let a guild of potters attend the Cæsar's progress."

The measure and the man prevailed : he had known the old court luxury and Nero's orgies prolonged to midnight, and the unnatural gluttony renewed when bellies were steaming with wine. No man of my own time was better trained in the science of gormandizing. He could decide at the first bite whether an oyster had been grown at

By emetics.

Circeii, on the Lucrine rock, or upon Rutupiæ's beds, and he would tell you a sea-urchin's origin at the first glance. *At Richborough.*

The emperor rises, and the dismissal of the council is the signal for departure to the senators whom the Great Captain dragged to his Alban citadel in fear and forced haste, as if he were to give them news about the Chatti or the savage Sigambri, or as if a despatch had arrived bearing the ominous sign of Haste. Would that he had chosen to spend in like fooleries the whole of that cruel time wherein he robbed the State of so many bright and famous lives, himself unhurt and unchastised. Yet the retribution did come after he grew to be a terror to the Great Unwashed. Here was the fatal error of a career drenched in gentle blood. *Domitian.* *German tribes.* *Of the Lamiæ.*

SATIRE V.

AN EPISTLE.

DINNER AT A GREAT HOUSE.

<table>
<tr>
<td>

1–11.
Remon-
strance
with a
professional
diner-out.

The mean-
ness of the
profession.
</td>
<td>

IF you are not ashamed of your choice and still
hold your theory that the whole duty of man is to
eat the bread of charity, if you can tolerate affronts
such as even Sarmentus or the cringing Gabba would
have resented at one of Cæsar's mixed dinner-
parties, I shall be afraid to trust even your sworn
evidence. Nothing can live harder than the belly ;
and suppose that you have lacked that precise
amount which is required to fill your vacuum, is
there not an empty beggar's stand? cannot you find
a bridge and half a mat ? Do you lay such store
by a dinner-giver's insolence? Is Hunger so im-
portunate, when it were less shame for it to crouch
in the streets and gnaw the scraps thrown to dogs ?
</td>
<td>

For begging.

Read *cum
possit.*
</td>
</tr>
<tr>
<td>

12–23.
Dinner an
inadequate
return for
the services
performed.
</td>
<td>

First of all, remember that in being bidden to
take your place you are receiving payment-in-full
for all past service. All you will reap from your
grand friendship is the meal ; and, few as his instal-
ments are, your patron charges them against you.
So if it suits his fancy after two months of neglect
to send for his dependant in order that an unfilled
</td>
<td></td>
</tr>
</table>

couch may not have its third place idle, "Give me," says he, "your company at dinner." Here is the crown of your hopes; what more do you want? Trebius has good enough reason for breaking his rest and letting his shoe-strings go untied; for he fears that all the crowd of callers will have done their round before the stars are settled for the day, or (yet earlier) while the icy wain of Boötes is wheeling its slow circling course.

Description of the dinner.

What a dinner it is after all! Wine that greasy wool would scorn to absorb, that makes the drinker mad as a dervish. The entertainment opens with raillery—to be followed very shortly by volleys of drinking-cups, casualties, and the wiping of wounds with crimsoned napkins. Such is the scene whenever the fight, once started between you and the troop of freedmen, takes Saguntine flagons for the missiles of its fury: meantime your host is drinking wine strained when consuls wore their hair long, and holds in his hand the juice of grapes which were trampled in the Social Wars. Though he would never send a mouthful to an ailing friend, to-morrow he will sip some rarity from the Alban or Setine Hills with its name and label obliterated by age and with the soot accumulated on its old jars, such wine as Thrasea and Helvidius would drink when they put on chaplets for the birthdays of Cassius and the Bruti.

Difference in the wines.

For linements.

About 90 B.C.

As republicans and as enemies of the authority of the Cæsars.

37–48. Difference in drinking vessels.

For Virro's own use there is embossed amber and goblets studded with emerald: but even gold is too precious for your hands; or if it ever is trusted to you, there is an attendant told off to count the

The host.

gems and keep an eye upon the points of your finger-nails. "No offence is meant," says he, "but the fine jasper there is famous." For Virro follows the fashion, and for the sake of his cups robs his rings of the gems which the favoured rival of jealous Iarbas once wore upon the face of his scabbard. The four-nozzled mug which you will drain is named after the Cobbler of Beneventum, with its battered face mutely crying "Broken glass to change for Brimstone!"

Æneas.

Jews exchanged sulphur matches for damaged glass vessels.

49–53.
Difference in the water.

If your patron's stomach is feverish with too much eating and drinking, water is fetched him that has been boiled and cooled again in Getic snow. Was I complaining but now that the wine was different? Why, there is privilege in waters.

Nero's invention.

53–65.
Difference in the servants.

Your cup will be served by a negro courier, or a bony-handed tawny Moor whom it would be ominous to meet at midnight as you passed along the tombs upon the Latin Road. Behind your host stands the choicest flower of Ionic youth, bought for a price exceeding all the riches of warlike Tullus, or of Ancus, or (cutting the list short) all the worldly wealth of the Seven Kings of Rome. Boys are dear nowadays, so you must look to a negro for your Ganymede when you feel thirsty. The lad who has cost so much money does not know how to serve poor men. (Indeed his beauty and his youth justify his airs.) When does he come your way? or answer to your call with the warm water or cold? Why, he is sulky at waiting upon an old retainer, and because yon

Superstitious horror of black objects.

have your wants and are reclining while he must stand.

63–79.
Difference in bread.
Every great house is full of bumptious slaves. Look how yonder fellow muttered when he handed the bread, hardly breakable as it was, only bits of lumpy meal grown mouldy, made to agonize your teeth and prevent their meeting. Soft white bread of the finest flour is reserved for the master. Let none violate that bread-pan's sanctity! Forget not to keep a watch over your hands. Suppose that you do take heart of impudence, there is some one at your elbow to make you drop the plunder.

"Saucy guest," he says, "kindly fill your belly from the usual tray, and learn to know the colour of your proper bread."

"Was it really for this," you cry, "that I have so often left my wife in bed, and raced across the heights of the frozen Esquiline under the fretting spring sky's vicious hail while the big drops of water were streaming from my cloak?"

80–85.
Difference in the fish.
Look at the lobster which is being carried to the host! what a length of body—too big for the dish! What a fine bed of asparagus it lies in! What a tail it turns up at the company as it is borne aloft by the hands of a tall waiting-man! There is a shrivelled crab for you, served on a mean plate, with half an egg for trimmings; what a dish to set before—a ghost!

86–91.
Difference in oils.
The master souses his fish in pure Venafran oil, but the sickly cabbage which is offered to the unhappy guest stinks of lamp-grease. Your sauce-boats are filled with the trash imported on

some negro potentate's beaky-nosed canoes;—very good reason why nobody at Rome goes into the bath with a Black Prince, and why his subjects at home are not afraid of snake bites.

Because the snakes are afraid to bite them.

92–106.
Luxury in fish-eating.

Your host will have a mullet which has been sent from Corsica or rocky Tauromenium, since all our own waters have been ransacked and long ago emptied under the ravages of gluttony; the busy nets of the Trade probe the depths of every neighbouring sea and will not allow our Tuscan fry to grow into fish. So the provinces supply our kitchen and export the presents for fortune-hunter Lenas to purchase and for his dear Aurelia to send—back to market. The lamprey set before Virro was the pride of Sicily's pool: for when the South Wind stays at home and sits down under cover to dry his dripping wings, the dare-devil nets brave the mid-waters of Charybdis. For you an eel is reserved, the first-cousin to a long snake, or perhaps a Tiber pike frost-bitten and spotted, a true riverside native, fattened on gushing sewage and a practised explorer of the vaults in the slums.

Because she prefers the money.

Near Sicilian coast.

106–113.
Parenthetic advice to the Host.

(Here I would say a few words to the host, if he would kindly give me hearing. Nobody expects such presents as Seneca would send to his humble friends, or asks you to emulate kindly Piso's or Cotta's lavishness. Once, indeed, men reckoned charity higher than honours and office. Now all we ask of you is to drop your rank at dinner. Do this, and follow the fashion if you will; be *your own* benefactor and retrench *your charities*.)

Before the host is the liver of a goose, a capon

big as a goose, and a smoking boar worthy of Meleager's steel. Then truffles will follow, if it be spring-time and if welcome thunderstorms provide the extra dish. "Libya may keep its corn," cries your Gourmand, "and release its oxen from the plough; only let it send the truffles."

To give your temper the last trial, you see a carver skipping and harlequinading all the time with his waving knife until he finishes his instructor's "exercise." Indeed, there are high rules of art which lay down one style for carving hares and another for chickens.

If you ever try to so much as open your lips, as though you had a third name of your own, you will be pulled out by the heels, like Cacus after Hercules had drubbed him. When does Virro drink to you or take the cup which has been touched by your lips? Which amongst you is so reckless or so desperate as to ask his Majesty to take wine? Yes, there are many words which may not be spoken by men who wear shabby cloaks. But if a knight's fortune came to you by gift of some god or of some "forked biped" great as God and kinder than Fate, how big your littleness would grow!—and the friendship of Vírro would grow too!

"Wait on Trebius," he would ṣay; "serve Trebius. Dear fellow, will you have a slice from that loin?"

No, it is the silver pieces that he compliments—they are his "dear fellows."

If you would be a power and courted by

Side notes:

114–119. Offensively luxurious eating of rich men.

120–124. Antics of professional carvers.

125–137. Nothing esteemed but riches.

The hunter in Calydon. Supposed to bring on truffles. Alledius.

Prænomen, nomen, and cognomen.

400,000 sests.

137-145.
Flattery of
rich persons
without
natural
heirs, and
(in a less
degree) of
all rich
persons.

powers, let there be "no young Æneas playing in your halls," nor a yet better-loved daughter. Barren wives make their husbands popular and valued. Still (now that you are rich) even if your good woman breeds and puts three boys at a birth into your paternal arms, Virro will be charmed with the lively brood. He will send for a green doublet, or tiny nuts, or a copper, if it is asked for, whenever the young touter comes to table.

145-148.
Difference in
"savouries."

Suspicious fungus for the humble friends : for the master a mushroom—but genuine, like those which Claudius ate before the one presented by his wife after which he gave up eating altogether.

A.D. 56.
Agrippina.

149-155.
Difference in
fruit.

For himself and his fellows Virro will order apples to be served—though the smell is all that you are to taste of them—such as enriched the year-long autumn-time of Phæacia, apples which you might think had been stolen from the African sisters. You will be regaled with the rind of such a crab as is gnawed on the Rampart by the creature in helmet and shield, who is learning under the whip how to pitch his javelin from the goat's hairy back.

As described
in Odyssey.
Hesperides,
guardians of
the golden
apples.
i.e., a
performing
monkey.

156-165.
All the
insults have
been inten-
tional.

You might think, perhaps, that Virro wishes to save expense. No, his object is to wound your feelings. What comedy or farce is funnier than "Stomach in Distress?" The meaning of his conduct is—if you know it not—to force you to pour out your anger in weeping and to gnash your long clenched jaws. Yourself, you think yourself a free man and a grand friend's guest He counts you the slave of his kitchen and its savoury odours. Nor is he far out in his reckoning.

Who so destitute as to tolerate such patronage a second time, if he had the right in childhood to wear the Tuscan jewel or the poor man's simple badge of leather ?

Badges of free-birth.

166–173.
Submission to them justifies them.

You are beguiled by the hope of faring sumptuously. "Think, he will give us that half-eaten hare," you say, "or a bit from the boar's haunch. Presently the little capon will come our way." For that is why you sit awaiting the word with your crust ready, untasted, and made ready for action.

To serve as spoon.

The deeper degradation which awaits the parasite.

He is right to treat you in this fashion. If you can endure the last insults, they are justified. One day you will shave your crown and let men thump it, nor will you be afraid of the heavy whip. Then you will really earn your dinners and deserve your friendships.

As a common clown.

SATIRE VI.

THE WOMEN OF ROME.

1-20.
There are no signs of chastity remaining except the tradition of its existence in the Golden Age.

ONCE (when Saturn was king) I believe that Chastity sojourned upon earth, and was visible awhile, in the days when a cold cavern gave men their humble dwelling-place and one common shelter enclosed the sacred Fire and Hearth-god, the cattle and their master; when the hill-man's wife made him his bed from leaves and straw and skins of the wild beasts about them. How different a woman was she from a Cynthia, or a girl whose bright eyes were troubled over her dead sparrow! She supported teats which could give their fill to lusty babes, and (often) she would be rougher than her acorn-reeking husband. Yea, life was not the same then, when the world was young and the heavens newly created; when, unbegotten and un-conceived, men were fashioned of clay or sprang from the riven oaks. Even under Jove's reign you will perhaps find many traces (or some traces) of the ancient chastity; none after the hair had grown on Jove's chin, or after Greeks had learnt to forswear themselves by one another's heads; but only in the days when cabbages and apples were safe from thieves, and men lived with their garden-plots un-

In the Golden Age.

The mistress of Propertius.

The mistress of Catullus, who lost her pet bird.

fenced. Step by step, Honesty soon withdrew to the gods above, and with her went Chastity, so that the two sisters were not divided even in their flight.

Astræa.

21-37.
Postumus Ursidius is exhorted not to persevere in his proposed marriage.

It is an ancient and time-honoured custom, Postumus, to defile a neighbour's bed and to brave the Spirit who consecrates the nuptial posts : every other sin was produced in good time by the Iron Age, but the firstfruits of adultery came in early with the generation of Silver. But forgetting this, and forgetting the times we live in, you are preparing your marriage covenant, settlements, and betrothal. The barber-artist is already trimming your hair, and perhaps the pledge has already passed from your finger. Once you had your wits, Postumus: can you then be a marrying man ? Tell me which Fury is driving you ? which of her snaky terrors ? Can you submit to any she-tyrant, when there is so much good hemp in the world, so many windows open at their dizzy elevations, and the Bridge of Æmilius offering its neighbourly relief ? Or (if you like none of the many ways of escape) do you not prefer to fondle the Pugio who does not treat you to curtain lectures, dun for dues, and rate your sleepiness or slackness ?

After the Iron Age.

Ribbeck.

38-59.
A man of less experience amongst women than Postumus might know better than expect to find purity at Rome.

But Postumus approves the Julian law, and is set on raising up a darling heir, even at the sacrifice of all the monster pigeons, bearded mullets, and other compliments from the market-place. Nothing is incredible when Postumus is pairing, when the most notorious cuckold-maker in Rome is really holding out his silly nose for the marriage-halter, though he has often been, like the

Imposing penalties on celibacy.

Presents from fortune-hunters to the heir-less.

7

unhappy Latinus, shut up in the "lover's box."
Moreover, you must know that Postumus looks
for the old-fashioned purity in his wife? Come,
doctors, rip the poor lunatic's vein right open!
Why, you fastidious creature! you must throw
yourself flat on Jupiter's Tarpeian rock, and
sacrifice a gilded heifer to Juno, *when* you have
found a modest matron. So scarce are the women
who are qualified to lay a finger on the fillets of
Ceres, or whom their own fathers would not be
afraid to kiss. If you will, then, weave the garland
for your doorposts, and stretch rich festoons over
your threshold. What? one man enough for your
Hiberina! Sooner will you force her to be contented with one eye.

There is a girl, it is true, living on the family
estate, who has a mighty reputation. Let her
make it good at Gabii or Fidenæ, by living the
same life there which she has led upon the farm.
Then I will believe in the family farm. Still, who
says that nothing went on among the hills or caves?
Have Jupiter and Mars forgotten their cunning?

In all the promenades can you find one woman
worth wishing for? do the benches of the whole
theatre hold one being whom you might love and
trust; one whom you could separate from the
rest? When womanish Bathyllus "breaks down" in
the Leda Pantomime, Tuccia cannot contain herself;
Appula "puts herself in his place"; and in quick
response Thymele heaves a long-drawn, wistful sigh:
yes, the simple Thymele learns her lesson. To
relieve their dulness, others assume the mask, wand,

Margin notes:

Perhaps the scene in a play acted by Latinus, cf. Sat. i. 36. Like Fal-staff?

i.e., who are chaste.

For a wed-ding.

The smallest country towns are no better than Rome.

60–81. The devo-tion of women to the voluptuous spectacles of the stage, and to the persons of the actors.

and drawers of Accius when the stage-curtains are packed away for Vacation and the theatres are shut and empty, so that no ranting is heard (except in the law courts), and when there are five long months between the two Festivals. The gestures of Urbicus in the Autonoë Burlesque draw laughter and earn him needy Ælia's affections; other women pay long prices for the favours of "legitimate comedians"; there are some who spoil a leading tenor's notes; Hispulla's fancy leans to tragedy. (Can you expect your mere man of letters to find a mistress?)

You are taking a wife only to make some harp-player, an Echion or a Glaphyrus, or some chorus-player like Ambrosius, the father of your child. Let us fix lines of woodwork along the narrow streets, and deck the posts and doorway with a huge laurel-tree, so that, under the gauze curtains and tortoise-shell, Lentulus may see his noble son and heir reproduce a gladiator's features.

Hippia, the senator's bride, followed her Bravo to Pharos and Nile and the storied walls of Lagus, so that Canopus itself cried shame on the wonders of Roman wickedness. Without a thought for home, for husband, or for sister, and without tenderness for her country, she hardened her heart and deserted her weeping children—deserted (which is much more startling) Paris and the play. Though she had been pillowed in down and luxury as a little girl in her father's house and had lain in cradles of fancy wooden-work, she laughed at the sea, as long ago she had laughed at honour (the

All tastes are catered for.

Advice to intending husbands.

82–113. *Even more monstrous was the infatuation of a lady of rank for a coarse gladiator whom she followed to Egypt.*

Popular actor.

Quintilian.

Wedding preparations.

i.e., in the cradle.

The popular actor in Domitian's time.

loss of which does not count for much among your women-about-town).   So she braved the tossings and the roarings of the Ionian waters with an unquailing heart, though she was to pass from Sea to Sea.   If there is a fair and honest reason for facing danger, chilly terror paralyses a woman's heart, and her unsteady feet refuse their support.   Her courage is only called up by base adventures. If a husband gives the word, it becomes a hardship to go on board; the bilge-water is noisome and the sky above her seems to reel.   A lady who elopes is never sea-sick, but the wife travelling with her husband covers him with vomit.   Your adulteress messes with the sailors, walks about the deck, and delights in handling the rough hawsers.

And what, after all, was the youth and beauty which captivated Hippia so that she consented to be called "the gladiator's girl?"   Already her Sergius had taken to scraping his chin, and a gashed arm had set him hoping for his discharge.   Upon his face, moreover, there were many blemishes—the scar (for instance) from his helmet, the huge wen between his nostrils, and the acrid rheum always trickling from his eye.   Still he remained a gladiator: this makes such as he more beautiful than Hyacinthus; this is what she thought better than family or fatherland, better than sister or husband. The steel blade is what they are enamoured of, and this very Sergius, had he accepted the wooden sword, would have sunk downwards to a husband's level.

But why trouble about the doings of a Hippia in

The perversity of the sex.

The coarse taste of bad women.

As a symbol of discharge. Veiento.

114–132.
The debased
lust of
Messalina,
wife of the
Emperor
Claudius.

a subject's home? Turn you to the omnipotent
gods-on-earth and hearken to the wrongs which a
Claudius endured. When his consort had discovered
that her lord was sleeping, this royal strumpet took
courage to change her chamber in the palace for
vulgar bedding, courage to put on the night-walker's
hood, and would start with one serving-woman for
retinue ; yes, she disguised her raven locks under
an auburn wig, entered the stuffy brothel with
its shabby coverlet, and took the empty stall
reserved for herself. Baring her gilded nipples
she took her stand under the letters of her alias
Lycisca, and exposed the body which gave birth to
Britannicus the Noble. There she entertained all
comers with graciousness (and exacted the fee); nor
did she shrink from the rude endearments of successive customers. Presently, when it was time for
the good man of the house to dismiss his staff, she
started laggingly, and (though she could do no
more) managed to be the last to shut her door;
with the passion still raging unappeased in her
heart she took her departure, overworked but un-
contented. With the defilement of dirtied face
and the filthiness of lamp-blacks, she carried the
stenches of the brothel to her marriage-bed.

133–141.
In spite of
their gross
superstition,
their
inchastity,
and worse
faults, rich
women are
tolerated by
their
husbands.

Why tell about love-potions, charms, or the
drugs mixed and administered to step-sons? Even
fouler are the crimes into which they are driven
by woman's domineering spirit ; and lust is the
least of their sins. Do you ask, then, why Cæsen-
nia's husband bears witness to her virtue? Because
she brought him ten times ten thousand sesterces

The
Emperors.

—that is his fee for proclaiming her an honest woman. It is not the arrows of love which wither him, nor its torch which scorches him. The shafts are barbed, and the fire is kindled in his heart, by the magic force of her money. She pays for the right of doing as she will, and she may make signals or write love-letters under her husband's eyes : rich wives of sordid husbands may live like single women.

Would you know why Sertorius burns with desire for Bibula? Sift the truth, and you will see that he loves his wife's beauty, not herself. Only let three wrinkles show themselves, let her skin become dry and shrivelled, let her teeth blacken or her eyes shrink, and the coarse upstart will cry out, " Pack up your baggage and begone. You have become loathsome to me, and you are always wiping your nose. Begone at once, and make haste about it. Your successor is coming, who is not a sniveller."

But before her charms are faded, she is hot and furious, rules her husband like a queen, and demands sheep-farms (with their shepherds) at one place, vineyards at another, and (besides such trifles !) all the slaves in town, bought by the prisonful. Anything which is not his own but some neighbour's must be purchased for her. Thus in the winter-month, when seafaring Jason and his

ship-shape Argonauts are shut and blocked against their frescoed walls by the whitened booths, she carries away rich spoil of crystal vases, goes on to the agates, and finishes with the famous diamond made more precious by having decked Berenice's

A fair called Sigillaria, held in a Temple of Neptune where the walls were frescoed with scenes from the adventures of Jason.

finger—the bribe which barbarian Agrippa paid for his sister's love in the country where bare-footed Royalty keeps the Sabbath holy, and where a time-honoured forbearance allows pigs to live long in the land.

161-183.
Such charms or merits as women may possess are more than compensated by their consciousness and arrogance.

"Is there not one out of so many whom I think worthy to be a wife?" Let her possess beauty, grace, and wealth, let her be a fruitful mother, let her point to rows of ancestors marshalled along her porticoes, and let her be of virtue sterner than any of the Sabine women (rushing with dishevelled locks and making peace between the armies):— that is, let her be the greatest rarity on earth, like a real black swan—who could tolerate Perfection in a wife? Give me some country maiden of Venusia rather than Cornelia herself, the mother of the Gracchi, if a contemptuous brow is to go with her lofty virtues, and if her family honours are reckoned in her marriage-portion. Away, if you please, with your Hannibalic victories and your stormings of the camp of Syphax—get you gone, you and all your Carthages.

As in pictures.

Achievements of her ancestors.

Humility in women inculcated by the sorrow which came upon Niobe for her pride.

"Apollo, have mercy," cried Amphion, "and Diana lay aside thy arrows. The children are innocent; slay the guilty mother." None the less, Apollo stretched his bow. So it was that Niobe carried to burial the bodies of her troop of children, and the father's with them—Niobe who thought herself grander than Latona's offspring, as well as more prolific than the White Sow. How can you prize a woman's virtue or beauty if she is always making a merit of them? The richest and rarest treasure

Found by Æneas with thirty young.

upon earth, it cannot give delight if the taint of
pride turns honey sweetness to the bitterness of
aloes. Where is the man so abject as not to
shrink from the woman whom he extols with
adulation, or not to detest her for the best part of
the day ?

184–199.
The odious
affectation of
Greek
phrases and
fashions.

There are some things small in themselves
which pass the endurance of husbands. What is
more nauseous than not a woman amongst them
being satisfied with her native charms unless the
Tuscan stuff has been manufactured into shoddy
Greek; the "home-grown Pelignian" into "pure
Athenian?" They talk nothing but Greek (though
it is a greater reproach for Romans to be ignorant in Latin). Greek is their language for alarm
or anger, for joy or trouble, even for the heart's
most secret confidences. Greek endearments are
the climax ! Still you may permit such fooleries
in girls. Shall the patter be still kept up by one who
is standing the siege of fourscore years and six ?
Greek words on an old woman's lips are rank
filthiness. How many times does naughtiness
like ζωή καὶ ψυχή crop up in her talk ? The language of chambering is aired in public. Appetite cannot but respond to the vile blandishing
notes which give tentacles to lust ; but it responds
only to subside in loathing. The words may be
spoken with all the softness of Hæmus or Carpo-
phorus, but every one of her years is recorded on
the speaker's face.

200–205.
The wasteful
expenses of

If you do not intend to love the woman con-
tracted and united to you by legal instruments, I

the wedding ceremonies.

can see no reason for marrying her ;—no reason for wasting the wedding supper or the sweet cakes (which you must bestow on your gorged friends at the final courtesies), or the fee which is paid for the first night's favours with the coins of Dacian and German victories which lie glittering on the rich plate.

Commemorative pieces struck by Domitian.

206-223. The uxorious husband must expect to be fleeced and bullied, and to have no voice in the management of his own household.

If you are possessed by a husband's fond devotion, and your soul is given over to one person's keeping, bow your head at once and put your neck to the collar. You will never find a mistress who has mercy on her lover. Though she catch the flame herself, she triumphs in torturing and spoiling her lover ; so that a good and model husband bears all the heavier burden. You will never bestow a gift without her consent, never effect a sale if she protests against it, or a purchase which she disapproves. She will dispose of your likings and dislikings : your friend must be turned away in his old age from the door which saw the first down on his chin. Though whoremongers and training-masters are free to make their own wills, and though that much of privilege is extended to the Arena, you will have to write down to dictation more than one rival's name in your list of heirs.

i.e., to gladiators.

Woman's cruelty and injustice.

"Crucify the slave !" she cries.

"What was his fault deserving the punishment ?" you ask. "Who gave the information ? where is the witness ? Give the man a hearing. Deliberation cannot be too slow when a human life is in question."

"Dolt !" she cries ! "so you call slaves human ?

Granted that he has done nothing : you hear my will and command. Let the wish be reason enough !"

So she queens it over her husband; but soon she abdicates her present throne, shifts from one home to another, and wears her bridal veil to tatters. Then she starts off again, and retraces the path that leads back to the bed which but now she scorned. She turns away while the decorations are fresh upon the doors, the draperies unremoved, and the boughs on the threshold still unwithered. This is how the numbers mount up, and how husbands are manufactured, eight in five years—an achievement worth recording on her tombstone.

You may abandon all hopes of peace so long as your wife's mother is spared. She initiates her daughter in the joys of stripping and spoiling husbands, and in the art of replying to the seducer's letters in a strain which is far from being innocent or girlish. She it is who cheats your watchmen or corrupts them ; finally, she summons the doctor to the side of her malingering daughter, and has the stifling bedclothes tumbled. Meantime, hiding in concealment and secrecy, the paramour frets and fidgets at delay whilst he makes ready for action. But of course you expect the mother to train her daughter to a purity not practised by herself. Why, the old bawd makes a profit by training a daughter to walk in her mother's ways.

As if the wife was feverish and could not see her husband.

There is hardly a case at law where the dispute was not raised by some woman. Manilia will be prosecutrix—if she is not defendant. They are

their own lawyers and draw out their own plead-
ings, and are quite ready to instruct a Celsus An eminent lawyer.
on the point at issue and the lines of argu-
ment.

246–267.
Women
forget the
delicacy of
their sex
and go into
training as
amateur
gladiators
(perhaps to
reduce cor-
pulence as in
the case of
Parisian
ladies).

We are all familiar with their purple wrappers
and "wrestling-ointment for the use of ladies." We
have all seen the "pupils'-post" taking its punishment whilst it is pierced by quick pikes and buf-
feted by the shield. Our matron goes through the
whole exercise, and establishes her right to blow a
trumpet at Flora's festival, except that she has set her
heart on real business and is in training for a fight
in earnest. What modesty can the woman show
who wears a helmet and turns her back upon her
own sex! She dotes upon a coat-of-mail; but for
all that she would refuse to become a man herself.
(Our sex's pleasures are less piquant.) What an
honour to your house if your wife's assets are put up
to sale—her belt, gauntlets, and plumes, with the
short left-legging! or what happiness if she turns
to a different field of exploit and sells her greaves!
(These are the delicate creatures who sweat under
the weight of gauze, whilst a silken vest galls their
flesh.) Mark you now! what a cry when she
strikes the blow home in the approved form! what
a massive helmet bows her neck! what a bundle of
legging-leather rests against her haunches! Now
enjoy your laugh when she puts away her arms and
sits down to do — what only women do sitting.
Answer me this question, you noble daughters of
the lines of Lepidus, Blind Metellus, or Fabius
Gurges—when did you ever see such a panoply

When women appeared naked.

Their conduct is worse than that of the low women with whom the gladiators themselves consort.

Ancient worthies.

upon any gladiator's wench? or hear the wife of Asylus grunting against the training-post?

A gladiator.

268-278.
Curtain lectures.

The wife's jealousy is a hypocritical screen for her own infidelity.

The bed which contains a wife is always plagued with disputation and mutual abuse, and it is the last place for a quiet night. Then is the time when she comes down upon her husband with more fury than a tigress robbed of her cubs; guilty as her own conscience is, she pretends to groan for him, curses his favourites, and invents a rival so as to bewail a grievance. Her tears are always plentiful and always ready in their place, awaiting the word to flow as she directs them. You believe that it is all her fondness, and flatter yourself, poor cuckold, and dry her tears with your kisses; but what notes and letters you would read if the jealous traitress had her desk opened!

279-285.
Even detection does not silence her tongue.

Or, again, suppose that she is caught in the arms of a slave—or knight.

Be kind enough, Quintilian, to plead some palliation.

As a rhetorician

"No, you have posed me," he replies.

The lady must plead her own cause.

"Long ago," she begins, "we struck the bargain that you should do what you liked, and that I could also please myself. Yes, you may cry aloud for heaven and earth to change their places; but I have my wants."

There is nothing on earth so impudent as a woman taken in the act. Detection lends her all the airs and indignation of injured innocence.

286-313.
Poverty, the old safe-

Would you trace these enormities to their source and origin? The women of old Latium were

preserved in purity by reason of their lowly estate.
Cottage homes could not be tainted with vice—
labour was too hard and the hours of sleep too short ;
women's hands were horny with plying Tuscan wool ;
and Hannibal was pressing onwards to the city, while
their husbands kept guard at the Colline fort. Now
we are labouring under the evils of a long peace.
More cruel than war, the yoke of luxury wreaks
its vengeance on the conquerors of the world.
From the day when poverty passed away from
Rome, every sin and crime has made its home
amongst you ; and your hills have been swamped
by Sybaris on one side, on the other by Rhodes
and Miletus, by Tarentum with its roses and riotous living.   Money was the bawd who first introduced our neighbours' vices ; enervating wealth
and corrupting luxury first debauched the generations.   Can there be nicety when lust and
sottishness are met together ? Lewd imagination
plays pranks with nature where a woman worries

huge oysters in the midnight hours, splashes the
foaming unguents into undiluted wine, and uses
the oil-pot for a drinking-cup, while her dizzy brain
sees the lights double, the roof reeling, and the
tables dancing.   After this can you fail to imagine
how the Mooress sniffs and sneers, or what Tullia
(foster-sister to that celebrated Mooress) says when

she passes the ancient shrine of Chastity ? They
make it the halting-place for their litters at night—
their place of convenience ; mock the holy image
with ingenious devisings, and play their unwomanish
antics under Luna's eyes.   Then they depart to

their homes ; but next morning when you go to visit a grand friend, you must pass through the trail which your wife has left behind her.

314-345. The atrocious travesties of religious rites.

The mysteries of the Good Goddess are open secrets :—the fife which sets the women going, the wine and music together which transport them, until they toss their loose hair in frantic fury and shriek aloud like Bacchantes to the God of Lechers. Priapus. What a furnace in their hearts ! what cries from their lips ! what convulsions in their bodies when the lust begins to throb ! Saufeia throws away her crown, makes a match with common prostitutes— and wins it ! but she bows in turn to Medullina's better style. Native merit counts above birth in the Ladies' Competition ! There will be no deceptions there, no make-believe, but true realism, such as would kindle Priam's time-extinguished ardours or Nestor's impotence. Here you may see lust which cannot wait its time ; the Woman pure and simple. The cry is raised, and repeated from every corner of the den—" The hour has come—bring in men." But the paramour is still asleep : she bids the young man take his hood and come at once. In default of him a raid is made upon the slaves. If there is no hope of them, a common water-carrier is hired and serves her turn. If he is missing, and men cannot be provided, lust will find out a way, nor will the woman make demur. Would that our time-honoured rites and public ceremonies might be celebrated without such desecrations ! But every Indian and Negro knows the name of the singing-woman who introduced a defilement (twice bigger than the volume which Cæsar attacked Cato with) into that holy place, where a buck-mouse feels that he is an intruder, and where a curtain is drawn (by order) over every painting which portrays the male form. But that dates from the day when men mocked not at heaven, and none dared to pass a jest on pious Numa's earthen cup and baked dish or the brittle platters fashioned from Vatican clay. Where is the shrine now which some Clodius does not enter?

Allusion to Clodius and to Cæsar's literary attack upon Cato, and (probably) his relations with Cato's sister.

Contrast the ancient piety which respected religious relics.

The profaner.

346–348.
It is hopeless to watch a wife.

I can hear the advice which my old friends are giving all the while : " Put the bolt up and shut her in." But who shall watch my watchers. My wife begins with them, wise woman !

349–351.
Vice is not the privilege of rank or wealth.

High or low, the vice of women is nowadays the same. Nor is she who tramps the dark paving-stones a-foot better than another who is borne aloft on the necks of stalwart Syrians.

352–365.
The foolish display made by poor women.

In order that Ogulnia may attend the games she must hire the very gown to her back :—the litter and cushion, the retinue and followers, the nurses and auburn-haired girl (to run on messages) must all be jobbed for the occasion. Nevertheless she lavishes the few remaining scraps of family plate and the last silver vessels upon greasy athletes. Many women feel the pinch of want at home, but not one of them respects the laws of poverty, or cuts her life to the given and settled measure. Men, however, do consider their interests (now and again), and the Ant has gradually taught them to be afraid of hunger and cold. Woman is a prodigal who does not see that her fortune is wasting away under her eyes, nor does she count the cost of her pleasures, just as though money would sprout again from the exhausted coffer and she could always be helping herself from an undiminished heap.

Thirteen lines omitted.

379-397. The lengths to which women were carried by their passion for public singers.

If your wife is musical, nothing can save the virtue of any man who has to trade upon his voice at the prætors' games. She is always fingering his instruments; and from one end to the other his lyre is studded with her gifts of sardonyx; she goes over every string with the tingling plectrum, stock-in-trade of languishing Hedymeles : that dear plectrum is her companion, her solace, and the pet which receives her kisses. One who was a daughter of the Lamian race and bore their exalted name went with her offering of meal and wine to ask Janus and Vesta whether her "Pollio" might hope to reward his harp-strings' efforts with the crown of oak-leaves? Could she do more if her husband were on a bed of sickness? what more for her own son, when the doctors shook their heads? She stood before the shrine and thought no shame to veil her head in the cause of a harp-player; she repeated the words in due ritual, and bent in pallor over the lamb's opened entrails. Tell me, I pray thee, Father Janus, tell me, thou most ancient of the gods, dost thou vouchsafe answer to such prayers? Time must hang heavily in heaven; there must be, so far as I can see, no business to be done amongst you gods if one woman is to take thy opinion on comedians, and another shall wish to recommend her favourite tragedian. The soothsayer's leg-veins will be swollen with over-work !

398-412.
The busy-body who considers herself posted in foreign politics and town scandal.

Better for her to be musical than to fly boldly about the whole town, face men's meetings, and show a steady eye and bold front to cloaked generals, while she lays down the law, with her husband in attendance. She is the person who knows what is going on all over the world—the policy of Thrace or China, the mystery between a young lad and his father's second wife, the constancy of one paramour and the general scramble for another. She will tell you the author and the date of a widow's misadventure, and what every woman says and does in consenting to a lover. She is the first to descry the comet which bodes ruin to the Armenian and Parthian kings ; she stands at the city gates to pick up the rumours and latest news :

Her canards.

some she invents for herself, and tells everybody whom she meets at the street-crossing that the waters of Niphates have risen against the inhabitants, and all the land in that region is covered with a vast deluge ; or that whole cities are tottering and the ground beneath them giving way.

In Armenia.

413-433.
The masculine woman.
Her brutality.

Even this pest is not worse to endure than the woman who makes it her custom to seize her humble neighbours and cut them with thongs in spite of their prayers for mercy. If her sound slumbers are broken by a noise of barking, " Bring the cudgels here, and be quick," she cries : she has the master beaten first, and the dog afterwards. She is dangerous to meet with her glowering face when

8

she repairs to the baths at evening. (For she waits
till evening before she gives the word of advance to
her oil-pots and her train-of-war.) She loves to

Her
vulgarity.

make a mighty bustle over the sweating of her
pores, after her wearied arms have collapsed under
the heavy dumb-bells, and the sly bath-man has

Hand-rub-
bing " (as in
Paris).

kneaded and patted the body of his patroness. Her
unhappy dinner-guests are being tortured all the
time with hunger and drowsiness. When at last she
does come, florid and thirsty enough for the whole
amphora of wine, which is set down at her feet brim-

Her gross-
ness.

ming with twelve good quarts, she drains two of
them before eating, just to make her appetite ravenous by their coming back again and pitching her
stomach's rinsings on the floor. There is a running
river on the marble pavement, and the golden ewer
reeks with the stench of wine : for she drinks and
spews like a long snake that has tumbled into a
deep barrel. This is how she turns her husband's
stomach, and makes him shut his eyes to keep
down the bile.

434-456.
The literary
woman.

A still more plaguy wife is one who only takes
her place at table to hold forth on the praises of
Vergil and sympathise with his frail, doomed heroine;
or contrasts and compares one poet with another,
putting Maro on one scale of her balance, Homer
on the other. Professors of literature and language

Her chatter
and over-
bearing
behaviour.

must bow to her, and the whole company is
silenced ; neither a lawyer nor auctioneer could
get a hearing—not even another woman. There
is such a noise of tumbling words that you might
think there were so many clattering dishes or jang-

ling bells. Let nobody trouble the trumpets or cymbals any more : one woman's lungs will be loud enough to deliver Luna from the troubles of eclipse. To drown the sound of the incantations supposed to cause eclipses. Pray that the woman who lies in your arms may not be ranked in any "school" of eloquence, or skilled in throwing off the neat arguments of a pregnant "Enthymeme." May there even be *some* things in books which she does not understand! I detest a woman myself who mutters and thumbs the precepts of Palæmon, and observes all the rules and principles of eloquence ; or lays the finger of a Dryasdust upon quotations which I never heard of, and criticises language in an uncultured woman-friend which would pass muster amongst men. It ought to be a husband's privilege to talk in slipshod sentences. Even in good things the sage declares, " Thus far only shalt thou go ; " whereas a woman who wants to be thought over-wise or over-eloquent may as well tuck up her tunic to clear her knees, kill pigs in honour of Silvanus, or pay her copper at the men's baths.

Her pedantry.

A rhetorician.

Ribbeck's arrangement.

As a man.

457-473. *The rich woman.* Nothing is forbidden, nothing seems wrong, to a woman after she has encircled her neck with a collaret of green stones and fastened big pearl-drops to her ears' elastic lobes. Nothing in the world is so unbearable as a rich woman. You will find her face made hideous and ridiculous under a thick paste of dough, or redolent of Poppæa's greasy unguents, which transfer their stickiness to her unhappy husband's lips. But to meet a paramour she washes her skin. Ah, how seldom does a wife wish to look her best in her own home? It is only

The art of beauty.

Nero's wife, a leader of fashion.

for the paramour's benefit that spikenard is procured and the rarities purchased which are transported from the land of the lithe Indians. In her own good time she reveals her face and takes the upper crust away; reassumes her features and pampers them with the precious milk for the sake of which she is followed everywhere by a retinue of she-asses—would be, if she were sent in exile to the Hyperborean regions. When a thing is coddled and pampered by successive liniments, and submits to sodden lumps of boiled meal, which will be its right name—Face or Ulcer?

474-507.
A fashion-able woman at home.

It will repay us to examine closely what our women are busied and concerned about for the livelong day. If the husband has turned his back in bed, it is

Her injustice to dependants.

death next morning to her girl-secretary; the tiring women strip their backs, and the chair-man is accused of being behind time and must pay the penalty for vicarious sleepiness. One back is *i.e., her husband's sleepiness.*

The flogging.

beaten with rods until they break, another crimsoned by the cat, and a third by thongs. (There are women who pay the Torturers so much per

Her callousness.

annum.) The mistress whiles away the thrashing by daubing her face and gossiping with friends, or pricing the golden border on an embroidered gown. The flogging proceeds while she checks the cross-entries in a long day-book. Still the flogging goes on until the wearied floggers hear her terrible "Begone" given in a voice of thunder when her inquisition is finished. Her government at home has all the barbarity of a Sicilian despot's court. If she has fixed a meeting and wishes her toilet to be extra-beautiful, if she is flurried for time and over-due in the garden or (more likely) at the bawdy shrine of Isis, unfortunate Psecas who is arranging the tresses has her own hair torn from its roots and the clothes stript from her shoulders and bosom.

Her spitefulness.

"Why is this ringlet straggling?" cries the mistress. In a moment the cow-hide is punishing the crime and sin of mis-twisting a curl. What was the fault of Psecas? how was the girl to blame because you did not like the shape of your own nose?

The arrangement of her hair is a matter which requires a solemn consultation of the authorities in the dressing-room.

Another maid stands at the left, drawing the hair out, combing it, and rolling it into a knot. Third at the council-meeting is a veteran, promoted to a sinecure amongst the wool-work after serving her time at the crisping-pin. Hers will be the vote first given; then the juniors of less experience will express their views, just as though it were a question which involved honour or life. The pursuit of beauty has become a serious business, and a woman's head-dress is a structure upreared by one layer upon another, story over-topping story. The front view will show you a very Andromache; the back is not quite so tall, and might belong to a different woman. But come —what would you have, when she has only received short measure in waists, and (without the aid of high heels) looks stumpier than a Pygmy girl, and has to tilt her little self on tip-toes to reach a kiss?

Aids to stature.

508-511. The estrange-

Not a thought for her husband all the time, nor a word of the expenses. Her life is as much apart ment of wife and husband.

from his as a next-door neighbour's; the only point of contact is that she abuses his friends and servants and strains his income.

511-541.
The super-stition of women ends in their houses being invaded by bestial im-postors.

Behold the entrance of frantic Bellona or Mother Cybele's chorus attended by the giant eunuch—him whose presence claims the reverence of neo-phytes in filthiness, who seized a potsherd years ago and gelded his flabbiness therewithal, him to whom common drummers must give precedence, him who veils his bloated cheeks under a Phrygian turban. Loud is the utterance which prophesies terrors for the advent of September's southern gales, unless she have erewhile purified herself with an offering of one hundred eggs, and pre-sented him with her cast-off russet gowns, in order that all the impending miracles and perils may pass into the drapery and give her an Indulgence which will clear her for the year.

The tasks and penances into which women are fooled.

She will break the ice in winter and go into the water; she will dip three times into Tiber at dawn and forget her terrors to bathe her head even in the roaring eddies; naked and shivering, she will crawl with bleeding knees over all the Plain of King Superbus—if the sanctified White Cow has so ordained. She will travel to the ends of Egypt and carry back the water drawn from Meroe's streams, only to sprinkle the shrine of Isis raised hard by our ancient "Sheep-fold."

Isis.

The gross-ness of the imposture.

She thinks that the real voice of her patroness is speaking with her upon earth. What a spirit and what a mind for gods to hold converse with by night! Such are the claims for highest and especial honours put forward by one who runs about the city amongst a pack of linen-wearing shaven-pates, and grins like the dog at the wailings of the people.   He is the mediator of pardon for a wife who sins upon the sacred days of penance, and incurs the grave penalty which is assigned to the unclean act, or if the Silver Serpent has been observed to wag its head.   His are the contrite weepings, his the professional mumblings, which prevail upon Osiris not to withhold his pardon— yielded (no doubt) to the seductions of fat goose and flat-cake.

As Anubis the Egyptian God

Another Egyptian God.

541-547.
The tricks of Jews.

After he has taken his departure, a palsied Jewess leaves her basket and wisp of hay to confide the mysteries which beggars thrive by—a crone who expounds the laws of Jerusalem but has nothing better than a tree to shelter her holiness, though she claims to be a trusty messenger from God on high.   She, too, manages to fill her fist, but it is cheaply filled.   Jews supply dreams to order on strictly moderate terms.

548-552.
Syrian and other Oriental adventurers.

A melting lover or a large inheritance from a wealthy bachelor is guaranteed by the Armenian or Syrian soothsayer after he has manipulated the yet reeking liver of a pigeon.   He peeps into the breasts of pullets, the bowels of a puppy—or (sometimes) of a boy.   He will carry out the crime just to lay the information.

Against his patron.

553-568.
The influence of Chaldæans has been increased by

Still greater is the confidence which Chaldæans inspire : women will believe that every word that is uttered by the soothsayer has come direct from the fountain of Ammon (at Delphi the oracles

the penalties inflicted on them.

are dumb and men are doomed to walk in the night of No Revelation). The first honours of humbug belong to the man—banished not once or twice only—whose friendly service and venal horoscope brought death to the great Roman whom Otho feared. Indeed, what creates the confidence in such ministrations is the clanking of a prophet's double bracelet of iron or his long sojourn in the custody of soldiers. No astrologer will be credited with a familiar spirit if he has not run near losing his head, or barely escaped with transportation to the Cyclades and a tardy release from confinement at Seriphus. Your virtuous Tanaquil is taking counsel about the funeral of a mother whom the jaundice is too slow in killing, *after* she has asked about your own ; about the day for following the bodies of her uncles and sister, and whether the gods will bestow the highest thing in their gift by sparing her paramour's life to outlast her own.

Seleucus.

Galba.

The subjects on which women appeal for revelation of the future.

Tanaquil, wife of Tarquinius Priscus, was skilled in augury.

569-581. Some women turn amateurs of astrology and guide their lives by it.

Still, she is not herself versed in the ominous signs of sulky Saturn or the happiest conjunctions for the star of Venus, in the months for making money and the seasons for losing it. But there is one worse than she whom you must avoid so much as meeting. The almanacks which she carries in her hands are worn away like the sweaty balls of amber. Counsel she does not ask, but has learnt to give it. She will refuse, if the ciphers of Thrasyllus recall her, to go along with her husband to his camp or on his homeward journey. When it is her fancy to take out the litter as far as the first milestone, his time for starting is fixed by her book.

Used to cool the hands.

An intimate of Tiberius.

If the corner of her eye itches after rubbing, she inspects her horoscope before she calls for ointments. Though she is sick in bed, no hour is so fit for taking nourishment as the one appointed by Petosiris.

Egyptian astrologer.

581-591.
Rich and poor alike resort to soothsayers.

If her means are humble, she will pace the ground between the goals of the racecourse on both sides, and entrust forehead and hand to the seer who demands one smacking kiss after another for refreshers. Rich women will receive their answers from the Phrygian or Indian augur whom they keep in service, some pundit learned in the astronomy of the universe, or some elder who purges the lightning's pollutions at the State's expense. Vulgar fortunes are told upon the Circus or the Rampart. A creature who displays the drooping gold upon her naked bust stands before the pillars and columns of the Dolphins, and asks whether she shall throw over the tavern-keeper to wed the clothesman.

As being ominous to the State.

i.e., a woman of the town.

?

592-602.
Why the use of abortives among rich wives is an advantage to their husbands.

Still such poor souls do face the risks of childbirth, and undergo, because they cannot escape, the labours of nursing. But you do not often see a lying-in mother on a gilt bedstead: so potent are the devices and drugs of the wise-woman who produces barren wombs and contracts for the murder of unborn children. But you should be glad of it, unhappy husband. You should yourself hand your wife the draught of nameless nastiness. If she consented to trouble and distend her body with bouncing children, you might perhaps find yourself father to a negro boy, and one day have to write in your will no name but that of the " coloured " son and heir of whom it would be ominous to catch sight early in the morning.

603–609.
The substitution of low foundlings in the places of noble children.

Now I come to the fraud of spurious children and the cheats often practised upon a husband's joyous hopes at those muddy ponds which supply a future Pontifex, priest of Mars, or a sham bearer of the Scaurus name. Fortune, the wicked hussy, stands by and laughs to see the naked infants. She cuddles them all and holds them in her lap ; then she puts them out to noble families, getting up a farce for her own amusement. These become the pets on whom she heaps her favours, and whom she brings forward (with a grin) as her own children.

610–626.
The administration of dangerous drugs by wives which cause dotage in the husbands.

Here is a man offering magic charms; there a dealer in Thessalian potions which enable wives to worry their husbands' souls and thwack their rumps with slippers. This traffic explains the sudden dotage—the fogginess of mind and utter forgetfulness of things that you have only just done. Still that would be bearable if you did not

Serious consequences, as in the case of Caligula's madness.

become a raving madman like Nero's uncle, for whom Cæsonia prepared an essence from the entire forehead of a staggering foal. (And every woman will follow whither an empress leads the way.) Thereon came a general crash and conflagration, such as might have been had Juno driven her husband into madness. So you will find less mischief done by Agrippina's mushroom, because that only stopped the beating of one

Superstitious horror of black things,

Where children were exposed to die, but might be picked up and palmed off.

Caligula.

dotard's heart and despatched him, with his palsied head and slobber-streaming lips, to—the nether heaven. But Cæsonia's potion brings fire and sword upon the world, and lays Senators and Knights in one bloody heap of lacerated bodies. Such the powers for evil which lie in one mare's belly and one witch's wickedness.

627–650. The unnatural crimes of wives and mothers.

A wife detests your bastards; let her encounter no check or restraint, and in a trice conscience enjoins her to murder the lawful step-son. Let every ward who is fatherless and rich lay my words to heart; let him be careful of his own life and distrustful of every meal. A mother's hand has charged the pastry with fever and lividness. He must have a taster for every dish that is offered by her who gave him birth, and every cup must be first sipped by his nervous dominie.

This is all my fancy (do you say?). My satire is wearing tragical high heels? I am trespassing beyond the bounds of precedent? opening my mouth as wide as Sophocles, and pealing out a note which is unfamiliar to the Rutulian hills and the skies of Latium? Would to Heaven that it were fiction !

They are not even concealed or denied.

But here is Pontia crying aloud, "Yes, I did the deed, I confess it. I got the aconite for my children, and the news is public property. It was wicked, if you will; but I did it with my own hands."

"Heartless viper, did you kill both children at one meal together?"

"I would have killed seven, had there been seven to kill."

They surpass the worst crimes of antiquity because the motive is baser.

We may believe all that Tragedy tells us about Medea and Procne's bloody deeds : I say no word against it ; and the two women passed in their own times for prodigies of wickedness. Still theirs was not sordid crime. The greatest of such prodigies claim less wonder when it is anger which inspires a woman's guiltiness. Then the heart rages and the soul is borne in headlong course, even as boulders which are rent away from their rock when the mass below them slips and the mountain - sides give way beneath the toppling summit.

651–661. The deliberate and heartless nature of the crimes.

The woman whom I shall never tolerate is she who reckons the gains and perpetrates a frightful crime in her right mind. Wives come to see Alcestis giving her own for her husband's life, and would gladly—by a parallel atonement—sacrifice a husband to prolong the lap-dog's life. Your morning walk will show you many a Danaid or Eriphyle, and a Clytemnestra in every street. The only difference is that the classical murderess had to use both hands to a clumsy and bungling hatchet, whilst the modern operation is performed by a delicate slice from a toad's liver. Still they use the cold steel also, if their Atreus takes warning by the insuppressible king of Pontus and begins his meals with an antidote.

As in the play of Euripides, adapted by Latin play-wrights.

Women who killed their husbands.

Mithra-dates.

SATIRE VII.

LITERATURE AND LEARNING AT ROME.

1-21.
The patronage of Hadrian removes the hardships of a literary life.

The shifts to which authors had been driven.

Encouragement to poets.

THE only hope and the sole object of our work lie in Cæsar. He alone turned to look upon the heavy-hearted Muses in the days when poets of real fame and note were making up their minds to turn lessees of baths at Gabii or bakeries at Rome, and when others saw no shame or degradation in becoming 'auction-touts; when famished Clio abandoned Aganippe's vale and shifted her quarters to the sale rooms. If you cannot catch a glimpse of any coin in the Pierian retreats, you should be thankful for a Machæra's name and livelihood, and (instead of starving) sell the trumpery for which men take their places in the battle of the bidders —jars, tables, cupboards, boxes, and old plays by Paccius and Faustus. This is better than to swear in court that you saw things which you never did see, though it is done by the pseudo-Roman knights imported with bare ankles from the Eastern Gallia.

Henceforth no man who sets the grace of words in tuneful measures and has tasted of the bay will be forced to undergo tasks unworthy of his art. Brave hearts, to work! Your sovereign's favour

Probably Hadrian.

An auctioneer.

Line 15 omitted as spurious.

i.e., as slaves from Galatia.

looks for you, cheers you onward, and only asks for an opening.

22–47.
No help is to be got from the private patronage of rich men.

If you think that protection of your fortunes is to be expected from any other quarter, and if it is with this idea that you are filling the sheet's yellow parchment, call at once for some bits of stick and make a gift of your writings to the husband of Venus, or stow them away for the worms to pulverize. The god of fire. Unhappy man, smash your pens and blot out the battle-scenes of your night vigils, if you are making lofty verses in a small closet, only to come forth as winner of some ivy leaves and a scraggy bust, the be-all and the end-all of your hopes. Wealth has learnt its lesson from avarice, praises genius (much as children praise a peacock's Argus-eyes), and that is the end of it. Meantime the years are fast ebbing which might nerve you for the sea, the helmet, or the spade. Soon weariness comes on the heart, and the old man curses himself and the Muse his mistress for the talent which leaves his back bare.

Even dilettanti refuse solid assistance.

Next learn the tricks which your patron plays to save his pocket, though to pay him honour you deserted the temples of the Muses and Apollo. He turns poet himself, bowing to none but Homer, and only to him because of the ten centuries between them ! If you are inflamed by Fame's witcheries and would give a recitation, he lends you a mouldy building. Here there is a room at your command which has been locked up for whole years, with its entrance looking like the gate of a besieged town. At the end of every row your patron manages to plant his claquers, and makes the most of his loud-lunged minions. But you will find nobody to give you the price of the benches, the tiers of seats upon your hired planking, and the chairs which set out the front rows until they have to be taken back. Yet we poets drive our trade, cut furrows in loose dust, and plough barren sand.

48-78.
The true poet must be raised above sordid wants as Horace and Vergil were.

If you would break away, you are held in a mesh by the inveterate force of a mischievous ambition, the poet's disease which is now become organic and established in your afflicted heart.

What, then, of the poet among poets? the man of finer gold than common : not a spinner of old worn themes ; not a stamper of stale figures at the vulgar mint—the man whom I cannot show you, but can only imagine? He must have a spirit free from care and unvexed by bitterness, eager for the woodlands and fit to quaff the waters of the Aonides. *Muses.* The songs of Pieria's grotto cannot be sung, nor the wand of Bacchus wielded, by gloomy Poverty that lacks the copper-pieces which humanity requires every day and every night. Horace had dined well when he sang his Io Bacche ! How can there be free play for your spirits unless song be your only care, and unless your hearts are borne along by the Lords of Verse and Wine, disdaining every *Apollo and Bacchus.* rival thought? Genius must not be flustered about providing its blankets if it is to call up the chariots and the horses, and the shapes of gods, *As in Æneid.* and the awful aspect of the Erinnys o'ermastering *The Fury Allecto.* the hero of the Rutuli. If Vergil had not had his *Turnus.* slave and a decent home, his Fury's hair would drop its snaky terrors, and his trumpet's deep note would be smothered.   Can we ask Rubrenus Lappa to walk with the classical buskin's grandeur, if *Atreus* puts his poet's dishes and cloak into pawn ? Poor Numitor has nothing to send to a friend, but he has enough for presents to Quintilla ; and the money was forthcoming to buy a ready-tamed lion which would devour loads of flesh.   But of course the wild beast costs less, and a poet's bowels hold more !

78–87.
Bare honour can only satisfy rich poets like Lucan.

It is very well for a Lucan amongst the statues in his gardens to rest contented with honour ; but for a Serranus or a starving Saleius, what is the value of all the glory in the world if there is nothing but glory?   When Statius has made Rome happy by fixing the day for a reading, there is a rush to hear his pleasant voice reciting the favourite *Thebaid's* lines; so strong the spell with which he holds their mind captive, so strong is the pleasure of the attending crowd.   But after he has made the benches rattle, his belly goes empty unless he sells his virgin *Agave* to the player Paris.

88–97.
No means of livelihood or promotion except by writing for the stage.

Paris it is who lavishes the honours of war upon poets, and encircles their fingers with the "honorary service " rings.   A player bestows what is refused by the nobles.   Do you look to a Camerinus or a Barea, or to the big patrician halls?   Why, it is pantomime makes the prefects, pantomime the tribunes !   Still you must not envy a poet who lives by the stage.   Where will you now find your patrons—a Mæcenas, a Proculeius or a Fabius,

Lappa's play.

A rich man.

His mistress.

The wealthy author of *Pharsalia.*

Favourite actor in Domitian's reign.

a second Cotta or another Lentulus? In their days genius received its due, and men advanced themselves by wearing pale faces and forswearing wine through all the Merry Month.

98–104.
Historians are no better off than poets.

Tell me next, historians, whether your work is more lucrative. It requires more time and wastes more oil. The sheets forget all bounds and run into the thousands, whilst the paper pile mounts to a ruinous height. Your mass of facts and the rules of your art will have it so :—but after all, what is your harvest? what do you reap after ploughing up the soil? Will any one give to the historian as much as he would give to a reader of the day's news ?

105–149.
The reputed gains of the lawyers are exaggerated.

But you say they are an idle tribe, loungers, un-practical. Then tell me how much is secured by the public services of lawyers and the big bundles of documents which go about with them. Their own talk is tall, and never taller than when there is a creditor to listen, or if they have felt a still sharper spur from the fidgeting client who brings his huge ledger to pursue a bad debt. Then our lawyer sets his big bellows to blow off gigantic lies, and covers his front with slobber. But if you want to know his actual gains, you may balance the estates of a hundred pleaders by a single Red Jacket's.

"The chieftains" are seated, and you arise like a white-faced Ajax to defend your client's status before a yokel Bench. Yes, you may strain and split your unhappy vitals, in order that you may see (for your labours) some branches of green palm erected to be the pride of your garret stairs. What

Saturnalia were held in December.

Driver in the chariot races.

As in the dispute for the arms of Achilles.

9

Empty com-
pliments and
shabby fees.
is the fee of eloquence ?   A joint of juiceless pork,
and a pot of tunny-fish, or some stale roots only fit
to be a blackamoor's rations, or five jars of wine
that have been carried the wrong way of Tiber—
one for each speech and a fifth thrown in.   If one
gold-piece has been realized, a commission is de-
ducted by your agent's bargain.

i.e., down
the Tiber, as
the inferior
Sabine wine
was carried.

Clients are
not attracted
by a pleader's
eloquence,
but by the
ostentatious-
ness of his
establish-
ment and
way of
living.
But an Æmilius will receive the full legal fee,
though we have been better pleaders.   For in his
porch there is a brazen car of triumph with four
tall horses, and a figure of himself mounted on a
mettlesome charger, poising his long bending lance
and squinting destruction.   Such grandeur brings
a Pedo to bankruptcy and a Matho to ruin,
and closes the career of Tongillius, who makes a
point of using a huge rhinoceros oil-horn to his
body and infests the Baths with his dirty mob.
The heavy litter-pole crushes his Mædian bearers
when he passes through the Forum on his way to
buy slaves and silver plate and agate-bowls and
mansions.

A noble
name.

Men of
inferior
position
aping their
betters.

Smart
advocates
The purple stuffs of Tyrian pirates are the
vouchers of his credit. Indeed, this is a trick which
is useful in the trade.   Purple advertises pleaders,
so do violet robes ; and it answers their purpose to
live in the bustle and display of wealth, though the
extravagance of Rome keeps no bounds.   Do we
put our hopes in eloquence ?   Nobody now would
give 200 sesterces to a Cicero if he did not flash a
monster ring.   The first thing to which a suitor
looks is whether you walk abroad between eight
slaves and ten retainers, the litter-carriers behind

you and the citizens ahead. This is why Paulus
hired a sardonyx ring to plead in, and this is why
he took bigger fees than Gallus or than Basilus.
Nobody expects to find eloquence wearing a thread-
bare cloth. When does Basilus get the chance of
bringing "a disconsolate mother" into court? To excite sympathy.
Eloquence in him would be impudence. If you
are determined to sell your tongue, take yourself
to Gaul or (better) to the African nursery for
sucking lawyers.

150-214.
The teachers of rhetoric have a hard life.

Are you a teacher of rhetoric? What a callous
heart you must have, Vettius, to stand by whilst
your crowded class is killing its "savage tyrants!"
The lesson which they have just read sitting they will
stand up to repeat in the same words, and they will
drone it all out line for line. "Cabbage, and cabbage
to follow!" It is death to the unhappy teacher.

The right treatment and the exact nature of a
case, the real point in issue, and the other side's
line of attack, are what everybody wants to know,
but nobody wants to pay the fee.

"Do you claim a fee?" he would say. "What
have I learnt?"

They are held responsible for the failure of stupid pupils.

And of course the blame is put upon the teacher,
because there is nothing thumping under the
young bumpkin's left breast, though my head
aches every sixth day with his "awful Hannibal."
Now it is one question, now it is another. "Shall
he march on Rome from Cannæ?" or "shall he
take warning from the clouds and lightning, and
wheel his drenched troops beyond reach of the
storms?"

The heart is spoken of as the seat of intelligence.

The subject of a rhetorical exercise.

"Bargain for what you please, and take it ; I
grant it on condition that his father listens to it all
as often as I must."

Such is the cry which comes at once from six or
more trainers of the young idea ; then they have to
fight a practical question and leave their "Ravisher"
at home.   Nor have they anything to say about the
"Mixing of Poisons" or "the Graceless Lover," or
"the Simples which can give back light even to
the blindness of long years."

So (if my advice is to have effect) the teacher
will take his own discharge and enter upon a
different walk in life, if he is obliged to leave his
academic retreat for the battlefield of the courts
so as not to sacrifice the value of a paltry corn-
ticket ! Indeed, that is quite a grand fee.   Ask
what Chrysogonus or Pollio receives for teaching
smart people's children, and you will tear up
"Theodorus on the Rudiments of Rhetoric."

Six hundred thousand sesterces spent on a bath !
and more on a colonnade for its owner to drive
under on rainy days ! (Would you have him wait
for fine weather, and spatter his team with the
fresh mud?   No ; let him drive here, because here
the mules' hoofs are kept clean and bright.)   On
the other side there must be a banqueting-room,
pillared on Numidian marbles and catching the
warmth of the winter sun.   No matter what the
house costs, there will be an artist to arrange the
courses and make up the dishes.   With all this
outlay, two thousand sesterces to Quintilian pass
for a handsome fee.   You will see that sons

are the cheapest things which their fathers keep.

Quintilian amassed a competence, but he was a 'lucky man,' and an exception to the general rule.

"How then" (ask you?) "is Quintilian possessed of all these pasture-lands?" Well, you must not press instances of startling careers. The *lucky man* is handsome and bold; he has wisdom, rank, and birth. The lucky man fastens the crescent-token on his senator's shoe; the lucky man is orator and debater too, and a fine singer (even if he has caught a cold). Much depends upon which stars

(The power of Luck.)

adopt you when you are just trying to utter your first cry and are still rosy from your mother's womb. If Fortune will have it so, the teacher becomes consul; or if she changes her mind again, the consul becomes teacher. Look at Ventidius or at Tullius—what do you see but the working of their star, and Destiny's mysterious force? Destiny will mount a slave upon the throne, and give a Triumph to the prisoner-of-war.

T., son of a slave woman became King of Rome. V., taken prisoner in Social War and advanced by Julius Cæsar.

Most teachers of rhetoric have reason to regret their choice of the profession.

Nevertheless, the lucky man is rarer than white crows; and many a teacher has cursed his profitless and barren stool. Witness the ends of Thrasymachus and Secundus Carrinas; and there was Another whom Athens beheld in poverty, and

Banished by Caligula. ? Unknown.

could yet withhold everything but the chilling draught of hemlock which she gave to Socrates. Gods above! make the earth lie gently and lightly on the spirits of our ancestors; let fragrant crocus and spring's ever-fresh treasures cover their ashes, because they wished a teacher to stand in the

They are no longer held in the respect which was

father's place. It was in fear of the rod that Achilles, though he was a big lad, learnt singing on

once accorded to them either by parents or pupils.

his native hills; nor was he the pupil to be tempted into laughing at his minstrel-master's tail.   But Rufus is not the only teacher nowadays who is flogged by his own class—the very Rufus whom it often called "our Gallic Cicero."

The Centaur Chiron. A Gaul who taught rhetoric. Read *quem*.

215–242.
The teachers of the rudiments of education lead lives of hardship. Their mean fees are reduced by the extortion of under-lings.

Who puts into the purse of Enceladus or learned Palæmon as much as their drudgery at grammar has deserved?   And whatever the amount be— less anyhow than the fee for rhetoric—the pupil's blockhead usher takes his snack, and the paymaster has a slice.   Palæmon, you must give way and abate your profit as if you were higgling over winter blankets and white rugs; only do not make a dead loss of having sat from the hour of midnight in a place which would be scorned by blacksmiths or instructors in the wool-teaseler's art.   Do not make a dead loss from the stink which came from all the lanterns of all the boys, while your Horace lost all his colour and sticky blacks dirtied Vergil's front.   Even so, there are few fees which do not require a "judgment" from the tribune.

Brought by the boys in the early morning.

They are expected not only to be posted in the minutiæ of literature, and to instruct the boys' minds, but also to form their characters and be responsible for their behaviour.

Nevertheless, let the parents make their hard conditions.   The teacher's rules of syntax must be fixed and firm; he must read history, and know all the classics as well as his own fingers and toes.   If he is asked at random on his way to the vapour-places or the baths of Phœbus, he must tell you the nurse of Anchises, or the name and origin of the step-mother of Anchemolus, or how many years Acestes lived, or how many jars of Sicilian wine he gave to the Phrygians.   You must require him to mould the soft natures of his pupils with the hand of

From the Aeneid.

an artist fashioning a waxen image; require him
to be a real father to the whole assemblage,
and to prevent their filthy sports and smutty
antics.

"It is no light task," you may well say, "to
watch the fingers of so many lads, or the eyes which
twinkle when the mischief has been done."

"Be diligent in this," the father answers; and
when the year comes round, you may have as
much as the people awards—to a winner in the
circus !

SATIRE VIII.

NOBLE BIRTH.

1-18.
Family honours are worthless if a man does not live up to the traditions of his ancestors.

WHAT are pedigrees worth? What good is it, Ponticus, to be counted in a long lineage and to display the painted masks of ancestors, or an Æmilianus standing on his chariot, the remaining half of a Curius, a one-armed Corvinus, and a Galba without his nose and ears? What profit to vaunt a Corvinus in your broad Roll, or in going down the family-tree to light at almost every twig upon grimy Masters of Horse (or a Dictator), if the life is wicked which you spend before the faces of Lepidi? What avail so many images of warriors if you are dicing all through the night-hours in presence of Numantia's heroes, and if you begin your slumbers at the morning-star's rising, once the signal for generals to advance their standards on the march? Why is a Fabius to take pride in Allobrogian honours and in the Great Altar just because he was born in the House of Hercules, if he is avaricious or a fantastic wanton far flabbier than Euganean lambs; if he brings shame upon the rough manliness of his ancestors by polishing his soft loins with Catina's pumice; if he traffics in poison and defiles his unhappy race with a condemned image?

Read *contingere.* Grimy from the smoke of the hearth.

Scipio Africanus reduced Numantia in 133 B.C.

Q. Fabius Maximus defeated Allobroges in 121 B.C.

Condemned to be destroyed.

19-38.
Virtue is the truest nobility.

Though the ancient waxen figures adorn every corner of your hall, Merit is the one and only title of honour. Let the virtues of a Paulus, a Cossus, or a Drusus be yours. Those you may put before the images of ancestors, and (when you are consul) those may take precedence even of the lictor's rods. What I demand first is inward goodness. If you earn by word and deed the name of one who is pure and resolute in right-doing, then I recognize the noble man. All hail to you, be you Gætulicus or Silanus, or whatever be your stock, if you are the rare and precious patriot vouchsafed to a rejoicing land. We would greet thee even with the cry of a nation greeting the new-found Osiris. Who will say that a man is noble if he is the shame of his own nobility, and bears no honours save a famous

Noble names unaccompanied by noble lives seem only to be given in derision.

name? We call a kept dwarf "Atlas," a negro boy "Swan," and a crooked, ugly wench "Europe." Lazy curs which have lost their coats from inveterate manginess, and lick the bowls of lamps for the dry sediment of oil, will answer to the names of Lion, or Leopard, or any other more ferocious roarer that walks the earth. Do you take warning, therefore, and be careful lest your Creticus or Camerinus be a name of scoffing.

The Egyptian Bull God.

39-70.
The lesson that there is no merit in nobility by itself is pointed by a personal application.

Whom was this lesson for? it is to you I speak, Rubellius Plautus. You are puffed up with the proud lineage of Drusus, as if you had done something to make yourself noble and bring about your own conception in a womb glorified by the blood of Iulus, instead of being born of a weaver-girl under the windy rampart. 'We are low creatures,'

i.e., descended from Æneas.

you say, 'dregs of the populace, not one of whom
can quote his own father's origin. But you are of
the line of Cecrops.' Long life to you then, and
may you reap lasting pleasure from your descent.

Merit is compatible with humble birth.

Nevertheless, amongst the lowest of the plebs you
will find the man of true Roman blood and genius,
one who is practised in pleading the causes of the
noble ignoramus ; and from those who wear the
garb of dependence one will come to disentangle
the knots of justice and solve the riddles of law.
Another with the young man's strength and the
warrior's vigour starts for the Euphrates, or the
Eagles which watch the subjugated Batavi. But
what are you except a son of Cecrops? a mutilated
figure-head like the Hermes block !—wherein are
you better, except that his head is marble whilst
you are an animated image?

Mutilated at Athens by unknown malefactors.

We do not value horses for their descent, but for the prizes which they win in races.

Answer me, son of Troy: who would speak of a
dumb animal's "blood" if it had no mettle ? No,
we only praise a fleet horse when he is an easy
winner in the circus, often glowing with victory
and exulting in the roars of applause. No matter
what grass he fed on, there is "blood" in the horse
whose stride distances the rest and who raises the
first dust-cloud on the plain. But the descendants
of Coryphæus and Hirpinus are made up as "selling
stock" if their chariots have seldom been driven
by Victory. There is no respect for sires, nor any
honour paid to ghosts, amongst our horses. They
are forced to change masters for mean prices, and
must gall their necks with tugging cart-harness,
like the sluggish cattle they are, only fit to grind a

Famous racers.

mill for Nepos.　Therefore, if you would have us admire not the rank but the man, produce something of your own for me to inscribe in your record, beyond those honours which we paid once and still pay to those whom you owe everything to.

71-86.
Exhortation to Ponticus to earn his honours for himself.

Enough for the young man whom report declares to be inflated and ready to burst with conceit at being Nero's kinsman.　In his rank of life we do not expect to find good sense.　But with you it is not so, Ponticus: I would not have men accord you the glories of the past if it makes you do nothing for your own future glory.　It is vanity to build upon borrowed honours, lest the pillars be withdrawn and the edifice fall with a crash.　Or it is like a vine sprawling on the ground and mourning for the elm which it has been torn from.　Be you a trusty soldier, a trusty guardian, an unblemished judge: and if ever you are cited as witness in a doubtful and disputed case (even though some Phalaris with his brazen bull commands you to be a liar and dictates the perjury), yet must you think the worst disgrace is to reckon mere existence better than honour, and for the sake of life to sacrifice what alone makes it worth living.　It *is* death to deserve death, though a man feast on ten score oysters from Gaurus and souse himself in a whole caldron of the perfumes of "Cosmus."

Sicilian despot.

The Roman "Truefit."

87-124.
A good governor must discard the traditions of pillage which have

When the Province of your hopes receives you for its governor, put the constraining curb on your wrathful passions, and likewise on your avarice; take pity on our pauperized "Allies"—Royalties reduced to their own skeletons with all the marrow sucked away!

disgraced the name of many Roman nobles.
Remember what the law lays down and the senate orders, what prizes await the upright governor, and how the bolt of retribution was hurled by the Fathers' sentence on Capito and Numitor—for robbing the Robbers! Yet what redress does the The Cilician bandits. sentence bring if Pansa takes away whatever Natta left behind him. No, Chærippus, look out for a An injured provincial. man to sell your rags, and hold you your tongue in good time. It is madness to finish up by throwing away your passage-money.

Once when our allies were flourishing (before they had long been conquered) the groaning was not so deep nor was the blow of their losses so heavy. Then every house was well stocked : there was money in huge piles, purples of Sparta, raiment of Cos ; along with pictures by Parrhasius and figures by Myro was the breathing ivory of Pheidias. Everywhere you might see much work of Polycletus, and few tables were ungraced by Mentor. But when our governors came home, Dolabella or Antonius or the profaner Verres, from their divers places, their deep ships would be carrying smuggled plunder—trophies of war won by the easier arts of peace. Now the little farm is seized, and our "allies" will be robbed of the few yoke of oxen, the scanty lot of brood-mares and even the single sire of the stock, the very gods of their hearths (if there be one attractive figure amongst them) or the one deity within the homestead. (Such things do duty amongst them for grand treasures, being the choicest which they own.)

It is not safe to drive the Perhaps you may despise the unwarlike Rhodians

provincials
into despera-
tion.
and the perfumed men of Corinth. What need
you fear from their depilated manhood or from a
whole nation of smooth legs? But beware you
of rough Spain, the Gallic region, and of the
Illyrian sea-board. Oppress not the farmer-folk
who feed Rome and leave it idle for the pageants
of the circus. After all, what prize will you win
great enough to reward such awful wickedness when
a Marius has so lately stript the poor Africans bare?
Let it be your first care that no intolerable wrong
be wrought on men who have all the courage of
despair. Though you may carry off the last ounce
of silver and gold, you will leave them buckler
and sword, helmet and javelins. When all else is
gone, a plundered nation has its arms.

Much of the corn came from Egypt.

125-145.
If you do
not practise
or permit
pillage, you
have earned
the right to
all the
honours of
nobility.

What I have declared is not a theorist's commonplace; you may believe that I am reading a leaf of
the Sibyl's sooth. If your retinue be guiltless, if
there is no "curled darling" to traffic in your
justice; if your wife has clean hands, and does
not prepare to go the circuit of the towns and
judgment-places that she may clutch at gold with
a harpy's crooked talons : then, if you will, count
the generations between yourself and Picus; and if
you take pleasure in exalted names, rank among
your ancestors the whole array of Titans, even
Prometheus himself; and pick a father for your
grandsire from whatever story-book pleases you.

Pre-historic king in Italy.

Otherwise,
your family
honours
testify
against you
and accen-
tuate your
infamy.

But if you are carried away in the headlong rush
of ambition and outrage; if you break your rods on
the bleeding backs of our allies; if you delight in
blunting the axes and over-working the headsmen,

then the honours of your own race come to rise up against you and hold a bright light over your infamy. In every human fault, the sinner's rank displays its vileness on a pedestal of shame. Why boast that your grandsire built the temple which your father's triumphal statue adorns, if you use it to follow the trade of a witness to forged wills? Why vaunt yourself to me, if you pull a Gaul's hood over your forehead when you start for the night's adultery?

146–182.
The low amusements and vulgar debauchery of a high-born official.

Fat Lateranus is hurried past the bones and ashes of his ancestors on a flying car, and (Consul though he be) himself chokes the wheel with his massive drag-chain. True, it is night-time; yet the moon sees it all, and the stars level their conscious gaze. When his year of pomp has come to an end,

Horsiness.

he will wield the whip in broad daylight and never flinch from meeting a venerable friend; he will challenge him with the driver's salute, and afterwards he will undo the hay trusses and measure out the barley for his tired cattle. Meantime, whilst, according to Numa's ordinance, he slaughters the woolly sheep and sturdy steer before Jupiter's altar, his only oath is by the Stable Goddess and

Epona.

the figures painted over the reeking stalls. But when it is his pleasure to repair to the night-houses, a greasy Jew (once a denizen of Idumæa's gate) runs and salutes his master and patron with all a host's fussiness, and with him comes Cyane, with her skirts tucked up and carrying a jar of wine for sale.

Youth is the only excuse for them, but

Some apologist will say, " I did the same things myself when I was a young man."

it cannot be
pleaded
here.

"So you did," I should reply, "but of course
you have given it all up, nor did you pet your fail-
ings afterwards." Let your adventures in wickedness be brief. There are some sins which ought to
disappear at the first touch of the razor. Allowance must only be made for boys.

But when Lateranus marches upon the mugs and
advertising curtains of the grog shops, his manhood is ripe for service, for guarding the Armenian
and Syrian borders or the frontier-lines of Rhine
and Danube. His prime might serve—to make a
Nero safe upon his throne! Despatch him, Cæsar, to
the Tiber's mouth; yes, despatch him—but you must
look for your general in the big tavern. You will find
him lounging beside a cut-throat, in a mixed company of sailors, thieves, runaways, hangmen, bier-
jobbers, and a eunuch priest sprawling behind his
idle cymbals. There you find all men free and
equal; no private property in cups, no distinction
in couches, nor privilege in tables. If you had a
slave like him, what would you do, Ponticus?
Why, you would turn him over to your Lucanian
farm or send him to the Tuscan prisons. But
amongst yourselves you "sons of Troy" have a
lenient code; and what would be disgrace for the
Unwashed becomes honour in a Volesus or Brutus.

Taverns.

Foul and shocking as are the examples chosen,
what when I tell you that there must always be
worse in reserve? Damasippus, when he had
wasted his substance, prostituted his voice to the
stage in order to act the Noisy Ghost for Catullus; and for his performance in the *Laureolus*, a

183–210.
Noblemen
descend to
yet lower
depths.

A writer of
mimes.
A character

Pantomime
acting in
public.

noble harlequin showed real agility, and deserved (in my judgment) something more than
a sham crucifixion.   But even so you must not
excuse the populace.   Still more brazen than his
must be the face of a populace, which sits and
looks on at the patrician clownery, which witnesses the antics of barefooted Fabii and laughs
at the Mamerci romping.   It matters not what
price our nobles accept, for their own extinction—
the price which they accept though no Nero is
compelling them, do not hesitate to accept at
the enthroned prætor's games.   Yet imagine that
the choice lies between cold steel and the stage.
Which is the better?   Can any man have so
quailed before death as to make himself a candidate
for Thymele's favours, a colleague of blundering
Corinthus?   But when an Emperor turns harper,
there is nothing strange in patricians acting pantomime.   What worse can there be except the gladiator's school? and here you have the real disgrace
of Rome—a Gracchus not even covered by the
mirmillo's armour nor fighting with the shield and
crooked falchion.   He curses such disguises, curses
and loathes them, nor will he hide his face under
a helmet.   Look, he wields the trident.   When he
has swung his arm backwards and missed his cast
with the dangling net, he shows his face uncovered
to the spectators, and all may recognize him as he
runs round the whole arena.   We may be sure of
the sacred tunic, since there is the golden ribbon
hanging down from his face and floating on his
tall priest's cap.   Yes, the " Pursuer " has suffered

Fighting in
in the arena
as gladiators.

who was
crucified in
the play.
Sometimes it
was played
by a criminal
who was
really
crucified.

On a high
car.

An actress
and actor.

A patrician
and a priest.
A gladiator
who was
covered with
heavy
armour
which would
disguise him.
He was
matched
against the
unarmoured
retiarius,
who carried
a net and a
three-
pronged
spear.

The

a shame more cruel than any wound in being matched against a Gracchus.

211-229.
Nero, who disgraced his noble birth by low acts, deserved to be dethroned in favour of Seneca.

If the people were to receive the right of free suffrage, who would be so depraved as to think twice about electing Seneca before the Nero who earned the Sack many times over and deserved more than one Serpent or a single Ape? Agamemnon's son committed the same crime; but circumstances alter cases.   Orestes acted under Divine guidance when he avenged the father who was murdered even as he drank the bowl of wine.   But Orestes did not pollute himself by the murder of Electra or his Spartan wife; he mixed no poisons for his kinsmen, never sang upon the public stage, and did not write " The Tale of Troy Town."   For what crime that Nero committed in all his heartless and bloody tyranny called, more than his poetry, for the armed vengeance of Verginius or of Vindex and Galba?   Such are the labours and such the accomplishments of the noble-born ruler who takes pride in exposing himself abroad in a shameful singing-tour and in having earned the Greek parsley crown.   Let him decorate his ancestors' statues with the trophies of his voice.   Let him lay the trailing robes of Thyestes or Antigone, let him lay Menalippe's mask, before the feet of Domitius; let him hang his harp upon the marble Colossus.

Punishment of parricides.

His crimes were not more shameful than his follies.

As Nero did.

Nero belonged to the gens Domitia.

230-268.
Noble malefactors are contrasted with low-born benefactors.

Catiline and

Where can anything be found grander than the lineage of Catiline and Cethegus?   Yet, as if they were of Gaulish blood, descended from Bracchati or Senones, they made fire and sword ready by night against the homes and temples of Rome, and

Gauls who invaded Italy and burnt Rome in 391 B.C.

his companions tried to wreck Rome.

Cicero, its saviour, was a self-made man.

dared deeds which might be punished with the "Shirt of Nessus." But the consul is at his post and checks your advance. He is but a self-made man from Arpinum, not a patrician, a provincial hardly admitted to the Roman knightage; still he posts armed garrisons everywhere for the panic-stricken city and is vigorous on all the Seven Hills. Thus he earned, in the civil dress and inside the city walls, a name and title higher than what Octavius won at Leucas in the plains of Thessaly after bathing his sword in repeated slaughters. Yes, and Rome was free, when she called Cicero the giver of her life, "the Father of his Fatherland."

Read *monte.*

Actium and Philippi (?)

Another man from Arpinum used to claim day-wages on the Volscian high-grounds after he had tired himself at his master's plough. His next promotion was for his skull to crack the knotted vine-stick (if he was idle and plied his pick-axe slowly at the camp entrenchments). Yet he is the man who confronts the Cimbrians at the most dangerous crisis of Rome's fortunes, and is the one saviour of the trembling state. So it was, when the ravens had flown down upon the slaughtered Cimbrians (finer corpses than they had ever found before), that only the second laurel was given to the colleague nobleman.

Marius and the Decii were not of noble birth.

Used by centurions to punish soldiers.

In 102 B.C.

The souls of the Decii were plebeian, and their name plebeian: yet the Gods Below and Mother Earth accepted them in sacrifice for all the Roman legions, all the Italian allies, and all the youth of Latium. The Decii were more precious than the souls which they died to save.

Three Decii were said to have sacrificed their lives to save the Roman armies in 340, 295, and 279.

Servius
Tullus.

Treachery in
the family of
the first
Brutus.

The son of a slave-girl won the robe and diadem
and fasces of Romulus, and was the last of the good
kings.   But the traitors who sought to open the
city gates to the banished tyrants were sons of the
consul himself, and the very men who should be
venturing some great exploit in the threatened
cause of liberty, such as might win the honour of
Mucius and Cocles, and the Maid who swam the
river which was then the boundary of Rome's
empire.   He who laid the villainous plot before
the fathers of the senate was a slave, but he
earned at his death the lamentations of the matrons.
The traitors met their due punishment from the
lash and first axe wielded for Rome's liberties.

Scævola.
Horatius
Cocles.
Clœlia.

269-275.
We should
look to a
man's life,
not to his
birth,
because the
origin even
of a noble
family is
either low or
shameful.

Better that your father be a Thersites (if only
you are to be like the grandson of Æacus and,
like him, wield Vulcan's arms) than that an Achilles
beget you in the likeness of Thersites.   The truth
is, if you are to trace your origin far back and
search it to its roots, your lineage is derived from
a sanctuary of ill-fame.   The first of your ancestors, whoever he was, was either a shepherd or a—
something which I will not name.

SATIRE IX.

A DIALOGUE BETWEEN THE POET AND AN UNFORTUNATE FRIEND.

1-26. *POET.* Pray tell me, Nævolus, why you are so often gloomy when I meet you, with a brow lowering like defeated Marsya's. What need have you for such a face as Ravola wore when he was caught with Rhodope in their amatory escapade? (None but slaves are thumped for licking dainties.) Not more woe-begone than yours was the countenance of Crepereius Pollio when he was going the round of the money-lenders and offering to treble the rate of interest, but could not find his fool. Whence come all these sudden crows' feet? Once, I know, you were happy in your modest fees for playing the amateur buffoon, and your dinner-table jests had a pleasant pungency and all the keen relish of town-bred talk. Now you are no longer the same man: your face is lumpish, your hair is like a thicket of dry sticks, and your skin has lost all the gloss which it once owed to warm liniments of Bruttian Paste. Your legs are slovenly and rough under their bushy growth. What right have you to be emaciated like a confirmed invalid who is being parched away under the regular visitations of a

In a musical contest with Apollo.

quartan fever? Just as one may detect pleasure, so may one detect anguish of the mind concealed in an ailing body. Either feeling wears its out-ward livery. So it is plain that you have reversed your objects and are running counter to your old scheme of life. It is not a long time (by my reckoning) since you were constant in your attend-ance on Isis, Ganymede, and Pax, at exotic Cybele's palace, and even at the temple of Ceres— for there are women on view at every temple now— and were better known for adulteries than Aufidius himself; nor (for all your slyness) did you confine your gallantries to the wives.

27-90. *Nævolus.* Many men thrive even at my trade, but I cannot earn a decent living. Now and again I come by a coarse cape only fit to save my toga— the dye stiff and harsh, and the texture badly combed out by some Gallic hand. My payment is in light money and base metal ! Man is the creature of luck, and no part is too private for luck to pene-trate. If his stars strike work, his best powers will be unknown and unavailing, though the slavering Virro has had the evidence of eyesight, and though pestering overtures are poured in by streams ; " for white flesh is a lodestone to lovers." Where, however, can you find the monster to out-match a Miser Debauchee ?

" First, I paid you so much, then on such a day so much, and afterwards on such a day you received so much more " — thus he checks the account and works out the balance.

" Produce the tally," I reply, " and let your

The " patron."

servants bring the ledger. On one side count the payments, only 5000 sesterces in all. Against them set the services performed."

Apostrophe to Virro.

Do you think that I have an easy and congenial task? The poor slave digging his field has a better soil to work on. But perhaps you always fancied yourself to be blooming, young, and beautiful, deserving all Ganymede's promotion! Will such men as you show mercy on a poor follower or a servant, if you are not generous even in your own corruptions? Imagine what a pretty creature to receive my offerings of green sunshades and big amber jewels on a birthday's anniversary or at the beginning of the vernal showers, whilst you loll upon the long sofa's cushions and play with the gifts set apart for the Ladies' Day! Who is it, you lecher, for whom you are keeping all your mountains, all your Apulian farms, and all the pastures which a kite would faint in flying over? You are gorged with riches from Trifolium's fruitful vineyards, from the eminence which Cumæ cowers under, and from the unpeopled hill of Gaurus. Who is there who fastens up more casks for storing the full-bodied vintage? Would it cost you much to reward your retainer's exhausted energies with a few acres of ground? Will yon cottage-home be so well bestowed (with its country lad, his mother, and his puppy playmate) if it become a legacy to your friend the cymbal-tinkler?

"Your begging is impudence," says Virro. But my Rent insists upon my begging, and my slave implores it—my slave as single as the big orb

Line 44 omitted.

Maternalia on March 1st.

A eunuch priest of Cybele.

The Cyclops.

of Polyphemus, the singleness of which saved the
life of cunning Ulysses. I must buy another slave,
for the one is not enough for my work; and the two
will both have bellies! What am I to do in the
nipping blasts of winter? In the cold gusts of
December how can I answer the appeal of naked
feet and shoulders? Can I tell them to "bear it
and look forward to the grasshopper's return?"

But suppose that you ignore and dismiss all
other claims—what price do you put upon the
loyal and devoted service, but for which your wife
would to this hour remain a virgin? You know
how exact your orders and how lavish your promises
were; more than once or twice your bride was
eloping when I caught her in my arms: she had
even smashed your marriage-tablet, and was just
signing a new one. I had a long night's work to
win her back, whilst you were whimpering outside.
The bed is my witness—and so are you, for you
heard what was being said and done inside. One
may find many houses where the bond of matri-
mony is weak, just about to be loosened and
all but undone, when it is once again made fast
by the adulterer's exertions.

Where will you turn and twist to? how begin
your plea or end it? Is it to go for nothing, quite
for nothing, you thankless traitor, that you have
issue in my son or daughter? For you are rearing
them as your own, and delight in dotting the
Public Record with the proofs of your manhood.
Yes, hang garlands on the doorposts! You have
become a father! I have given you the answer to

rebut slanders with ; and you owe to me all your privileges as a father—your rights as heir and legatee, and your claims upon such pleasant things as forfeited bequests. There will be many extras beside to go along with the Forfeits, if I ever make up your family to the Number Three.

Persons without children were restricted in their succession to residuary legacies. Jus Trium Liberorum.

90-91.   *Poet.* You have good reason, Nævolus, for your indignation. What does he bring forward in defence ?

92-101.   *Nævolus.* He ignores me, and is looking out for a two-legged ass to take my place. But remember to guard the secrets which have been entrusted to no ear but yours, and bury my complainings in the silence of your own heart. It is a deadly thing to make a depilated fop your enemy. The very man who trusted me with his secret not long ago, is now become all fire and fury, as if I have published my knowledge abroad. He does not think twice about taking up a sword or cracking your skull with a bludgeon, or putting a lighted torch to your doorway. It is not a matter to ignore or laugh at, that the market-price of poisons is never beyond his powers of purchase. Therefore you must keep my words secret as the meetings of the council on Mars Hill at Athens.

102-122.   *Poet.* Why, it is rank bucolic innocence to think that there can be any secret about a rich man's life. Though the slaves hold their tongues, the cattle, the dog, the doorposts, or the statues would find voices. You may shut the windows, draw curtains over the openings, fasten the doors, you may have everybody in bed and nobody sleeping near;—but anything which a rich man is doing at chanticleer's second signal will be known before daybreak to the nearest tavern-keeper, who will hear the news improved by the fancy of secretary, cooks-in-chief, and carving-men. Is there any charge which such as they are slow to formulate against their masters when they retaliate with slander for the strap? Besides them you may count upon some unwelcome sot for marking down his man and emptying his tippler's talk into the victim's ear. Yes, make to them the request which you were just now making to me—ask them to hold their tongues! Why, they would liefer be blabbing your secrets than drinking the Falernian wine in measure such as Saufeia would swallow as her sacred duty.

There are many good reasons for living in virtue, but none better than to be enabled to ignore your servants' tongues—for the tongue is their most unruly member. But worse than any is that master's plight who is bondsman to them whose being he maintains at his proper charge and cost.

123–129.   *Nævolus.* If your object was to teach me to ignore my servants' tongues, your words were wise but vague. Adapt your counsel to my own case of wasted time and blighted hopes. The fleeting bloom of youth, our scanty portion in this prison-house of sorrows, is chafing to be gone. Even as we quaff the wine and are calling for roses, perfumes, and sweethearts, age is creeping on us with its stealthy stride.

130–134.   *Poet.* Be not alarmed. So long as the Seven

Hills stand firm on their foundations, you may always count upon the supply of customers for your vices. Thither they will come by the ship-load and carriageful, the fops who dare not give an honest scratch to the hair on their heads! There are better strings than the old one to your bow. Do you but fortify your vigour by chumping simples!

135-150.   *Nævolus.* Such lessons may be left for Fortune's favourites. The Destinies who rule my life are well content if my wants are fed by the sweat of my body. Gods of the humble home which I call mine, whom it is my wont to honour with scraps of frankincense or with meat-offerings and flimsy garlands, tell me, when shall I put away enough to rescue my declining years from the beggar's mat and staff? A little income of some 20,000 sesterces from sound securities; some vessels of silver (plain, but good enough to be condemned by censors like Fabricius); and two stout fellows from the Mæsian gang, to job out their necks and set me down in comfort in the brawling Circus. May I also own one stooping silversmith, and one other artist who will turn out a batch of family portraits to my order. This is all that I ask, since I must always be a poor man. A mean enough petition it is, and not even hopeful. For when Fortune is besought in my name, her ears prove to have been stopped with wax borrowed from the very ship which was saved from the Sirens' spells because the oarsmen were deaf.

Of Ulysses.

SATIRE X.

THE VANITY OF HUMAN WISHES.

1–18. Men set their hearts on what will bring them to death or ruin.	IN all the countries of the world (from Gades to Aurora and the Ganges) there are few men who can put aside the mists of error and distinguish true from widely different benefits. How seldom does Reason inspire the wish or fear! How seldom do you start with so lucky an idea as not to repent when you have accomplished your effort or desire! Whole households have been upset at once because the gods (in their goodness) had hearkened to the inmates' prayers. Prizes which are sought in camp and forum bring damage to the winners. In eloquence and flowing language many a man has found his own ruin. Muscle and girth of chest were fatal to Him who put his trust in them. Many men are smothered by money which they have piled together with overmuch taking of thought, or by the bulk of a revenue surpassing other fortunes even as the whale of Britain is bigger than dolphins. So it is in the reign of cruelty (and when there is a Nero to give the order) that Longinus and too wealthy Seneca's large gardens are invested, and the palace home of

i.e., from West to East.

Milo of Crotona tried to split an oak-tree, and got his hands wedged in the wood.

The philosopher condemned for conspiring.

Lateranus is besieged, by cohorts in full strength; against Nero. but a garret lodging is seldom visited by the soldiery. As police.

19-27. **The dangers to wealth from crime.** If you have started on a journey by night, though the vessels of silver which you take are few and plain, you will go in fear of sword and bludgeon, and tremble when the shadow of a reed flickers in the moonlight. But an unencumbered traveller will troll his song in the highwayman's face. In most temples the first, and in all the most familiar, prayer is " Riches—let my wealth increase, let my money-chest be the biggest in the Forum Banks." But remember that the draught of aconite is not put into cups of earthenware: you need fear it only when you take jewelled goblets or bowls with the ruddy gold glowing under Setia's wine.

28-53. **The life of man is a farce which might well move the laughter of Democritus.** Do you see now that it was well for one of the Democritus. Wise Men to laugh, while the other shed tears, Heraclitus. whenever he put one foot forward and planted it out-of-doors? Jeering, indeed, and dry chuckling come easily to any man : but the wonder is where enough moisture was pumped from for the other's eyes. Democritus, however, used to shake his sides **Nothing is more laughable than the** with continual laughter, although the cities which **would-be grandeur of Roman pageants.** he knew had no purple robes to show him, nor striped togas nor fasces nor litters—nor the Court of Justice. What if he had seen the prætor perched on a tall chariot, raised aloft in the middle of the dusty Circus, wearing Jupiter's Tunic and carrying the Spangled Toga's Tyrian drapery on his shoulders, with a huge encircling Crown too big for one human neck to support? (Indeed it makes the public slave sweat, who is taken on the car to hold it and placed alongside of the Hero to keep his conceit down.)　To this picture add The Fowl mounted on its ivory Sceptre : and in front, on one side trumpeters ; on the other, a long line of homage, sons of Romulus dressed in their whitest, and become the Hero's friends—or friends of the charity which is stowed away in their money-boxes. But even before there were such doings, every contact with mankind was food for laughter to Him whose wisdom is the proof that men of genius and exemplars for future ages may be bred under a foggy climate in the native land of mutton-heads.　He could make merry over the business as over the pleasures of his fellow-men : sometimes over their tears even, while (for himself) he told Fortune to go and be hanged, and pointed at her with the finger of scorn.

All the petitions, then, for which Piety enjoins us to daub wax on the knees of gods, are either idle or mischievous.　Some men are overthrown by their very greatness because it cannot escape the envy of Power : they are overwhelmed by the long and grand record of their own honours.　Down their statues come, and go after the tugging rope. The very chariot wheels are smashed by the smiting axe, and the innocent horses have their legs broken.　Already the flames are hissing ; forge and bellows are melting the head once worshipped by the people.　Sejanus is one crackling mass !　Presently the face which ranked second in all the world is manufactured into jugs, foot-pans, frying-pans,

Margin notes:

The Aquila.

Democritus.

54–113.
The vanity of ambition illustrated by the fall of Sejanus.

Wax tablets containing prayers.

Of the triumphal statues.

The favourite and minister of Tiberius.

and chamber-pots. Put up the laurel-boughs over your doorways! chalk the big ox white, and lead him to the Capitol! Sejanus is being dragged away by the Hook! It is a sight to see, and the joy is universal.

Conversation between two time-servers *after* the fall of Sejanus.

"What lips he had! and what a face!" cries some one. "If you believe me, I never liked the man. But tell me what charge overthrew him? who was the informer? what the evidence? who the witness?"

"No such thing," it is answered. "A long and rambling letter came from Capreæ." Where Tiberius was living in seclusion.

"I am glad of it, and that is enough for me."

Does one ask what the spawn of Remus say about it? Why, they follow Fortune's lead, and curse the fallen—that is the way of them. The lower orders of Rome. All the same, if Nortia had prospered her Tuscan, and if An Etruscan goddess. the old ruler had been caught napping, in that very Reference to the origin of Sejanus. hour the Roman People would have hailed Sejanus as their Augustus. It is a long time, dated from the day when votes were first withdrawn from When Tiberius deprived the people of the right of electing magistrates. the market, since the People shook off public spirit. Once the dispenser of authority, office, and commands, it renounces its pretensions and sets its heart anxiously on two things only — food and pageants free.

"I hear that there will be many deaths."

Another conversation (*before* the fall of Sejanus) as to impending trials.

"No doubt about it. There is room enough in the furnace. At the Mars altar I met my friend Brutidius looking rather pale. I am much afraid that our Ajax, if he is beaten, will take revenge on *i.e.,* if Tiberius fails to weak supporters."

secure the conviction of the other persons involved in the conspiracy.

" Then let us run in haste, and trample Cæsar's enemy while he is prostrate on the bank. But let the slaves see it done, lest one of them should deny it and drag his terrified master with neck throttled into the claws of Justice."

Better than to pay the price which ambition requires is the peaceful security of humble office in a country town.

Such were the comments on Sejanus ; such the furtive murmurs of the crowd. Do you then covet the *levées* of Sejanus ? Would you be as rich as he was ? and able to set one man in the chair of office and another at the head of armies ? Be guardian to a ward like the Cæsar perched with his pack of Chaldeans on Capreæ's cliffs ? You wish, no doubt (and why should you not wish ?), to command the pikes and cohorts, the knights-at-arms, and the imperial guard. Even those who have not the will would have the power, of inflicting death on their fellows. Yet what distinction or what success is worth the winning, if the meed of pleasure is to bring an equal meed of woe ? Would you wear the state robe which once decked yonder draggled corpse ? would you not rather be a High Mightiness at Fidenæ or Gabii to adjudicate on the imperial standard, and to break up swindling measures like the shabby magistrate at depopulated Ulubræ ?

Tiberius.

So, then, you admit that Sejanus mistook the right objects of desire ? Wishing for too much honour and demanding too much wealth, he was building a tower of many stories only to lengthen

The violent ends of great men.

the fall—the fearful force of that downward impetus. What overthrew a Crassus, a Pompeius, and him who brought the Romans in submission

Julius Cæsar.

to his lash? What but scrambling and pushing for the topmost place? what but the cruel kindness of the gods in hearkening to ambition's prayers? Yes, few are the kings started on their downward road to Pluto without murder and violence, few despots by a bloodless death.

114-132. *The vanity of eloquence illustrated by the fates of Cicero and Demosthenes.*

Every lad not too old to worship the Minerva image (bought by his single copper-piece) or to be attended by the slave urchin carrying the tiny box of books, sets his heart, and all through the Five Days' festival keeps it, on the eloquence and glory of Demosthenes and Cicero. Yet that eloquence was the ruin of both orators: both were given over to destruction by the rich flood of their own genius. And "Genius" found his head and hands cut off, whereas no feeble pleader has ever drenched the rostra with his blood.

As patroness of learning.

Festival of Minerva.

Cicero.

"*Blest state, regenerate in my consulate!*" If the orator had been no better than the poet, Cicero might have laughed at the swords of Antonius. Myself, I would rather claim the doggerel verses than the brilliant honours of that marvellous philippic which comes second on the roll! So, again, it was a cruel end which snatched away him to whom all Athens would listen in amazement as he rushed on in his might, yet kept the crowded benches well in hand. Only because he had been born in the disfavour of Heaven and under an evil star was he sent to the rhetoric school away from the coals and tongs, away from the anvil and yellow flames of the sword foundry, where his father's eyes had grown purblind from the dross of red-hot ore.

One of Cicero's bad verses.

Against Antonius.

Demosthenes.

133–146.
The vanity of military glory.

Spoils of war—the breastplate fastened as trophy to a tree's trunk, the cheekpiece hanging loosely from a battered helmet, the war-chariot with shattered pole, the stern-end of a defeated trireme, and the gloomy captive figured overhead upon the arch of triumph — are thought better than all human blessings. Such the height to which the captains-of-war, Roman, Greek, and Barbarian, had lifted up their spirits! such their impulse to danger and toil! So much stronger is the thirst for glory than for Merit! Who, indeed, woos Merit for its own sake if its rewards are taken away? And yet a country has ere now been ruined for one or two men's ambition, for the lust after honours and inscriptions that will only be fastened upon stones which mount guard over the ashes but are not strong enough to hold together against the tough malice of a wild fig-tree's fibres. Verily there is a last day even for the tomb.

147–167.
The exploits and ambition of Hannibal ended·in suicide.

Put Hannibal in the scales, and how many pounds of flesh will you find in the famous general? Here you have all that remains of one who cannot be confined within a continent lashed on one side by the Mauretanian Ocean, on another reaching to the warm Nile and downwards again to the Ethiop tribes and the land of tall elephants. He extends the frontier beyond Spain, and springs across the Pyrenees. When Nature confronts him with her Alpine snows, he splits the rocks and breaks open the hills with floods of acid. Already he lays his hand on Italy, yet presses on to further conquests. "All has been as naught," he cries, "unless the

11

soldiers of Carthage force the gates of Rome and my banner is planted in the Subura's heart."

It was a grand sight, and a grand subject for a picture, the one-eyed captain sitting his African monster! What then is the end of it all? Fie on Elephant. Glory! Why, he is beaten himself, and flees in hot haste to exile. There the mighty man, the novel suppliant, crouches at the palace-doors of a king, Antiochus of Syria. until it suits him better to dance his attendance on a Bithynian sultan. The spirit which once made Prusias. havoc of the world will not get its quietus from sword or sling or javelin, but from one small ring whose poison shall wipe out Cannæ and avenge the 216 B.C. carnage. Onwards then, poor fool ; race across your cruel Alps—to become the hero of school-boys and the subject of "Prolusions"!

168-173.
Alexander the Great met an inglorious death.
Pella's hero finds one earth too small, and chafes Alexander. in wretchedness within the world's cramping limits as if he were cribbed between the cliffs of Gyaros or tiny Seriphus. Nevertheless, after he has made his entry into the city of brick-bakers, he will find Killed by a tile at Babylon. room enough inside a coffin. Only death discovers the littleness of human bodies.

173-187.
The fabulous exploits of Xerxes ended in a disgraceful *fiasco*.
An old article of faith is the flooded ship-way through Mount Athos, and so are all the lying sallies of Greek history—the bridging of the sea by the selfsame fleets until it made a solid road for The bridge of boats. wheels, the failure of deep rivers and the swallowing of whole streams (when the Mede broke his fast), with all the other drunken flights of singer Sostratus. But (after Salamis) what was the manner of return 480 B.C. for him whose wont it had been to wreak the fury of

a savage by whipping the winds—though they had
never undergone such dishonour in the jail of
Æolus — for him who put fetters even on the
Shaker of the Earth.   It was grace and mercy that
he did not also inflict the branding-iron ! (Any
god would be proud to be such a master's humble
servant !)   Well, what was the manner of his return?   With a single ship, over waves of blood,
through bodies blocking his prow in masses.   Such
was the price exacted by the glory which had been
besought with so many prayers.

Poseidon.

188-216.
The vanity
of long life.

The dis-
figurements
and
incapacities
of the aged.

"Grant me length of life, Jupiter; grant me
many years"—that is your only prayer, whether
your face be healthy or overcast with pallor.   Yet
how grievous and unremitting are the woes of a
prolonged old age.   Imagine your face become
ugly and beyond comparison disgusting, all your
features vanished, your skin changed into ugly
leather, your cheeks flabby and wrinkled like the
withered jowl which a matron monkey scratches in
Numidia's vast and leafy forests.   There is variety
amongst young men : one is fairer than the other,
that other fairer than a third ; or one is far stronger
than the other. But the old all wear one uniform—
limbs as shaky as their voices, pates worn to
smoothness, and noses running like a baby's.   The
poor soul must mumble his bread with toothless
gums; and he has become so loathsome to his
wife, his children, and himself, that he would
turn the stomach of fortune-hunter Cossus.   The
sluggish palate has lost its old relish of food and
drink—sex being a sense long ago forgotten.   Or

if a trial is made of it, the flesh reveals its weakness, a weakness which no prurient arts can stimulate. What better hope can there be for decrepid lust? (Have we not, moreover, good reason to look shyly at the lechery which pretends to passions that it cannot gratify?) Look now at the damage done to another organ. An old man takes no delight in the music of a harper, howsoever famous, not even Seleucus or the stage fops in their dazzling cloaks of gold. It matters not whereabouts he is seated in the theatre, since he can hardly hear even the braying horns or crashing trumpets. The slave must shout aloud for his master's ear to catch a caller's name or the time of day.

Perhaps for extortionate purposes.

217-239.
The diseases of age.

Then, again, the blood is poor in his chilled body, and gets its only warmth from fever. Diseases of every kind form in fiendish chorus and dance about him. But if you ask me for their names, it would take longer than to give you the list of Hippia's paramours or the patients sacrificed in one autumn to Themison's quackeries; the partners swindled by Basilus or the wards by Hirrus; the customers exhausted in one day by the lankey Mooress, or the pupils debauched by teacher Hamillus. It would be quicker to run through the roll of mansions now possessed by the man whose razor once grated against my young stubble. One old man you may see paralyzed in shoulder, loin, or hip; another blind of both eyes, and jealous of those who have sight in one; the bloodless lips of a third are receiving food from a servant's fingers, whilst

The mental weakness of the mouth, which once showed all the teeth at

old men
subjects
them to
unworthy
bondage.

sight of dinner, gapes in helplessness, like the nestling swallow welcoming its famished mother's well-stored beak: but worse than any bodily decay is mental failure, forgetfulness of the names of servants or the features of the friend and companion at last evening's dinner—forgetfulness of the children begotten and reared in the father's house. They are cut off by a heartless will from their natural portions, and the whole estate passes to the "Virgin Harlot," so potent are the persuasions of that ingenious mouth which for many a past year had done duty at the brothel cell.

240-257.
The family
afflictions
which come
upon old
men.

Even if the mental powers do not decay, the old man must follow sons to the grave, and behold the dear wife or brother on the funeral pyre and the ashes of sisters packed in urns. This is the penalty exacted from long-livers—havoc in the family time upon time repeated, and an old age spent amid afflictions in constant mourning and black weeds. The king of Pylos was (if one puts Nestor. any trust in classic Homer) an instance of long life only second to the crow's. And we must suppose that he is happy because he has put off his death for so many generations, begins to reckon his century, and drinks new vintages so often! But listen, I beseech you, how he rails himself against the rules of Fate and curses his own long-drawn thread of life, when he looks upon his son Antilochus, once a bearded and gallant warrior but now flaring on the pyre. Hear the old man put his question to all the friends about him—"why am I lingering to this day? what sin have I done

to deserve so long a life?" The same words
were spoken by Peleus mourning for the ravished
Achilles, and by him who had a father's right to   Laertes.
mourn for the wave-tossed Ithacan.   Ulysses.

258-272.
The vanity
of long life
illustrated
by the
disastrous
close of
Priam's
career.

Priam might have gone down to the shades of his
ancestors in honour and glory, as king of the grand
old Troy, with Hector and his brothers to support
his bier amid the wailing of noble women, with
Cassandra to lead the strain of sorrow and Polyxena
to rend her raiment, if only he had died at another
time before Paris had laid the stocks for his desperate cruisers. What then did he profit by length
of days? He saw his fortunes overturned, and all
Asia falling before fire and sword. That was the
hour when the palsied warrior flung aside his
turban to bear arms, and tumbled before great
Jupiter's altar—like a worn-out ox, long ago scorned
by the graceless plough, submitting a lean and
wretched neck to the farmer's knife. Be that as it

His wife
was more
unhappy.

might, his end was human: but the wife who out-
lived him came to snarling and barking in the image
of a dog.

273-288.

I pass over the King of Pontus and Crœsus   Mithri-
(warned by the eloquence of Solon the Just to look   dates III.
to the last lap in the race of life), and I hasten on
to Roman instances. It was length of days which

The sad end
of the
glorious
career of
Marius.

brought Marius to exile, imprisonment, concealment in Minturnæ's marshes, and the bread of
beggary in the streets of conquered Carthage.
Where could the world, where could Rome, ever
have shown greater happiness than would have
been his, had he given up his ghost in triumph

amid the pomp of war, just after he had led round
his line of Teuton prisoners and just before he
stepped down from the car of victory?   Campania

Pompeius
was more
unfortunate
than the
Catilinarian
conspirators.

(in its prescience) had granted to Pompeius the
fever which should have been prayed for; but the
multitude of cities and a people's prayers prevailed
against it.   So it came about that he was saved by
his own and the city's fortune only to be conquered
and robbed of his head.   This agony and retribution were escaped by Lentulus; Cethegus fell
unmutilated; and Catilina lay with his body un-
divided.

50 B.C.

63 B.C.

289-323.
The vanity
of beauty.

Its dangers
for girls.

When a fond mother sets eyes on a temple of
Venus, she prays in whispered accents for handsome sons, but speaks more boldly in her daughters'
names, so that she ends by being dainty in her
petitions.

"Why should you rebuke me?" she cries.   "Does
not the mother Latona take delight in her Diana's
beauty?"

Yes, but Lucretia's fate is a lesson against covet-
ing such charms as hers; and Virginia would be
glad to bestow hers upon a Rutila and take the

The heroine
of the tale
about
Appius
Claudius.

The worse
dangers
which it
brings upon
boys.

hump in exchange.   Surpassing beauty in a son
keeps his parents in constant agony and alarm
—so rare it is for modesty and beauty to dwell in
peace together.   Yea, though purity of life be the
heirloom in a family of the rough old Sabine type,
and even if Nature herself (who is stronger to help
than any watch or ward) opens her generous hand

The tempta-
tions of a
handsome
youth.

to give him the greatest of her boons, chastity
of spirit and a face which flushes with modest

blood, still the lad must not keep his manhood. The lavishness of the seducer's vice does not even shrink from tampering with his parents. Such is the boldness of corruption! On the other hand, no ugly boy was ever mutilated by a tyrant in his cruel stronghold, nor did Nero ravish a young bandy-legs or a scrofulous and pot-bellied hunchback.

His probable career, sinking from bad to worse.

Go you, then, and rejoice, if you can, in the beauty of a son whom peculiar perils are awaiting. He will become the town adulterer, and live in fear of penalties which he owes to the angry husbands; nor will he be so much luckier than Mars as never to fall into a trap. And sometimes outraged Honour enforces more than any law allows to honour—death by the knife, stripes from the bloody scourge, or perhaps the "Mullet-clyster." At first your Endymion will pick the partner of his sin. Afterwards, when a Servilia has offered money, he will give himself even to the woman whom he loves not, and strip her of the very clothes from her body. Be she high or low, she thinks no sacrifice too great for her passion, once it is excited; for passion is the focus of a soiled woman's whole life.

An instrument of torture.

324-345. The dangers of purity.

Do you ask, what harm can beauty do where there is purity? Ask, rather, what profit had Hippolytus, what profit had Bellerophon, from his stern resolve? Why, Phædra flushed like a woman insulted, and rejected Sthenobœa glowed with an equal flame; and both of them gathered themselves for the leap of vengeance. Woman's fury reaches its climax when hatred is spurred on by shame.

The fate of
Caius Silius,
who was
enticed into
a mock
marriage
with
Messalina.

Take your choice of the counsel which you would give to the youth whom Cæsar's wife marks down to become her "husband." Best and fairest of Rome's gentle blood, the unhappy youth is carried away to perish under Messalina's basilisk eyes. The bride is seated and waiting with her yellow veil prepared; the purple coverlet for the nuptial bed is spread in the gardens for all to see; the dowry of one hundred thousand sesterces will be given in time-honoured fashion; and witnesses will be present with the augur.   Perhaps

Apostrophe
to Silius.

you thought that this matter, Silius, would be the secret of a few confidants.   No; she will not have a make-shift wedding!   Tell me your decision : if you will not consent, you must die before candle-light; if you do the sin, you will gain a brief respite, until the common talk of town and populace finds its way to the Emperor's hearing.   He will be the last to learn the disgrace of his own house.

Greater
fortitude on
his part
would have
been
unavailing.

For that interval go and do her bidding, if you put such a value on the few days of life.   But whatever course you think is the better (or the worse), still you must sacrifice that fair white neck of yours.

346-366.
The moral
of this Satire
is for Man to
leave his fate
in the hands
of Heaven.

Do I cut man off from every prayer?   If you would have my advice, you will leave it to the gods to decide what is right and useful in human fortunes.   The gods will give us not what we desire, but what we most need.   Man has a better friend in Heaven than in himself.   Driven on by passion, and led by the blind guidance of a masterful desire, we set our hearts upon marriage and the hope of offspring.   But the gods know—how the

Messalina,
wife of
Claudius.

wife and children will turn out! Still, if you really must pray for something, and must go to the shrines with your offerings of tripe and white porker's consecrated sausage-meat, let your petition *His only prayer should be for virtue.* be for a healthy mind in a healthy body. Pray for a brave heart, which knows not the fear of death, and ranks length of life lowest among the gifts of Nature, strong in the sufferance of appointed labours, innocent of wrathfulness and lust, and counting the trials and cruel labours of a Hercules better than the loves and revelries and feather-beds of Sardanapalus. The prize which I offer you can win for yourself. The only path which leads to peace of mind goes by way of Virtue. Wheresoever Wisdom abides, there, Fortuna, thou hast no power of thine own. It is we who make a goddess of thee, and give thee thy mansion in the skies.

SATIRE XI.

LUXURY AT ROME.

(AN EPISTLE TO A LUXURIOUS FRIEND.)

1–8. Rutilus, the typical spendthrift, turns gladiator to earn his living.

IF Atticus dines richly he passes for a sumptuous man, but Rutilus for an idiot. Nothing is greeted with louder public laughter than a pauper prodigal. Rutilus is the one topic of every dinner-table, bath, lounge, and theatre. For though his sturdy young frame is glowing with blood, and might support a soldier's helmet, the story is that he intends—not by, but not against, our "Tribune's" orders—to put his hand to the harsh terms and rules of the Gladiators' school.

Title assumed by the Emperors.

9–20. The recklessness which leads such men to ruin.

There are plenty like him, men for whom the dodged creditor is wont to lie in wait just at the Fish-market's entrance, men who live for nothing but their palates. The neediest wretch amongst them dines in all the better style and comfort, though he is as sure to come down as a wall which shows daylight between its cracks. But before the crash comes they scour all the elements for a relish, and never let their desires be balked by prices; and a closer view shows that the cost and pleasure are enhanced together. So they do not boggle about raising the (predestined) loan by

pawning their silver dishes and a mother's chipt
bust, or about wasting four hundred sesterces
upon a savoury mess for the importunate crockery
platter.   This is the road which brings them to
the gladiators' hotch-potch.

21-45.
Expenditure
must be
proportional
to income.

The same thing may be right for one man to get,
and for another wrong.   What is wastefulness in
Rutilus wears a good aspect in Ventidius, because
his fortune backs it up.   Will not my contempt be
justified when a man knows by how many feet
Mount Atlas overtops the other Libyan altitudes,
though he has not learnt the ratio between a
pocket-purse and an iron-bound safe?   *Know*

Men must
take stock
of them-
selves.

Thyself is a maxim direct from Heaven which
should be fixed and worn in the heart and memory,
whether you are looking for a wife or a seat in the
" Holy Senate."   Even Thersites is wiser than to

The braggart
of the Iliad.

claim that breastplate of Achilles which sat so ill
upon Ulysses.   Or if you take it upon you to argue
a knotty point of law with important issues, put
the question to yourself and answer it—What are
you? are you a strong speaker, or like the wind-
bags Curtius and Matho?   We must take the
measure of ourselves and test it in little and big
things alike.   Even in the buying of fish, you must
not wish for a mullet when your money will only
cover a gudgeon.   What is the end which awaits
you, with your gluttony expanding as your purse
contracts, when your family fortune and estate
have been submerged in a stomach big enough to
hold income, solid plate, lands, and herds?   A
capitalist of this kind must (last of all) part with

his Ring, and our Pollio takes to beggary with his finger naked. The fear which should lie before a prodigal is not the untimely pyre nor early funeral —worse than death should be the fear of prolonged existence.

46-55.
The Prodigal's progress ends in dishonour.

These are the regular gradations : first at Rome, the loan at interest, spent under the lender's eyes. When nothing is left except a paltry trifle and the usurer grows uneasy, the next thing is defaulting and a change of quarters to Baiæ and its oysters. For there is no more shame nowadays about running away from engagements than moving your residence from stifling Subura to the Esquiline Hill. Your exile's only trouble and only regret is to have missed one whole year of Circus pageants. Not a drop of blood is left him to blush with ; and Honour flees amid derision from a city where few men seek to hold her back.

56-76.
Juvenal invites a friend to share his own humble fare.

Sybarite, this day you shall see whether I do not bear out my pretty profession in practice, life, and fact, but am a secret gormandizer (though I swear by a diet of beans), and whisper "sweets" in my servant's ear when I call aloud for "porridge." When you come upon your promised visit, I shall be Evander and you shall be like his Tirynthian, or like his other guest (not, indeed, so grand as he, but still a blood-relation of the gods, who ascended to heaven by way of water as the other had by

The dinner described.

fire). Now listen to your dinner, which I shall not cater for in the markets. You shall have the fattest kid from my own farm at Tibur, innocent of grass, never yet bold enough to have gnawed the

The emblem of rank.

Hercules and Æneas were entertained with plain fare by Evander. Hercules was burnt and Æneas drowned.

lowly twigs of osier, and with more milk in his body than blood; asparagus from the high ground, which my bailiff's wife has laid aside her distaff to gather; monster eggs, still warm from their envelopes of hay, served with the pullets who laid them; grapes, kept for a part of the year, but fresh as on the vine; Signian and Syrian pears from the same basket as apples which might vie with Picenum's fruit. Though they smell so fresh, you need not fear them, since the winter frost has purged them of their dangerous autumn acid.

77–99.
The plain living of ancient Rome.

This was once upon a time quite an extraordinary repast for the senators of Rome. Curius would pick from his garden-plot with his own hands, and cook at his humble hearth, vegetables which are rejected nowadays by a dirty ditcher working in heavy fetters, who carries in his mouth the flavour of sow's womb eaten in the stuffy cook-shop. Once it was the fashion to save for a feast the chine of dried pork that hung from the wide rack, and to serve kinsmen with fat bacon only as a birthday treat, with any fresh meat from the sacrifice added. To attend such a banquet, a kinsman who had thrice supported the honours and active duties of a consul, as well as the dictator's office, would do a short day's work, shoulder his spade, and trudge home from the mountain-farm which he had bought to order. When men lived in awe of such censors as a Fabius, Scaurus, Fabricius, and unbending Cato; when, indeed, a censor himself quailed before his colleague's rigour, nobody thought it part of his

Simplicity in household furniture.

Defeated Pyrrhus 275 B.C.

In 204 B.C. one Censor was condemned by the other.

own business and concerns to know the quality
of the tortoise-shell floating upon the sea's waves
and destined to become a bright and shining
supporter for a "Trojan noble's" couch.   Beds
were small in those days, and the sides unadorned ;
the bronze front displayed the cheap ornament of
a crowned donkey's head, which the saucy bump-
kins used to mock at.   The food in those days
was, of course, simple, like the houses and
furniture.

100-110.
There was
no
æstheticism
in the army.

The soldier was rough then, not an amateur of
Greek art ; and at the sacking of a town, if in his
portion of the spoils he came upon cups by a great
designer, he would break them up for trappings
to please his horse or for his embossed helmet
to confront the doomed enemy with a figure of
the savage monster forced by Rome's destiny to
minister to Romulus the milk of kindness, or with
the twin Quirini seated underneath the rock, or
with the naked form of Mars descending with
shield and spear and just hovering between earth
and air.   There was not an ounce of silver save
what gleamed upon the armour, so they used to
serve their porridge on Tuscan pottery : a happy
world, in fact, such as might arouse envy in a
jealous nature !

The Wolf.

Romulus
and Remus.

111-116.
The very
statues of
the gods
were made
from clay,
but Rome
nevertheless
enjoyed the
favour of
Heaven.

Yea, the godhead in the temples was nigher to
man ; and a voice was heard by midnight in mid-
city, when the Gauls were marching from the ocean
and the gods took upon themselves the work of
prophets.   Such the monition and such the loving-
kindness which Jupiter would vouchsafe to the

fortunes of Latium when he was still fashioned from clay and undefiled by gold.

117–135.
The extravagance of costly dinner tables was unknown.

The dinner-tables of those days were made at home, and carved from native woods. This was the purpose for which the timber was stored if an old walnut-tree happened to be overthrown by the east wind. But your modern Dives can take no pleasure in dining, and finds the turbot and venison tasteless or the perfumes and roses nauseous, unless his huge round table rests upon a mass of ivory and an open-throated rampant leopard, fashioned from the teeth which are transported from Syene's station, from the land of the fleet-footed Moors or yet swarthier Indians, or shed in Nabathæa's forest when they have grown too big and cumbrous for the monster's head. This is what gets up the appetite and gives vigour to the

The modern prevalence of ivory ornaments, which are more precious than silver.

stomach. (A pedestal of common silver would be like wearing finger-rings of iron.) Have I not reason to be shy of a purse-proud guest who contrasts me with himself and looks down upon my slender fortune? Not so much as a single ounce of ivory is mine—no dice or counters made of that substance; nay, the very handles to my knives are of bone. But (all the same) they never taint the victuals or spoil the pullet's flavour.

136–148.
The fantastical carving of game will not be reproduced at Juvenal's dinner, nor the roguery

Nor, again, will you find a carver whom all the College must bow to, a pupil from Instructor Exquisite's house, where big sows' udders, hares, boars, antelopes, Scythian pheasants, flamingoes, and Gætulian goats are set out—a rich repast (of elm-wood) for the blunt knives to hack at until all Subura rattles. My raw youngster has never been trained, and has not learnt to snick away a steak of wild goat or a guinea-fowl's wing. His only guilt is petty larceny in the scraps. The common bowls (which were bought for a few copper-pieces) will be handed by a lad dressed roughly but protected from the cold, not a slave imported and purchased at a fancy price. You must call in the vulgar tongue when you call to him.

My staff of servants are all dressed alike; their hair is cut short and not curled, and only combed because there is company to-day. One is son of a rough shepherd, another of a cowherd; yonder lad, sighing for the mother whom he has not seen for a dreary while, and thinking wistfully of his cottage-home and the kids his playmates, has the gentle face and gentle purity which should belong to them who wear the blazing purple. (He does *i.e.*, free-born youths. not go to the Baths with his voice cracked and his puberty forced by precocious vices; he has not yet given his arms to the depilator, nor does he walk in the terrors of mock-modesty.) He will serve you with wine which was strained upon the very hills which he comes from himself and under whose shadow he has played. For the wine and butler are natives of the same country.

You might expect, perhaps, to have your naughti-ness awakened by a girl from Gades in a singing ballet, and to clap your hands while dancing women sink to the floor with quivering thighs. That is a sight which the bride with a husband at her side sits and watches, though a man would be

12

ashamed to describe it in her presence. (It is the
stimulant for sluggish blood and the rich man's
aphrodisiac. But the other sex feels sharper pleasure than ours ; their natures rise higher, and the
passion which made its entry at eye and ear throbs
quickly through the system.) Such fooleries can
have no place in my humble home. The music of
rattling castanets, accompanied by words too gross
for a harlot standing uncovered in a stinking
brothel, and the enjoyment of dirty songs, with the
divers inventions of lust, must be reserved for one
who has marble floors to lubricate with wine which
he is too dainty to swallow. (We make allowance
in his case for rank ; but gambling is disgraceful,
and so is adultery disgraceful—in the middle class !

But a simple reading of classical poetry. When the self-same things are done in high life
we call them spirited and smart.) At my dinner
to-day the amusement will be very different : a
reading from the author of the Iliad and verses,
which dispute his honours, written by majestic
Maro : poetry which the intoner cannot make or
mar.

183–192. Juvenal exhorts his friend to forget the troubles of domestic life. Come now, for once away with business, and
let your cares wait. Treat yourself to a pleasant
recreation, since you will have the chance of keeping a whole holiday. There must not be one
word spoken about money matters, nor one splene-
tic thought swelling in your secret heart because it
is your wife's way to go out early and return late,
bringing suspicious creases in her wet muslin, with
her hair tumbled and her face and ears flushed.
At my doorway you must at once drop all your

troubles; forget your servants with all their break-
ages and damages, and above all forget the
ingratitude of friends.

193–208.
The general
holiday
of the
Megalesian
games will
be a good
opportunity
for spending
a long day
with
Juvenal.

The
excitement
of the
people
backing their
favourite
" Faction "
in the chariot
races.

The people meantime are celebrating the pa-
geant of the Napkin, the holy rite of the great
goddess from Mount Ida.   The prætor is sitting
in state, as if it were a Triumph, high above the
horses which are eating up his substance; and the
whole of Rome (if I may call it so without offending
this huge and unwieldy populace) is to-day packed
within the Circus; and the din which strikes my
ear proves that Green is the winning colour.
For if it lost the day, you would see this city
in such grief and consternation as when our consuls
were vanquished on the dusty field of Cannæ.
Be this a spectacle for younger men, who have a
better right to cheer and offer rash bets and take
their seats beside smart girls.   It is for shrivelled
skins like ours to absorb the warm spring sun
and escape from the costume of the streets.   Even
now, though it wants a good hour of noon, it is
not too early for you to walk to the Baths with an
unabashed brow.   But you could not do it on
each of the Festival's five days, because even
holiday-making is followed by profound weariness.
The zest of pleasure lies in moderation.

The
" Napkin "
was dropt
as the signal
for the start.

SATIRE XII.

THE STORM AT SEA ENCOUNTERED BY CATULLUS.

(AN EPISTLE TO CORVINUS.)

1–16.
The sacrifice which Juvenal has prepared in honour of the escape of his friend Catullus from the storm.

IT is a morning, Corvinus, more pleasant to me than my own birthday. The turf of my festal altar is waiting for the victims promised to Heaven. White as snow is the lamb which is being led in honour of the Queen Goddess, and another as [Juno.] spotless shall be given to her who wields the Gorgon mask upon her shield. But the sacrifice [Minerva.] reserved for Tarpeian Jupiter is tugging viciously at the far end of a taut rope and tossing his head; a mettlesome calf indeed, ripe for temple and altar, and worthy of the wine-spray, ashamed of pulling his mother's bag any longer, and beginning to bully the oaks with his sprouting horns. If my purse might open as widely as my heart, I would have a grown bull dragged along, more corpulent than Hispulla and lazy from his mere bigness—not pastured on my own country-side, but with throbbing veins which told of the rich Clitumnus herbage, and a neck which wanted a big slaughterman to chop it. So would I celebrate my friend's return whilst he is still trembling and fresh from perilous adventures and wondering at his own salvation.

17–36.
Mock heroic account of the storm.

Besides the dangers of the waves, he has gone scathless through strokes of lightning. The whole sky was muffled in one pall of black cloud, when a flame flashed upon the yard-arms. Not a man but believed that he had been struck himself; still dazed after the shock, not a man but thought that no wreck could match the terrors of that flaring canvas. (There are always all these harrowing details—when a poet brews the storm.) Let us pass on to the next form of peril. Once again give me your attention and your sympathy, though what is coming is of a piece with what went before—the dreadful but familiar sequel which is recorded in many a temple by votive pictures. (Everybody knows that it is the Storm-goddess who boils our painter's pots!) Well, the conventional disaster came upon my friend Catullus. When the hold was half-way filled with water, and the waves were pitching first one side, then the other, of that crazy tree which did duty for a ship, and when the gray-haired skipper's science was unavailing, Catullus offered to compound with the winds at a loss, following the example of the Beaver, who makes a gelding of himself in the hope of saving his life at the sacrifice of sex—so conscious is he of the virtue in his loins!

They painted ship wrecks.

A valuable secretion, "castoreum."

37–51.
The terror of Catullus becomes for once in a way a passion

"Overboard with my possessions, over with them all!" cries Catullus, who was ready to fling away his greatest treasures—purple raiment soft enough for fops like Mæcenas, as well as woollen stuffs which

stronger than avarice.

.were dyed golden on the sheeps' very backs by the natural powers of Bætica's rich herbage, assisted by its climate and its famous river's alchemy.　Not even his silver plate was he slow to abandon—the platters fashioned by Parthenius, the mixing-bowl which held three gallons and might quench the thirst of Centaur Pholus or the wife of Fuscus;

Ironical commendation of Catullus.

baskets beside, and dinner-plates without number; a multitude of embossed cups once drained by the Schemer who bought Olynthus at a price.

Philip of Macedon.

What other man lives, and in what corner of the world, who has the (moral) courage to value person more than precious metals? salvation more than property?　There are many who do not make fortunes as the means of living, but—in their wilful blindness—only live to make the fortunes.

52–61.
The sacrifice of the cargo failing to lighten the ship, the sailors are reduced to cutting away the mast.

Most of the household wares are thrown away; still the sacrifice does not raise the good ship in the water.　In the urgency of trouble it came to putting axe to mast and so escaping from the strait.　A forlorn hope indeed, when we must mutilate a ship to save her.　Go you, then, and commit your life to the winds, because you have put your trust in hewn timber and are parted from death by four (or at most by seven) finger-breadths of deal planking. Again, consider what must go on board along with your sack of bread and fat wine-flagon—a set of hatchets for use in dirty weather !

62–74.
The storm abates, and the ship sights Alba Longa.

Well, when the sea had been smoothed in repose, when our passenger's luck had turned and his destiny prevailed over wind and wave, when the Spinster Sisters began to work in White Thread

The Fates.

and reel off better portions in their joy and loving-kindness, and when a wind got up not much stronger than a gentle breeze, the wretched make-shift of outstretched garments and (on the fore-sail only) some rags of canvas gave a start to the disfigured prow. When at last the wind. dropt by degrees, light returned, and with it hope of life. Then they sight the lofty peak which Iulus loved, the abode for which he abandoned his step-mother's Lavinium, and which took its name from the White Sow—that miracle of maternity which gladdened the Trojan Wanderers and rejoiced in the unexampled honour of thirty paps.

75-82.
She enters the artificial harbour constructed by the Emperor Claudius.

At last the good ship makes her way between the Moles over their watery enclosure, behind the Tuscan "Pharos" and those arms of wall which are first stretched out to sea right away from Italy and then elbowed inwards to the shore, making an anchorage more wonderful than any which Nature has provided. Well, crippled as his bark was, the captain steers for the smooth water inside the sheltered basin quiet enough to tempt pleasure-boats from Baiæ. There the sailors shave their pates in token of deliverance, and delight in spinning long yarns of perils past.

83-92.
Thanksgiving of the sailors and of Juvenal for his friend's safety.

Ho, then, mates! keep ye reverent silence and reverent thoughts; cover the shrines with garlands and the knives with meal-offering, and deck the soft altars of green turf. I will follow you anon, and will duly perform what is the chief rite, ere I return home where my humbler images of brittle, glistening wax receive their own tiny chaplets.

Alba Longa.

Lavinia.

A.D. 42.

Here I shall propitiate my private Jupiter and make burnt-offering to my family gods, and scatter the violets, blue, white, and yellow. It is a smart scene; my doorway has put up tall laurel boughs, and does its festive duty with daylight lamps.

93-110. Juvenal is not seeking to ingratiate himself with Catullus so as to secure a place in his will.

The arts of fortune-hunters.

Away, my friend, with your suspicions. The Catullus for whose home-coming I am setting up all these altars has three little ones to be his heirs. Tell me, pray—I pause for a reply—who would invest the value of a sickly, blinking hen upon so unprofitable a friend! No, that is an absurd out-lay. Not a quail will ever go to sacrifice for the man who has issue. But if childless (and wealthy) Gallita or Paccius show a symptom of malaria, their porticoes are hung from end to end with vows recorded and duly set up. Men arise who vow a

Elephants at Rome.

hecatomb of oxen—not of elephants, only because there are none here on sale, and because such mon-sters cannot be bred in Latium or anywhere in our climate, but are imported from the Land of Dark Skins before they come to browse upon the fields and forests of our Rutulian Turnus and range the imperial parks—not to take their orders from a subject. Remember that their ancestors were fol-lowers of the Tyrian Hannibal or the Generals of Rome, or the Molossian Monarch, and used to

Pyrrhus.

carry whole cohorts on their backs at a time—hosts by themselves, and moving towers of de-struction.

111-127. The extravagant sacrifices offered by

So it is not the fault of Novius or Pacuvius that ivory is not dragged to the altar and offered as the only victim which can satisfy such important

The fortune-hunters.

fortune-
hunters for
rich friends.

household gods and—their very humble servants. Gods of
Gallita and
Paccius. One of our worthies, if you allow him to make the sacrifice, will promise the finest and fairest carcase from his drove of slaves, or set the sacrificial wreath upon the brows of his page and maid; and, if this Agamemnon has an only daughter in Agamemnon
consented to
sacrifice
Iphigenia to
save the
Greek fleet,
but she was
redeemed by
the animal
put in her
place. the bloom of girlhood, he will resign her to the They would
even give
their own
flesh and
blood. altar, though he looks not for a second conjuring atonement by the Poet's hind. All praise to my countryman : an inheritance is worth more than the safety of a fleet. If the invalid has slipt past the Funeral Goddess, he will fall into our fisherman's weel; and (for a service so truly marvellous) he will unmake his old will and (perhaps) leave everything to Pacuvius without mentioning one other name. Our heir will strut in triumph over his defeated rivals; so you see that he has a goodly reward for slitting his Iphigenia's throat.

128-130.
But their
gains are not
worth
winning.

Long life to Pacuvius, say I—longer than the days of Nestor. Let his possessions be great as Nero's ill-gotten plunder; let him heap up mountains of gold—and let him be no man's friend, nor any man his friend.

SATIRE XIII.

THE PUNISHMENT OF SIN.

(AN EPISTLE TO CALVINUS.)

1-4.
General remarks upon the power of conscience.

EVERY act framed after a bad model is condemned by its own author. Punishment begins in the Court of Conscience, which never acquits a guilty man, although shameless partiality may have prevailed before the prætor in his treacherous ballot.

5-10.
The injury was slight in itself and an every-day matter.

What do you think is the public feeling, Calvinus, about the sin and crime of this late breach of trust? To begin with, the fortune which you came in for is not so slender that you will be overwhelmed by the pressure of an ordinary loss. Nor, again, is yours a rare misfortune, but a familiar and quite commonplace adventure, drawn hap-hazard from Fortune's heap of chances.

A friend had received money in trust and then denied his obligation.

11-22.
Practical knowledge of life, a more useful teacher than abstract philosophy, should have reconciled Calvinus to this blow.

A truce to idle lamentations. Manly sorrow must not waste heat, nor outgrow its cause. Is it so hard a thing for you to bear the smallest fraction of trouble, that you bubble and blaze inwardly just because a friend will not meet his solemn obligation? Does that astound one who has turned his back on threescore years, and was born when Fonteius was consul? Do you reap no

i.e., in 59 A.

better profit from such a long experience of life?
Philosophy, we know, can vanquish Fortune, and
her sacred writings contain grand maxims. Still,
we cannot deny the happiness of those pupils in
life's practical school who have learnt to bear its
drawbacks and not to fret under the collar.

23-37.
Virtue is so
uncommon
in these
wicked times
that it is a
mark of
puerility or
second child-
hood to
expect to
find it.

Which is the day of rest observed so holy as to
bring no swindler to light? no treachery or fraud?
no contempt for scruples in the race for wealth?
no earning of money by dagger or poison-box?
Rare, indeed, are good men—almost outnumbered
by the gates of Thebes or the rich Nile's mouths.

i.e., less than
seven.

We are living in the Ninth Epoch, and among a
generation worse than the Age of Iron; one for
whose wickedness Nature herself cannot discover
or assign a title from any of her metals. Yet we go
on making our appeals to the honour upon earth
and in heaven, loudly as Orator Fæsidius is ap-
plauded by the mouths which he feeds. Hang the
boy's bauble to your old neck! Are you really
ignorant of the charms which lie in other people's

Some rich
man eager to
win forensic
applause.
The " bulla "
worn by
young lads.

(Decay of
the old
religious
faith.)

money? Do you not really know what public laughter
your innocence excites when you ask any living
man not to become a perjurer, but to believe that a
God is present at temples and crimsoned altars?

38-52.
Religion has
been
corrupted by
anthropo-
morphic or
ridiculous
fables.

Once upon a time aborigines lived in that simple
faith, before banished Saturnus laid aside his diadem
for a farmer's pruning-hook, when Juno had not lost
her maidenhead, and Jupiter was still living in the
seclusion of Cretan caves; before there were big
dinner-parties up above the clouds, and before the
Trojan Pet or the buxom wife of Hercules filled

Ganymede
and Hebe.

the wine-cups, or Vulcan drained his nectar without first cleansing his arms from the griminess of his Liparean blacksmith's shop. Every god then used to eat his meals at home—nor was there such a mob of gods as nowadays; and the modest Pantheon of star-promoted deities did not lie so heavily on the shoulders of unhappy Atlas. That was before the kingdom of Nether Gloom had been allotted; before the time of Pluto and his Sicilian consort; before the Wheel, the Furies, the Stone, and black avenging Vulture, when the ghosts led a merry life without kings in hell.

The tortures of Ixion, Sisiphus, and Tityus.

53-59.
The modesty and respectfulness of primitive times before the introduction of cereals.

Shamelessness passed for a wonder in these days; and men thought it was a heinous crime, only to be expiated by death, if a youth kept his seat before an old man, or a boy (though at his own home he could feast his eyes on more strawberries and bigger acorns) before his whisker'd senior. Such was the honour paid to four years' start in life; so equal the sanctity yielded to reverend age and to the downy chin!

60-70.
Honesty has become a miracle.

Now if a friend does *not* disavow the trust, but restores a battered pouch with all its rusty contents, his good faith is a prodigy which deserves a place in the "Etruscan Records," and must be expiated by a lamb in chaplets. When I see a good and incorrupt man, I think that he is a freak of nature —like a boy-centaur, or breeding mule, or like the fishes which some plough is startled to unearth. He makes me as uneasy as if there had been a shower of stones, or a long cluster of bees swarming on a temple roof, or as if a river had carried

As a miracle portending mischief.

down to the sea an unnatural eddying stream of rolling milk.

71–85.
The loss of Calvinus is comparatively small. Worse frauds are committed every day, and supported by elaborate perjury.

Do you complain because your ten thousand sesterces have been embezzled by a profane fraud ? What say you when twenty times that sum (confided in the same private fashion) has been lost by your neighbour; and a still larger amount by some third person, one which had scarcely been packed within the four corners of an ample money-box ? So easy and natural a thing it is to set the evidence of gods at defiance when their secret is not shared by some human witness. Mark the steady tone of our liar's No ! behold his false, yet unflinching, eye !

Curious oaths.

He takes his oath by Sol's rays and Tarpeian Jupiter's bolts, by the spear of Mars and the shafts of Cirrha's Seer, by the quiver and arrows of the Virgin Huntress, by the trident of the Ægean Father Neptune; he throws you in the bow of Hercules and Minerva's lance along with all the other weapons kept in stock in the magazines of heaven. More than that : if he is a father, our Thyestes cries, " If ever I had that money, may I eat the head of a late lamented son, boiled and soused in Pharos vinegar."

86–105.
The unscrupulousness of an atheist is not worse than an orthodox believer's self-sophistication.

Some put human life amongst the accidents of chance, and believe that the universe moves without a Ruler, for the alternations of light and season are regulated by blind force. So they feel no qualms when they place their hands upon whatever altars you pick out. Another man has in his heart the fear of penalty following upon sin. He believes in gods—still he does his

About £85.

Apollo and Diana.

perjury.   This is how he reasons with himself:—

"Let Isis pass what sentence she will upon my "body: let her strike the rattle of wrath against "my eyes, if only I may keep my hold, even at "the cost of blindness, upon the money which I am "disavowing. That is a recompense worth consump-"tion, mouldering sores, and withered limbs.   Not "even a runner like Ladas, if he were a poor man, "would think twice about praying for gout (with "riches) unless he stands in need of Anticyra's "specific and the attention of Archigenes.   What "advantage is there in a pair of heels honoured for "their lightness, or from sprigs of Pisa's olive-crown "—on an empty stomach?   The wrath of the gods "may be stern, but certainly it works slowly. When "will my turn come then, if they make it their busi-"ness to punish all sinners?   Or perhaps I shall "find a god of mercy. Sins like mine are pardoned "every day. The same transgression brings different "fates upon different men.   The reward of one "man's iniquity is the cross, while another earns "the crown."

This is how they harden their hearts against the first tremors of guilt.   Soon, if you call upon your doubter to go with you to the sacred shrine, he steps ahead, and is ready to drag you along himself and insist upon his ordeal.   The world gives credit for a good conscience when great effrontery backs a rotten cause.   Yet the man is acting a farce like the truant slave of waggish Catullus. You protest (unhappy you!) enough to shout down

The Egyptian deity imported to Rome.

"The unjust profit is worth the penalty."

"But that penalty will be long in coming if the gods have to punish all the sins in the world."
"Perhaps they will pardon this sin."
Honesty is not always the best policy."

Helle-bore (for insanity). The mad doctor.

The athletic prizes.

106–119. Effrontery passes for conscious honesty.

The vanity of appeals to the deaf ears of Heaven.

A play writer.

a Stentor, or perhaps as loudly as the Mars in
Homer :—

"Dost thou hear him, Jupiter, yet makest no sign
with thy lips though thou shouldst have sent forth
a voice from thy mouth, albeit bronze or marble?
Else, why do we open our paper parcels and lay
the burnt-offerings of piety upon thy cinders, along
with slices of calf's liver and white pig's chitter-
lings? For what I can see, we need make no
difference between your statues and the figure of a
Vagellius !"

Perhaps an inarticulate speaker.

120–125.
Preface to the consolatory part of the epistle.

Now accept the antidote of comfort which can
be given even by one who has studied the doctrines
neither of Cynics nor Stoics (divided only in point
of vestments), and is not an admirer of the vegeta-
rian Epicurus in his garden-plot. Let fashionable
doctors treat critical cases; but you may entrust
your bleeding even to an apprentice of Philippus.

Probably a notoriously incompetent physician.

126–142.
The injury of Calvinus does not deserve much lamentation, although money is the one thing which has a sure place in men's hearts.

Show me that your injury is unparalleled for
vileness in the whole world, and I say not a word;
nor do I forbid you then to thump your breast with
clenched fists, or to batter your face with the open
palm. (After a bereavement etiquette requires a
man to keep his door closed, and there is louder
wailing and uproar in a house for lost money than
lost relatives. There is no sham sorrow over this
misfortune; nor is it enough to slit the outside hem
of your tunic, or to vex your eyes with reluctant
moisture. They are honest tears which weep for
the dear departed gold.) But if every Court in
Rome is crowded with plaints like yours, and if
you see defendants, after documents have been

Barefaced
perjury in
open court.
quoted time upon time on the other side, still declaring that the bond is not worth the wood on which it is inscribed—although they are confronted with their own Hand and Seal (which they treasure in ivory caskets as the Premier Sardonyx)—do you consider, my dainty friend, that you are to be placed above the common lot of man because you are The White Hen's son, whilst we are the vulgar chickens from unlucky eggs? Perhaps an allusion to some fable.

Turn your eyes to the greater crimes, and yours becomes a commonplace wrong which can be met without uncommon spleen. Think of hiring an 143-156.
Conspiracy
to murder.
Incendiar-
ism. assassin, or laying the sulphur for malicious arson and starting the first flames at the inmate's exit-door. Sacrilege. Think of men robbing temples of cups oxidized by venerable age, public gifts of a nation, and crowns bestowed by some king of olden times. If rich booty fails, a petty profaner rises into view, who scrapes the thighs of gilt Hercules, and peels the gold-foil from Castor. (Need he have scruples when we make nothing of smelt- Perhaps to be re-cast. ing a Thunderer whole?) Think of the com- The trade in poison. pounders and traffickers of poison, and of one who Parricide. deserves to be carried to the sea in an ox-hide with an innocent unhappy ape to share his close Drowned in the same sack as the parricide. quarters.

157-173.
Human
nature is
seen in its
true colours
in the
Criminal
Court.
This makes a tiny fraction of the total wicked-ness which the City Warden Gallicus hears recited from the morning star's rising until the light sinks again. The student of human nature need not travel beyond that chamber. Spend a few days there, and when you come away, tell me,

Crime is the staple product of Rome.

if you dare, that your own is a hard case. Who is surprised at goître among the Alps or, in Meroe's island, at a woman's breast being bigger than her ⟨In Egypt.⟩ lumpish baby? Who was ever startled at a German having watchet eyes and yellow hair, or twisting his curls into a greasy tuft? The reason is that the type of one is the type of all. A Pygmy soldier in dwarf's armour marches against a sudden onslaught from the hurtling cloud of Cranes. Presently he is outmatched, clutched, and borne aloft in the cruel birds' crooked talons. Here the sight would shake you with laughter; but there is no laughing (though such combats are watched intently) in a place where no soldier in the whole cohort stands more than " one foot nothing."

174–192. The vanity of seeking satisfaction by legal process.

"Shall there be no punishment (do you ask?) for that perjured soul, for that infamous fraud?"

Suppose that he has been taken off in the heaviest irons and put to death according to our own sentence. (What further satisfaction could wrath demand?) Still, your deficit remains what it was, nor will your trust-money ever be made good. You will only get an odious satisfaction by spilling a few drops of blood from the mutilated corpse.

The vanity of revenge for its own sake.

Do you say that "Revenge is dearer than life itself?" Why, that is like fools whose passions take fire at nothing or at trifles. No matter how petty the occasion, it is good enough for their anger.

Revenge is unworthy of a philosopher, being what belongs to a woman or

No, you will not find your maxim among the sayings of Chrysippus, or gentle Thales, or the Elder ⟨Socrates.⟩ who lived near honey-sweet Hymettus and even in his cruel fetters refused to share with his traducer the hemlock meted out to himself. (One by one, blessed Philosophy divests man of most vices and all errors, and gives him the first lesson in right-doing.) Yes, it is the dwarfed, weak, and mean spirit which takes delight in revenge. Here is the proof put closely :—retaliation is Woman's special pleasure !

But why do you think that men have escaped when they live in terror of the awful knowledge residing in their own hearts and are scourged by silent lashes from the whip which is wielded by Inquisitor Conscience ? It is a punishment heavy indeed, and far more cruel than any which stern Cædicius and Rhadamanthus can devise, night and day to carry the condemning witness in your own soul.

A man of Sparta received answer from the Pythian prophetess that one day he should not escape for taking thought to withhold a trust and support his cheat by a false oath. (He came to ask what the god thought, and whether Apollo advised the act.) So he made his restitution—but from terror, not from honour. Still he became a testimony that all the oracle's words were words of truth and worthy of that famous temple, for he was blotted out, he and all his house, and (however distant in their lineage) all his kinsmen with him.

Such is the punishment for the mere desire of unrighteousness. The man who harbours an unspoken thought of wickedness has all the guiltiness of sin. What comes to pass if he has carried out his purpose ? Haunting anxiety does not rest even

when he sits at table. His throat is parched and
feverish, and the unmanageable morsel swells as he
chews it, but he cannot retain the wine to dilute
it. Unhappy wretch ! he is disgusted by Alba's
old and precious vintage. Offer him a choicer
kind, and puckering wrinkles are gathered upon
his brow, as on one grimacing after sour " Falernian." If his trouble has humoured him with
a short slumber at night-time, and his limbs, after
being tossed over the whole bed, are at last rest-
ing, at once there rises before him the temple and
altar of the offended deity, and—what more than
all bathes his soul in a cold sweat—the Vision
of Yourself—a ghostly and gigantic form, which
terrifies the coward and forces him to make confession.

223–228.
His
superstitious
terrors.

These are they who quake and grow pale at
every flash of lightning ; and thunder makes them
faint even at the sky's first rumbling. For they
believe that the fire is not falling to ground by
accident or stress of weather, but is sent in wrath
and coming to judgment. If the first storm has
done no damage, they look for the next in yet more
grievous terror, as though the present calm was
but respite for a time.

229–235.
His fanciful
ailments.

Moreover, if they have felt a twinge in the side,
followed by feverish wakefulness, they think it is a
disease sent upon them by some offended deity—
such they believe are the stones and javelins which

His
hopelessness.

gods fight with ! They have no heart to vow a
bleating sheep at the altar, nor to promise a cock's
comb to their own Lares. What hope is vouchsafed

to the guilty man in sickness? What victim is not nobler than the soul which it would atone for?

236-249.
His repentance is transitory, and cannot hold its ground against ingrained badness.

Unstable and fickle as the heart of wicked men is at most times, there is steadiness enough while the sin is being done. It is after the guilt has been completed that they begin to have glimmerings of right and wrong. Stubborn and unteachable, the heart nevertheless turns once more to that life which it has just condemned. Where is the man

Sooner or later he will come to grief.

who has ever stopped short in misdoing, or regained the blush once banished from his hardened brow? Who is the man whom you have ever seen

This will be the fate of the unfaithful friend of Calvinus.

contented with sinning once only? Some day our own Traitor will put his feet into the snare, and make acquaintance in a dark dungeon with the Hook, or with the Ægean rocks and cliffs which are thronged with Crime's banished heroes. You shall exult in a detested being's bitter punishment, and confess with gladness at last that every god has ears to hear and eyes to see with.

SATIRE XIV.

THE HOME INFLUENCE.

(AN EPISTLE TO FUSCINUS.)

1–14.
The example of parents is the cause of their children's evil actions.

THERE are many things, Fuscinus, deserving evil report and putting an indelible blotch on purity, which children get as a lesson and legacy from their own parents. If an old man takes delight in ruinous dicing, his bauble-wearing heir becomes a young gambler after him, and fights the same battles with toy weapons. Nor can a young man's relatives hope for better things of him if he has learnt from a prodigal father, and been in-

The lesson in gluttony.

structed by a grey-haired gormandizer, to peel truffle-skins, flavour mushrooms, and souse floating becaficoes in "the family sauce." When his *Eodem (quo pater).* seventh year has passed away, and before all his second teeth have grown again, though you may station ten Long-Beards to instruct him on his right, and another ten on his left hand, his desire will be to eat his dinner every day in grand style and to perpetuate his culinary honours.

15–25.
The lesson in cruelty.

Does Rutilus inculcate gentleness of spirit and forbearance towards trivial faults? Does he consider that Master and Slave are compounded from the same matter and like elements? Is he not rather an instructor in cruelty, if he takes delight in the tingling resonance of stripes, and thinks that no siren can discourse music like the scourge's ; if he is an ogre and cannibal in his trembling household, finding his great happiness in the torturer's visits, when red-hot irons are scorching a misdemeanant in the matter of two towels? What is the teaching to the young mind from a father who exults in the clanking of fetters and becomes ecstatic over branded slaves and farm-prisons?

25–30.
The lesson in adultery.

Do you expect Larga's daughter not to be an adulteress, if she finds it the work of minutes to give you the latest list of her mother's lovers, no matter how quickly she speaks, or at what rate she strings the names together? Even as a virgin she was made an accomplice ; and now she fills her own little tablets at the mother's dictation, and sends them to her lover by the regular sodomites.

31–37.
The influence of a bad home is only defied by young persons of rare strength of mind.

It is but human nature that a bad example in our own homes corrupts our minds with special ease and quickness, because it approaches us with strong credentials. Its influence may, perhaps, be trampled under foot by one or two young natures on which the Maker has spent the labour of love and—superior clay. All the others follow their fathers in the way in which they should *not* go, and are dragged along the familiar track of old misdoings.

Prometheus.

38–49.
The fear of setting a bad example should be a motive to

Therefore hold aloof from sin. There is one, if no other, strong reason for this, in the fear that our own crimes may become examples to the sons of our loins, since all men are apt pupils in

virtue, because children are quick to get the knowledge of evil.

baseness and wickedness. In any nation and under any climate you may find a Catilina, but a Brutus or his Uncle nowhere. Let no sound or sight of shame pass the threshold which leads to a young boy's home. "No admittance (do you hear?) for young persons from the whoremonger's, or for toady vocalists who do not go home till morning." Children have a claim to the deepest respect. If you are meditating any baseness, do not rate their understanding too low; but let the sin in your heart be turned aside by thinking of your baby son.

Cato of Utica.

50–58. A bad father loses his right to rebuke or punish a bad son.

If he has done anything in after-life to merit the Censor's indignation, and proved his resemblance to yourself in more than face and figure by showing the morals of his father's son and following your lead until he beats your badness, you will be hard on him (no doubt) and rebuke him with harsh outcry, and make up your mind at last to alter your will. How can you put on a father's aspect and claim his rights, when there are worse sins upon your own grey hairs, and your brainless head must pay its long overdue visit to the draughty cupping-glass?

For brain affections.

59–63. The visit of a friend is the signal for setting a man's house in (external) order.

When a guest is expected, there will be no peace for anybody in your household.

"Sweep the floor and bring out the pillar's polish. Down with the dusty spider and all its cobweb. One of you rub the plain silver while the other does the chased."

Thus the master raves, threatening and brandishing a rod.

64–74.
But there is no such anxiety to keep it inwardly pure for the sake of the children in it.

So you fluster yourself, deluded man, not to have your friend's eyes offended at his entrance by the dirt of dog's droppings in the hall, or by the splashings of mud against the vestibule, though such faults can be put right by one slave-boy with one half-peck of saw-dust. What you do not trouble yourself about is for your own son to see his home pure and without spot or blemish of sin. We only thank you for having given a citizen to

Responsibility of a father to the State.

your country and people if you make him fit to belong to that country, useful to its soil, and useful in works of peace and war. His future depends very much upon what qualities and character you are forming in him.

74–85.
Character is formed by training. This is illustrated by the disgusting food on which storks and vultures are brought up, in contrast with the nobler game which young eagles are taught to hunt.

Young storks are brought up on snakes and lizards which come from lonely wastes, and so they go hunting the same vermin when they use their own wings. Rotting cattle, dogs, and criminals are the prizes with which a mother vulture hurries to her brood, and she gives them part of her carrion. This of course becomes the young vulture's food when he grows a big bird in turn and caters for himself and makes a nest upon some tree of his own. But the noble birds who wait upon Jupiter chase hares and hinds in the wild forest; such is the game which they store in their eyrie: but when the matured eaglets soar upon the wing, the pricks of hunger turn them straight upon the game which they first tasted after their shells were cracked.

86–95.
The building mania of a

Cetronius was a man of bricks and mortar, and reared his mansion Follies, some on the indented shore of Caieta, some on Tibur's highest peak, others on Præneste's high-grounds; the marbles which he brought from the far ends of Greece outshone the temples of Fortune and Hercules, even as the eunuch Posides put our Capitol to shame. By housing himself in this fashion, of course Cetronius diminished his means and made a hole in his fortune; still the remnant mounted to a pretty figure. But the whole of it was squandered by his crazy son in raising fresh mansions and using rarer marbles.

father is exaggerated by his son.

A favourite of Claudius.

Some men who have been blessed with a Sabbatarian father are worshippers of nothing but the Clouds and Sky God, and see no difference between human flesh and the pork which their fathers abstained from; and in good time they shed their foreskins. Having learnt to ignore the laws of Rome, they study, keep, and reverence all the articles of Jewish Jurisprudence which are recorded in the mystic roll of Moyses:—never to point out the road to any but observers of their own rites, and to help none but the circumcised in the search for water. But the blame of it all is with the father who wasted every seventh day and cut it adrift from all the business of life.

96–106. The Judaizing corruption of Rome begun in the father and developed further in the son.

Young men take to every other fault of their own accord. Avarice alone they are trained to practise, even against their wishes. This is a vice which conceals its nature under the guise and shadow of a virtue, being of a sour mien and wearing a solemn face and habit. We do not hesitate to praise an avaricious man for being thrifty and

107–118. The worst influence of a bad father is the inculcation of a disagreeable vice like avarice.

keeping a better watch over his own goods than if they were trusted to the dragon sentinels of the Hesperides or of Pontus. More than that, the man whom I describe is reckoned by vulgar folks a first-rate performer in the art of money-getting. His (they say) is the skilled labour which increases fortunes. Indeed, it does increase them—in one way or another; and hammers them out upon its unresting anvil over a never extinguished furnace.

So avarice passes for a happy state of mind with a father who worships wealth and thinks that misfortune is but want of fortune. So he exhorts his sons to walk in its ways and hold fast to his own doctrine. Vice has its own rudiments which he instils early in life, and he makes his sons learn shabbiness in little things (afterwards advancing them to the vista of boundless avarice). He punishes his servants' bellies with short commons, and even stints his own appetite; for he never has the heart to use up all the mouldy fragments of skyblue bread, and will save minced meat from one day to another in the hottest of September, and put away beans in summer-time for resurrection at to-morrow's dinner, along with the scraps of salt fish or half a stale shad, and count every fibre in the cut-leek before he seals it in the cupboard :— all to make a dinner which a beggar from the Bridge will decline with thanks.

What avail the riches earned by all these tortures? It is stark madness and plain lunacy to live like a pauper for the sake of dying rich. All the time that the money-bag is swelling almost

The respectability of this vice.

119–134.
The systematic education in avarice begins with petty economies.

135–140.
It is useless to humour an appetite which grows by what it feeds on.

Who guarded the golden apples and the golden fleece.

to bursting, the lust of gold waxes stronger with every piece added to the store (whereas not-having means not-wanting).

140–155.
Land-
hunger.
Since one estate is not enough, you buy a second mansion. You delight in extending your land-mark, and yet you think that your next neighbour's cornfield is still bigger and richer. You make an offer for it also, with all its plantations and the
High-
handed
injustice.
canopy of silver olives over its high-ground. But if the owner will not come round to any price, some dark night you turn famished oxen with over-worked and underfed mules upon his green crops ; nor do you fetch them back before the whole field has disappeared within their ravenous bellies as cleanly as if the reapers had been at work. It is hard to reckon how many persons are complaining of such treatment, or how many farms have been forced into the market by such outrages.

Indifference
of the land-
grabber to
public
opinion.
"But what comments it would arouse ! (does any one say ?) What a trumpet blast of scandal !"

"What damage does that do me ? (answers he !) A fig for the praises of all my neighbours in the country-side, if I must earn them by reaping scanty crops from a meagre estate."

156–171.
Ironical
congratula-
tion upon
the new
acquisition.
Happy man ! No doubt but he will ever after be exempted from disease and feebleness, freed from grief and trouble, and receive a longer and happier portion of life, if he has once become
Small estates
satisfied the
wants of
early
Romans.
the holder of as much land as was ploughed by the whole people of Rome—in the days of King Contemporary of
Romulus. Tatius. (Later on, again, the soldiers, who were enfeebled by age, and had gone through Punic

battles or faced the Molossian swordsmen of savage Pyrrhus, received in the end scarcely two jugera of land apiece as the recompense for all their wounds. Nor did they ever think that the price of their blood and sweat was less than their deserts, or that a thankless country had broken her faith. Such was the allotment which satisfied the wants of the father and his cottage company—the wife lying in child-bed, and four romping lads (one of them a slave boy and three young masters), whilst great pots of porridge were steaming at the hearth, a late and special dinner for the big brothers on their way from trench or furrow. (Such a bit of ground is not enough for a modern garden.)

Of Epirus. Less than two acres.

172-178. The unscrupulousness of avarice.

Here is the origin of most crimes. There is no sin in the heart of man which has led to more compounding of poisons or more plying of daggers than the ravenous lust for unbounded wealth. Whosoever would be rich would be rich quickly. How can there be respect for Laws, how can there be shame or awe, when avarice will not wait?

179-188. The primitive simplicity of the old Italian life shown in a farmer's advice to his children.

"My sons, do ye live contented with your cot- "tages and high-land farms"—so would say the Marsian, Hernian, or Vestinian elder. "Let us "earn by the plough bread enough for our board. "That is a life pleasing to the rustic gods, whose "helping aid gave us the corn which we love so "well, and taught us to despise the acorn of our "fathers. No man will seek to do the forbidden "things, if he is not ashamed to wear long farmer "boots throughout the time of frost, and keeps out "the east wind by sheep-skins turned warm side

"inwards. What leads men to wickedness and
"shame is that purple stuff from foreign countries,
"whatever it may be, which we do not know in
"these parts."

189–207.
Contrasted
with this is
the modern
father's
restless
ambition for
his son to
get
eminence as
a pleader,
military rank
and pay, or
(in default)
to make
money by
coarse
trades.
This was the young man's teaching in ancient
times. Now the son is roused in his bed on
a winter midnight by his noisy father. "Take
"your tablets," he cries; "wake up, my lad!
"Practise pleading, read up the rubrics of ancient
"statutes.   Or send in your memorial for a
"centurion's staff.   But mind that Lælius marks The
commander
who made
the appoint-
ment.
"your unkempt hair and shaggy nostrils, and
"admires your breadth of chest.   Down with
"Moorish huts and British forts, so that your
"sixtieth year may bring you to the lucrative
"'Eagle.' If you dislike long years of camp work,
"and if the mixed notes of bugles and trumpets
"disturb your bowels, invest in something which
"you can sell again at one-third profit.   Have no
"nicety about wares which may not come on the
"city side of Tiber.   Do not imagine that there is
"anything to choose between unguents and hides.
"No matter what it comes from, profit never stinks.
"Let this maxim be always on your lips (it might
"have been composed in heaven, even by Jupiter
"himself) :—

    "'Getting money is man's task; how he gets it,
"none will ask.'"

This is what boys learn from the nurse crone
when they are crawling babies, and what girls are
taught before their A, B, C.

208–255.
This is how I might address a parent who was

How
Juvenal
would
answer such
a father.

The father
can afford to
wait his
time, and he
will see his
son become
a promising
criminal.

insisting on such a lesson : " Tell me, foolish man,
" who bids you be in such a hurry? I warrant
" that the scholar will better his teacher. Go in
" peace : you will be surpassed even as Telamon
" was outdone by Ajax, and Peleus surpassed by
" Achilles. Make allowance for a young beginner.
" The essence of matured wickedness has not yet
" spread through his system. When he begins to
" comb a beard and apply the razor's edge, he will
" grow into a false witness, and supply cheap
" perjury with his hands laid on the foot and altar
" of Ceres. You may look upon your son's wife as
" dead and gone if she has passed his threshold

The son will
murder his
own wife for
the sake of
her money.

" with the death-warrant of a dowry. Whose
" (think you) will be the fingers to smother that
" sleeping girl?—Yes, the money for which you
" think that land and sea must be traversed will
" come to him by a shorter cut. Great crimes are
" easy in doing.

" 'I never told him,' you will say one day, ' to
" do this act ; I never gave him such counsel.'

These crimes
lie on the
father's head
because he
started his
son on the
career of
crime.

" Nevertheless, you are the root and source of
" his corruption. The man who has inculcated
" love of wealth, and brings up his sons by sinister
" teaching to be avaricious men and double their
" fortunes by chicanery, gives his team their heads
" and loses all control of the reins. One may call
" him back, but he cannot pull up. He rushes on
" regardless of the warning voice or of the turning-
" post behind him. No man is contented to limit
" his sins by your allowance. A wider latitude is
" taken without leave asked. When you call a

"son foolish for giving to his young friend, or
"raising and supporting a needy kinsman, you are
"teaching him to become a swindler, and to stop
"short of no crime whatever in winning that wealth
"for which the love in your heart is strong as was
"the Decii's towards their country, strong as the
"affection of Menœcus to Thebes—if Greek tales
"are true. (For that is the wonderful place where
"ploughed land produces from dragon's teeth
"whole legions of men with shields complete, who
"set about fighting grim battles as soon as they
"appear, just as if their trumpeter has not been
"forgotten.)

"Well, you supplied the sparks, so you will see
"the flames blazing far and wide and making
"universal havoc. Nor will your own pitiful self
"escape. The lion cub will raise a roaring in his
"pit and make an end of his trembling keeper.
"The astrologers may have reckoned your nativity:
"but your son will find it tedious to await the slowly
"working spindles of Fate, and death will come
"before your thread of life has been snapt. Already
"you block his way and defer his hopes. The
"young man is kept in tortures by your uncon-
"scionable and superhuman age. Pay a visit to
"Archigenes at once and buy the Mithradates
"Mixture, if you wish to pluck next autumn's figs
"or to handle the roses of spring. We want some
"specific which may be taken before every meal
"by kings—and fathers."

It is a ravishing spectacle which I show you, far
outdoing any theatre or any of the glorified

Margin notes:

(Juvenal's scepticism about Greek legends and history.)

The wickedness inculcated upon the son will end in the father being poisoned unless he takes precautions.

256-275. The amusement

Sacrificed their own lives to satisfy the gods instead of the whole army.

The story of Cadmus.

A doctor. Antidote against poison.

which is given by contemplation of the struggle for wealth, keen and dangerous as the combats in the arena, and farcical as stageplays.

Prætor's displays. Look at the risk of life involved when a man is adding to his substance, loading his bronze-bound chest with treasure, and getting the gold-pieces (which have had to be banked at vigilant Castor's temple ever since Mars lost the helmet from his head—ever since the Public Protector could not keep his own property). You may give up the scenic shows of Flora, Ceres, and Cybele. The farce of real life is much broader fun. Is there more diversion of the mind in the chucking of human bodies from a spring-board, or in the inevitable tight-rope walker, than in watching

Comparison of the merchant and the rope-walker.

you—taking regular quarters and making your home on a Cilician boat to become the regular sport of north-wester and south-wester, adopting a low and vulgar trade in stinking bales and making it your pride to have imported oily raisin-wine and wine-jars (Jupiter's fellow-countrymen) from the classical shores of Crete? The poor fellow who risks life at every setting down of his heel earns his victuals by the wages, and the tight-rope is his one mainstay against cold weather and emptiness. Your fool-hardiness is but to make up your thousandth talent or hundredth mansion.

275-283. The extravagant adventures by sea undertaken for the sake of money.

Turn your eyes to the docks and the masses of timber which block the sea: half the world lives now on board ship. Shoals of sail will go whithersoever they are beckoned by the chance of profit. Not only will they bound across Carpathian and Gætulian waters; but leaving Calpe far in the rear, they will hear the sun hissing as he sinks in the Pool of Hercules. You have a fine recompense

Gibraltar.

As the furthest West.

indeed in being able to come home with stuffed money-bags, and in exulting over a bloated purse after your adventures among the sea-serpents and mermaidens' sweethearts !

284–302.
The infatuation of avarice amounts to insanity.

Madness takes many forms. One lunatic in the arms of his own sister quails before the torch-lit faces of the Furies. Another smites an ox, and thinks that the bellowing is coming from Agamemnon or the Ithacan. A man may do no damage to his own tunic and cloak; but he is " not fit to manage his own affairs " if he packs his ship to the very brim with merchandise, and has nothing but planking between himself and water, when the only object of all this hardship and danger is bits of silver chopt into little images and superscriptions.

Orestes.

Ajax.

The foolhardy merchant laughs at the warnings of the sky.

Enter Clouds and Lightning. " Loose all cables !" cries the proprietor of " cornered " wheat and pepper. " There is no mischief in the colour of the sky or that strip of blackness. It is only summer thunder."

He is shipwrecked and driven to beggary.

Thou fool, this night perhaps thou shalt be pitched from thy shattered timber; shalt be overwhelmed and buried, still holding by hand and mouth to thy belted purse. Yes, the man whose desires were not contented with all the ruddy sand which is rolled along by the waters of the Tagus and Pactolus, will be perforce contented with a few rags to hide his shivering nakedness, whilst he begs for coppers as a shipwrecked mariner who has lost his vessel, and picks up his living by showing a picture of the storm.

303–310.
The safe-keeping of riches is worse than earning them.

What has been won with such hardships brings worse fear and trouble in the keeping. The charge of a great fortune is a wretched thing. Wealthy Licinus has a row of fire-buckets made ready and a cohort of slaves mounting guard all night, so terrified is he for his amber vessels, statues, marble pillars, and tables of tortoise-shell. But no flames attack the bare Cynic's tub. Break it, and he can make a new house next day, or the old one will stand again by the help of some lead.

Diogenes.

311–314.
Alexander realized the vanity of ambitious desires.

When Alexander beheld that Shell and its famous inmate, he felt how much more blessed a thing it was to want nothing than to desire all the world and be predestined to suffer dangers great as the glories won.

315–331.
It is easy to draw a line beyond which the desire of gain must not pass.

Wheresoever wisdom abides, Fortuna, thou hast no power of thine own. We it is who make a goddess of thee and give thee thy mansion in the skies. But if any man asks my counsel, I will declare what is the right limit of an income: enough to meet hunger, thirst, and cold—what contented Epicurus in his plot of garden, and was accepted by the household gods of Socrates before him. (The voice of Philosophy is always at one with the voice of Nature.) Do you think that I am cramping you and using too rigid patterns? Then add a tincture of modern life. Get such a capital as the law of Otho honours with a place in the Fourteen Benches; or, if that contracts

If it does pass beyond it wil never stop.

your brow and shoots out your lips, make yourself a knight twice or three times over. If your breast-pocket is not satisfied yet, but opens its mouth

Fourteen benches in the theatres were reserved for "Knights," i.e., men

wider, your soul will never be contented—not with the fortune of Crœsus nor the Persian Empire, nor with all the riches of the Narcissus whom Emperor Claudius humoured in all things, obeying his orders even when bidden to put his own wife to death.

possessed of 400,000 sesterces.

A favourite freedman.

Messalina.

SATIRE XV.

CANNIBALS IN EGYPT.

(AN EPISTLE TO VOLUSIUS BITHYNICUS.)

WHO but knows, Volusius Bithynicus, what strange gods are worshipt in demented Egypt? One district says prayers to the Crocodile, another is abased before the snake-gorged Ibis. On the ruined site of Thebe the Hundred-gated, where disfigured Memnon twangs the invisible chord, the long-tailed Ape has an image of burnished gold. Cats are holy in one place, and the Fishes of the River in another. Whole towns pay honour to the Dog, but not a man in them to Diana.

It is a sin and defilement to crunch leeks and onions. (Is not this a religious people which grows gods in kitchen-gardens?) Every dinner-table in the land abstains from woolly creatures, and it is reckoned sinful to slaughter the she-goat's offspring. Man's flesh it is lawful to eat of.

When Ulysses at the banquet told his own cannibal story to amazed Alcinoüs, he found that some of the guests showed wrath against him—or ridicule, more likely, as a gasconading liar.

"Why does nobody pitch this fellow into the

the
Phæacians
when
Ulysses told
them than
any other of
his
marvellous
adventures.

" sea? he deserves the agonies of a real Charybdis
" —this inventor of Læstrygonian and Cyclops
" monsters ! Why, I would sooner believe in his
" Scylla, or in the opening and shutting of his
" Sky-Blue Rocks, his wine-skins of decanted winds,
" or in his Circe touching Elpenor with a dainty
" stroke and turning him and all his crew into
" grunting hogs. Did he reckon that Phæacians
" had such empty skulls ? "

Cyanean
Rocks.

Such might well have been the words of one
who had remained sober, and had taken his liquor
modestly from the Corcyrean bowl. For the
Ithacan's was only one man's story without a
witness behind him.

i.e.,
Phæacian.

27-32.
Juvenal's is
a modern
instance,
which out-
does the
horrors of
tragedy
because the
sin was not
one man's
but a whole
nation's.

My own tale will deal with marvels, but they
are modern as the consulship of Juncus, and were
done in the land beyond the sultry walls of Coptus.
It will be the tale of a nation's crime, and worse
than ever walked the tragic stage. From the
Deluge downwards, not one drama trails its
draperies over the boards which has a Nation for
its Villain. I present you with a type of brutal
wickedness developed by our own generation.

33-46.
The ancient
feud between
Ombi and
Tentyra has
its roots in
religious
bigotry.

There is an old and immemorial quarrel between
the neighbour towns of Ombi and Tentyra—an
undying feud whose fires are unquenched to this
day, a wound which will never be closed. What
intensifies the mad passions of both peoples is the
mutual jealousy of either for the other's deities,
because each thinks that there must be no gods
but its own gods. So the feast day of one people
seemed to the enemy's elders and chieftains a

In Egypt.

chance not to be foregone, lest the hours should
be spent in joy and merry-making, lest the raptures
of a special banquet should be realized, when tables
were spread at every temple and cross-way, and the
carousing couches lay night and day where they
had been set—sometimes until the light dawned
on them for a seventh time. (Egypt is a rough
country, but its hordes of savages can—if I may
trust my own eyes—vie with far-famed Canopus
in their riotous living.)

Moreover, it would be an easy victory over men
well-drunken, stuttering and staggering from strong
liquor.　Look at the two pictures :—One, of males
dancing in crowds to a negro's piping, unguents
(or what did duty for them), flowers, and brows
crowned with many a chaplet; the figures in the
other are Famine and Malice.　The first outcome
of their boiling passions was the voice of reviling.
This was the signal for the fray.

Shout answers shout, and the two masses meet,
wreaking their fury with naked fists for weapons.
Not many jaws remained unbroken, and you could
hardly find one, if you could find any, undamaged
nose in the whole battle-field.　Already up and
down the two hosts you might see faces mutilated,
features disfigured, bones laid bare under the
gashed cheeks, and fists dripping with the blood
from eye-balls.

But this is only play—or so they think—and
nothing but a children's make-belief engagement,
since there are no dead bodies underfoot. (True
enough, there would be no good in mobs fighting

by the thousand if they are all to be survivors.) So the onset waxes more furious. Presently, they begin to hunt for stones along the ground, aim with their arms, and hurl the rioter's natural weapons :—not, indeed, such as the boulder which Turnus and Ajax wielded, nor like the mass wherewith the son of Tydeus smote Æneas on the hip, but only such as can be flung by the modern and degenerate biceps. (For the human type began to dwindle even in Homer's own time. Earth's present nurslings are weak as well as wicked men, so that they have become not merely odious but funny in the sight of any god who has deigned to look at them.)

After this digression let me come back to the track. When one party, being helped by reinforcements, makes bold to draw sword and point arrow for renewal of the combat, the others with one consent present backs in rapid flight, and are pressed by the heroes who dwell by Tentyra's canopy of palm-trees. One amongst the runaways, who is forcing his pace in the excess of terror, trips and is taken prisoner. Thereupon, he is carved into many steaks and portions—so that the multitude may have satisfaction from the only dead man. The victor rabble gnaws his bones and eats him up to the last scrap. They do not cook him in the boiling-pot or on roasting-spits. They think it slow and tedious to wait for a fire, and satisfy themselves with raw corpse. (Here we may well be thankful that they did not pollute that Flame which Prometheus ravished from the highest

Margin notes:

Stones are used.

(The degeneracy of mankind.)

Diomede.

72–87. Mock heroic account of the devouring of a prisoner.

From Ombi.

Of Tentyra.

They would not wait to cook him, which was at least one profanity spared.

Heaven and gave to the Earth. Element, I congratulate thee, and believe that thou too art overjoyed.)

87–92.
Their horrid gusto.

Well, the man who could make himself set his teeth in corpse never relished any other meat so well. Make no subtleties over this infamy, and raise no question whether the first man found the flavour pleasant in his gullet. Anyhow, the one who waited to the very last, when all the carcase had been quite used up, scraped his fingers along the ground, and got a twang of the blood.

93–103.
The case of the besieged defenders of Calagurris, who were forced to eat their own wives and children.

Once upon a time—so legend says—the Vascones eked out life upon similar support. But theirs was a different case. They could plead the persecutions of Fortune, stress of war, desperate disaster, and the agonizing famine of a prolonged siege. This diet ought to excite your compassion (in the example which we are taking for the moment), insomuch as it was not before they had used up every green plant, every living beast, and every last resort of maddening starvation ; it was when their pale, gaunt faces and wasted limbs moved pity even in the enemy's heart, that this people (whom I spoke of) were driven to rending the limbs of other human beings by a hunger which made them ready to devour their own.

Spanish partizans of Sertorius who died 72 B.C.

103–112.
Their extreme want was their sufficient excuse, though Juvenal says ironically

Is there any man, is there any god, who will refuse pardon to these Mighty Fallen? to their agony and superhuman suffering? to sinners who could be forgiven by the spirits of them of whose bodies they were eating? (We, of course, have a better light from the maxims of Zeno, who holds

Read Viribus.

The Stoic.

that Rome is enlightened enough to know that there are things better worth having than life. The doubtful advantages of the universal influence of Greek culture.

113-131. No such excuse for the Egyptian cannibals.

that self-preservation is a rule not without exceptions. But how could Cantabrians be Stoics? at least how could they be such in the ancient days of Metellus? Now, indeed, every country has its own Athens, either Greek or Roman-Greek. Glib Gaul has taught Britons to become pleaders of cases, and Thule talks of engaging a rhetoric-teacher.)

Spaniards.

Such or suchlike is the excuse for that gallant nation whom I have spoken of, and for the people of Saguntum who equalled them in valour and loyalty, whilst their fall was greater. But the atrocity in Egypt is worse than at the Altar of Tauris. She who instituted those hideous rites—if we are really to put faith in poets' stories—does no more than slaughter her human victims, and they need fear no worse maltreatment after the knife. What was the disaster which forced these wretches to their crime? Where was the urgent famine or beleaguering host which compelled them to brave such loathsome and unnatural sin? If there were

Sacred to Artemis.

viz., the Tentyrates.

(A reason for their act suggested ironically.)

(The contemptible life of Egyptians.)

a drought on the land of Memphis, could they bring worse odium upon the Nile for its sulkiness? A frenzy which fell not on dread Cimbrians, never yet on Britons, on grim Sauromatians or savage Agathyrsi, is allowed to madden this mob of good-for-nothing cravens, who delight in rigging crockery gondolas with canvas strippings, and bending over the little paddles of their gaudy pots. You will never devise a reward proper to this iniquity, nor find a punishment meet for this nation which gives like and equal rank to Anger and—Appetite!

131–142.
Compassion is the highest human attribute.

Nature shows that she bestows her tenderest hearts on mankind because she has bestowed on them what is the highest of human sentiments, the gift of tears. So it is she who bids us weep for the friend pleading his claims and answering accusations in the mourner's garb—for the ward who is bringing a swindling guardian to justice with the tears streaming down a face which almost hides its own sex under the long girlish locks. It is Nature who calls up the groan when a fair young maiden's funeral meets us, or when some child too small for the flames of the pyre is laid away underground. Where is the good man, fit to carry the mystic torch and such as the priest of Ceres would have him be, who thinks that any suffering of his fellows does not touch himself?

142–158.
It is the final purpose of human intelligence, and the most perfect development of civilization.

Sympathy puts Man above the Brutes. For its sake, man alone of all beings has been endowed with a grand intellect, a power of rising above his human self, and an aptitude for grasping and wielding knowledge ; for its sake he has brought down from its heavenly citadel that understanding which is denied to the stooping creatures whose eyes look earthwards. He, who in the beginning fashioned us and them alike, only gifted them with the power of life; but He gave us living power, so that the affection between men, one towards another, might teach us to seek help and give it ; to gather them who lived apart into one people ; to abandon the primitive groves and leave the forests which our fathers inhabited ; to build us houses ; to set each our own home against another's dwelling-place, so that the confidence of union might make our slumbers peaceful because a friend's home was nigh ; to wield weapons in defending a fellow-countryman fallen or staggering under a heavy blow ; to sound a public trumpet for the battle signal ; to live together under the same fortress, and to make the gates fast with a common key.

159-163.
Degenerate humanity is shamed by the example of wild beasts.

Now there is better harmony amongst the serpents ;—one savage creature is tender to a brother spotted like itself. When did a strong lion ravish a weak one's life ? what forest has seen a boar dying by a larger boar's tusks ? Ravening tigers of India keep a lasting peace one with another ; and there is agreement amongst savage bears.

164-174.
The guilt of shedding man's blood has been surpassed by the recent act of cannibalism.

For Man it is not enough that he has drawn the deadly steel from the anvil of wickedness, though the primitive blacksmiths were but used to forging harrows and hoes and tired their arms over mattocks and ploughshares ; nor did they know how to hammer out the sword-blade. Now we behold peoples whose wrath is not sated by the slaughter of an enemy, and who can imagine that his breast, shoulders, and face are articles of diet. What then would Pythagoras say ? or (rather) where would he not flee away to, if such prodigies of sin were beheld by one who abstained from every sentient being's flesh, as if it were a fellow-man's, and restrained his own stomach in its choice of Beans ?

Pythagoras as believing in the transmigration of souls.

SATIRE XVI. (INCOMPLETE OR FRAGMENTARY).

THE SOLDIER'S LIFE.

(AN EPISTLE TO GALLUS.)

1–6.
The advantages of a military career.

But even in that much depends upon luck.

WHO could reckon up, Gallus, the prizes which are won in a soldier's lucky trade? Why, it will be a happy star that beholds me pass within the camp gate—if I go to a favoured station. Yes, one hour of Fortune's kindness is better worth having than credentials to the god of war written by his goddess sweetheart, or by her, his mother, who rejoices in the sandy shore of Samos.

Venus and Juno.

7–12.
The exemption of soldiers from the jurisdiction of ordinary courts.

First let me speak of the benefits shared by the whole Service, not the least being that no wearer of the toga would dare to commit a battery upon you. Indeed, if he were the party battered he would keep his own counsel, nor would he dare to call the prætor's notice to the teeth which you had knocked out, the black lump and swollen lividness upon his face, or the one remaining eye over which the doctor shakes his head.

i.e., no civilian.

13–25.
The civilian cannot get justice against a soldier in the military courts, even if he has the incompetent judge on his own side.

If he wishes for redress, he can see nothing of the judge who is appointed except a big bench with booted heels and magnificent calves. We observe the laws of our fathers and the practice of Camillus, that no soldier be party to a lawsuit be-beyond the camp boundary and away from the standards.

"I suppose, then" (do you say?), "that officers do perfect justice between soldier and civilian. I shall not go without my redress if I show good cause of complaint."

The soldiers will take up the cause of their comrade and use violence, and make you repent of your legal victory.

No doubt; but the whole cohort is against you, and all the maniples with one consent take measures to make "*your damages*" exemplary and more grievous than the first outrage. For a man who has only two legs to kick with, it is conduct worthy a stubborn mule like orator Vagellius to run against so many boots and such a mass of hobnails.

25-35. No chance of getting testimony in favour of a civilian.

Who would go so far from the city to support you? who is the faithful Pylades who would cross the rampart? No, let us dry our tears at once; let us not worry friends who will only plead excuses. When the judge has said the word, "Call up your witness," only let the man (be he who he may) who saw the blow given say, "I saw that blow," and I shall think he has a right to wear his beard and hair in the fashion of our forefathers. It is quicker work to bring forward a suborned witness against a man of peace than honest evidence against the interests and honour of a soldier.

Only a quarter of a mile.

The devoted friend of Orestes.

i.e., long.

35-50. The delays of the civil courts are contrasted with the special arrangements made for giving prompt justice to soldiers.

Look, now, at different prizes and different profits which come by swearing the soldier's oath. If a roguish neighbour has robbed me of the valley or meadow-land in my family farm, and removed the consecrated stone which lay as a landmark betwixt himself and me and received my yearly sacrifice of flour and flat-cake, or if a creditor refuses to refund a loan and declares that the bond is not worth the wood on which it was inscribed, I must wait for the year to come round which is to make a start upon the public list of causes. Even when the time comes there are a thousand vexations and as many delays, and on each occasion nothing is done except to make ready the judgment seat. Even when glib Cædicius is putting off his cloak and leaky Fuscus is really taking his last precaution, we are parted from the encounter which we were primed for, and must fight our battle by the tedious rules of the legal ring. But the heroes who are covered by armour and encircled by the belt have any day accorded to them which they have fixed upon. Nor in their case are the wheels of justice teased by a long drag-chain.

51–60.
Partial exemption of soldiers from the *patria potestas*.

Soldiers, again, are the only persons who can make wills in a father's lifetime; for it has been ruled that money won by service in war is apart and separate from the property over which a father keeps full powers. So you may see Coranus (who goes about with the standards and earns his soldier's pay) being caressed and courted by a father now palsied with age. Here is one who is promoted by well-earned favour, and finds that noble work brings

Promotion in the army.

its own reward. Indeed, it seems to be for the commander's interest that the brave should also be the luckiest men, and that all who rejoice in medals and chains should——

*   *   *   *   *

The rest of this satire either has been lost or was never written.

FINIS.

JAMES THORNTON'S

𝕷𝖎𝖘𝖙 𝖔𝖋 𝕻𝖚𝖇𝖑𝖎𝖈𝖆𝖙𝖎𝖔𝖓𝖘

CHIEFLY EDUCATIONAL,

MANY IN USE AT THE HIGHER SCHOOLS AND UNIVERSITIES.

CONTENTS.

Also sold by { SIMPKIN, MARSHALL, & CO. } London.
{ HAMILTON, ADAMS, & CO. }

A Catalogue of these Publications with fuller descriptions, some notices from the press and specimen pages, will be issued shortly, and will be forwarded gratis on application.

JAMES THORNTON *desires to direct attention to the accompany-ing List of* EDUCATIONAL WORKS, *many of which have now attained a wide circulation.*

The Authors and Compilers are mostly scholars of repute, as well as of large experience in teaching.

Any notices of errors or defects in these publications will be gratefully received and acknowledged.

The Books can generally be procured through local Booksellers in town and country; but if at any time difficulty should arise, JAMES THORNTON *will feel obliged by direct communication on the subject.*

MISCELLANEOUS.

THE LATIN PRAYER BOOK OF CHARLES II.; or, an Account of the Liturgia of Dean Durel, together with a Reprint and Translation of the Catechism therein contained, with Collations, Annotations, and Appendices by the Rev. CHARLES MARSHALL, M.A., Chaplain to the Lord Mayor of London, 1849–1850; and WILLIAM W. MARSHALL, B.A., of the Inner Temple, late Scholar of Hertford College, Oxford. Demy 8vo. cloth, 10s. 6d. [*Recently published.*

'Is a distinct and important contribution to the Evangelical side of the Sacramentarian controversy.'—BRITISH QUARTERLY REVIEW.

'We have great pleasure in commending this work as a learned and valuable contribution to our liturgical literature.'—RECORD, *November 3, 1882.*

CANONS OF THE SECOND COUNCIL OF ORANGE A.D. 529. With an Introduction, Translation, and Notes. By the Rev. F. H. WOODS, B.D., Fellow of St. John's College, Oxford. Crown 8vo. 2s.

RECORD of the UNIVERSITY BOAT RACE, 1829–1880, and of the COMMEMORATION DINNER, 1881. Compiled by GEO. G. T. TREHERNE, O.U.B.C., and J. H. D. GOLDIE, C.U.B.C. With Illustrations, 4to. cloth, 10s. 6d.; or, printed on large hand-made paper, with China paper impressions of the Plates, price 30s. (only 250 copies printed, each numbered and initialled).

NEW AND REVISED EDITION, bringing the work up to 1884. 8vo. cloth, 6s.

An UNDERGRADUATE'S TRIP to ITALY and ATTICA in the WINTER of 1880–1. By J. L. THOMAS, Balliol College Oxford. Crown 8vo. 5s.

THE LIVES AND EPISTLES OF GIFFORD AND BUNYAN. By the Rev. T. A. BLYTH, B.A., Queen's College, Oxford.

[*In the press.*

The RECENT DEPRESSION of TRADE, its Nature, its Causes, and the Remedies which have been suggested for it; being the Oxford Cobden Prize Essay for 1879. By WALTER E. SMITH, B.A., New College. Crown 8vo. cloth, 3s. 6d.

LAW, HISTORY, & POLITICAL PHILOSOPHY.

THOMAS HOBBES, of MALMESBURY, LEVIATHAN;
or, the Matter, Forme, and Power of a Commonwealth. A New
Reprint. With a facsimile of the original fine engraved Title.
Medium 8vo. cloth, 12s. 6d.
A small edition of 250 copies only, on Dutch hand-made paper,
medium 8vo. 18s.
Students' Edition, crown 8vo. cloth 8s. 6d. *[Just published.*

'In matters of reprints, such as this is, it is always well to retain as much as possible
the old spelling, and the old form of printing. By this means we are constantly
reminded that we are reading a seventeenth century writer, and not a nineteenth ; and
hence students will apply more checks to their process of reasoning than they might be
inclined to do if the book were printed in modern form. This is, we are glad to say,
applicable to the present excellent reprint, which is issued in old spelling, and contains
in the margin the figures of the pagination of the first edition.'
THE ANTIQUARY, *October* 1881.

' We have received from Mr. James Thornton, of Oxford, an excellent reprint of
Hobbes's "Leviathan." The book is one which is not always easy to obtain ; and a satis-
factory reprint at a reasonable price may do more to advance the knowledge of Hobbes's
philosophy than one of the condensed handbooks which are now extensively popular.'
WESTMINSTER REVIEW, *January* 1882.

THE ELEMENTS OF LAW, NATURAL AND POLITIC.
By THOMAS HOBBES, of Malmesbury. The first complete and correct
Edition, with a Preface and Critical Notes. By FERDINAND JOENNIES,
Ph.D. To which are subjoined selected pieces of unprinted MSS.
of THOMAS HOBBES. *[In the press ; ready in October.*

BEHEMOTH ; or, The LONG PARLIAMENT. By THOMAS
HOBBES, of Malmesbury. For the first time Edited after the
Original MS., with many Additions and Corrections. By FERDINAND
JOENNIES, Ph.D. *[In the press.*

REMARKS on the USE and ABUSE of SOME POLITICAL
TERMS. By the late Right Hon. Sir GEORGE CORNEWALL LEWIS,
Bart., sometime Student of Christ Church, Oxford. A New Edition,
with Notes and Appendix. By Sir ROLAND KNYVET WILSON, Bart.,
M.A., Barrister-at-Law ; Reader in Indian Law, and late Fellow
of King's College, Cambridge ; Author of ' History of Modern
English Law.' Crown 8vo. 6s.

An ESSAY on the GOVERNMENT of DEPENDENCIES. By
the late Right Hon. Sir GEORGE CORNEWALL LEWIS, Bart., sometime
Student of Christ Church, Oxford. A New Reprint. *[In the press.*

QUESTIONS and EXERCISES in POLITICAL ECONOMY,
with References to Adam Smith, Ricardo, John Stuart Mill, Fawcett,
Thorold Rogers, Bonamy Price, Twiss, Senior, Macleod, and others.
Adapted to the Oxford Pass and Honour and the Cambridge Ordinary
B.A. Examinations. Arranged and edited by W. P. EMERTON, M.A.,
D.C.L., Christ Church, Oxford. Crown 8vo. cloth, 3s. 6d.

MONTENEGRO : being the Stanhope Prize Essay for 1884. By
WILLIAM CARR, Commoner of University College, Oxford. 8vo.
paper covers (106 pages), 2s. 6d. *[Just published.*

LAW, HISTORY, AND POLITICAL PHILOSOPHY—
continued.

DE CONJECTURIS ULTIMARUM VOLUNTATUM.
Dissertatio pro Gradu Doctoris in Jure Civili. By Wolseley
P. Emerton, D.C.L., Christ Church. 8vo. sewed (110 pages,
2s. 6d. [*Just published.*

An ABRIDGMENT of ADAM SMITH'S INQUIRY into the
NATURE and CAUSES of the WEALTH of NATIONS. By
W. P. Emerton, M.A., D.C.L. Crown 8vo. cloth, 6s.

This work (based on Jeremiah Joyce's Abridgment) originally appeared
in two parts and is now republished after careful revision, with Additional
Notes, Appendices, and a Complete Index.

The above can be had in two Parts. Part I. Books I. and II. 3s. 6d.
Part II. Books III., IV. and V. 3s. 6d.

OUTLINES of JURISPRUDENCE. For the Use of Students.
By B. R. Wise, B.A., late Scholar of Queen's College, Oxford;
Oxford Cobden Prizeman, 1878. Crown 8vo. cloth, 5s.

This book is intended to be a critical and explanatory commentary upon
the Jurisprudence text-books in common use; and it endeavours to present
a precise and coherent view of all the topics upon which these touch.

'The student of jurisprudence will certainly find the work suggestive and helpful.'
THE ATHENÆUM, *July* 15, 1882.

OUTLINES of ENGLISH CONSTITUTIONAL HISTORY.
By Britiffe Constable Skottowe, M.A., late Scholar of New
College, Oxford. Crown 8vo. cloth, 3s. 6d.

The object of this book is to assist beginners in reading Constitutional
History by arranging in order outlines of the growth of the most important
Institutions.

An ANALYSIS of the ENGLISH LAW of REAL PRO-
PERTY, chiefly from Blackstone's Commentary, with Tables and
Indexes. By Gordon Campbell, M.A., Author of 'An Analysis of
Austin's Lectures on Jurisprudence,' and of 'A Compendium of
Roman Law.' Crown 8vo. cloth, 3s. 6d.

An ANALYSIS of JUSTINIAN'S INSTITUTES of ROMAN
LAW, with Tables. [*In preparation.*

A CHRONOLOGICAL SUMMARY of the CHIEF REAL
PROPERTY STATUTES, with their more important Provisions.
For the Use of Law Students. By P. F. Aldred, M.A., D.C.L.
Crown 8vo. 2s.

ELEMENTARY QUESTIONS on the LAW of PROPERTY,
REAL and PERSONAL. Supplemented by Advanced Questions on
the Law of Contracts. With Copious References throughout, and
an Index of Legal Terms. Crown 8vo. cloth, 3s. 6d.

The SPECIAL STATUTES required by Candidates for the School
of Jurisprudence at Oxford. Fcp. 8vo. sewed, 2s. 6d. With brief
Notes and Translations by a B.C.L. Cloth, 5s.

OXFORD STUDY GUIDES.

A SERIES OF HANDBOOKS TO EXAMINATIONS.

Edited by F. S. PULLING, M.A., Exeter College.

THE object of this Series is to guide Students in their reading for the different examinations. The amount of time wasted at present, simply through ignorance of the way to read, is so great that the Editor and Authors feel convinced of the necessity for some such handbooks, and they trust that these Guides will at least do something to prevent in the future the misapplication of so much industry.

Each volume will be confined to one branch of study, and will include an account of the various Scholarships and Prizes offered by the University or the Colleges in its department; and will be undertaken by a writer whose experience qualifies him to speak with authority on the subject.

The books will contain extracts from the University Statutes relating to the Examinations, with an attempt to explain them as they exist, and advice as to what to read and how to read; how to prepare subjects for examination, and how to answer papers; a few specimen questions, extracts from the Regulations of the Board of Studies, and a list of books.

THEOLOGY. By the Rev. F. H. Woods, B.D., Fellow of St. John's College. Crown 8vo. cloth, 2s. 6d.

ENTRANCE CLASSICAL SCHOLARSHIPS. By S. H. Jeyes, M.A., Lecturer in Classics at University College. Crown 8vo. cloth, 2s. 6d.

'It is quite refreshing to find a guide to an examination that so thoroughly discourages cram.'—SCHOOL GUARDIAN, June 20, 1881.

'This is a smart book, and a useful comment on the present method of awarding scholarships. There is a certain frank cynicism in much of the advice, as when Mr. Jeyes remarks, It is no good wearing out your trousers in a study chair, if you do not set your brains to work;" or that it "is quite useless to play at hide-and seek with examiners who are familiar with every turn and twist in the game;" and there seems little doubt that a clever boy, coached by him on his method, would get a scholarship.'—SPECTATOR, Aug. 27, 1881.

'Mr. Jeyes has provided parents and teachers with an excellent manual by which to guide their sons or pupils in preparing for University Scholarships...... He gives directions as to the best way of preparing for the different sorts of papers.....and also for the best way of tackling with the paper when confronted with it in actual examination. The observations are of the most practical kind...... The book is well done, and ought to be useful.'—THE ACADEMY, June 18, 1881.

HONOUR CLASSICAL MODERATIONS. By L. R. FARNELL, M.A., Fellow of Exeter College. Crown 8vo. cloth, 2s. 6d.

'It is full of useful and scholarly suggestions which many hard-reading men will be thankful for.......With hints as to the line of reading to be adopted, and the books to be taken up so as to make the most of their tim' ' and to read to the best advantage.'

SCHOOL GUARDIAN, *November* 4, 1881.

LITERÆ HUMANIORES. By E. B. IWAN-MÜLLER, M.A., New College. [*Shortly.*

MODERN HISTORY. By F. S. PULLING, M.A., Exeter College. *Will be published as soon as possible after the new scheme is finally sanctioned.*

NATURAL SCIENCE. By E. B. POULTON, M.A., Keble College.

JURISPRUDENCE and CIVIL LAW. By W. P. EMERTON, M.A., D.C.L., Christ Church. [*In preparation.*

ARITHMETIC.

Just published.

ARITHMETIC for SCHOOLS. Based on principles of Cause and Effect. By the Rev. FREDERICK SPARKS, M.A., Mathematical Master, the High School, Plymouth, and late Lecturer of Worcester College, Oxford. Crown 8vo. cloth (416 pages), 4s. 6d.

It may perhaps appear somewhat rash to add another to the many text books on Arithmetic already in use. It is believed, however, that the present work will be found to contain some features sufficiently distinctive and valuable to warrant its appearance.

The chief aim of the work is to place prominently before the student the fact that the principle of 'cause and effect' is as applicable to Arithmetic as to other sciences, and that by working on this plan he may obtain his results in about half the time required by other methods. In each division of the subject this is shown by a typical example worked out in full, followed by ample exercises, with examination papers at regular intervals. The more complex parts of fractions and decimals are introduced later, so that the pupil may reach as early as possible the more interesting part of his work, the arithmetic of ordinary life. The so-called 'inverse rules' are learnt at the same time as the 'direct rules,' and thus the difficulties of proportion wholly disappear. A careful selection of questions set by the Universities, Civil Service, and Army Examination Boards, and other educational bodies, has been placed at the end of the volume.

The ANSWERS to the above are published in a separate form.

CLASS BOOKS.

MELETEMATA; or, SELECT LATIN PASSAGES IN PROSE AND VERSE FOR UNPREPARED TRANS-LATION. Arranged by the Rev. P. J. F. GANTILLON, M.A., sometime Scholar of St. John's College, Cambridge, Classical Master in Cheltenham College. Crown 8vo. cloth, 4s. 6d.

The object of this volume is to furnish a collection of about 250 passages, graduated in difficulty, and adapted to the various Examinations in which ' Unprepared Translation' finds a place.

' The work is nicely got up, and is altogether the best of the kind with which we are acquainted.'—THE SCHOOLMASTER, December 3, 1881.

' We find this collection to be very judiciously made, and think it one of the best which has yet been published.'—EDUCATIONAL TIMES, April 1, 1881.

Forming a Companion Volume to the above.

MELETEMATA GRÆCA; being a Selection of Passages, Prose and Verse, for unprepared Translation. By the Rev. P. J. F. GANTILLON, M.A. [*In the press.*

SELECTED PIECES for TRANSLATION into LATIN PROSE. Selected and arranged by the Rev. H. C. OGLE, M.A. Head Master of Magdalen College School, and T. CLAYTON, M.A. Crown 8vo. cloth, 4s. 6d.

This selection is intended for the use of the highest forms in Schools and for University Students for Honour Examinations, for whom it was felt that a small and compact book would be most serviceable.

' The selection has been made with much care and the passages which we have more particularly examined are very appropriate for translation.'
SCHOOL GUARDIAN, June 7, 1879.

LATIN and GREEK VERSIONS of some of the SELECTED PIECES for TRANSLATION. Collected and arranged by the Rev. H. C. OGLE, M.A., Head Master of Magdalen College School; and THOMAS CLAYTON, M.A., Trinity College, Oxford. Crown 8vo. 5s. [*Just ready.*

This Key is for the use of Tutors only, and is issued on the understanding that it does not get into the hands of any pupil.

For the convenience of Schoolmasters and Tutors these Versions are also issued in another form viz. on separate leaves ready for distribution to pupils, thereby saving the necessity of dictating or copying. They are done up in packets of twenty-five each, and not less than twenty-five sets (= 76 packets) can be supplied at a time. Price—Thirty-five Shillings net.

DAMON; or, The ART of GREEK IAMBIC MAKING. By the Rev. J. HERBERT WILLIAMS, M.A., Composition Master in S. Nicholas College, Lancing; late Demy of Magdalen College. Fcp. 8vo. 1s. 6d.

This small treatise claims as its merit that it really teaches Greek Iambic writing on a system, and this system is based on no arbitrary analysis of the Iambic line, but on the way in which the scholar practically regards it in making verses himself.

A Key, for Tutors only. Fcp. 8vo. cloth, 3s. 6d.

CLASS BOOKS—*continued.*

SHORT TABLES and NOTES on GREEK and LATIN
GRAMMAR. By W. E. W. Collins, M.A., Jesus College. Second
Edition, revised. Crown 8vo. cloth, 2s.

ARS SCRIBENDI LATINE; or, Aids to Latin Prose Composition.
In the form of an Analysis of Latin Idioms. By B. A. Edwards,
B.A., late Scholar of Jesus College, Oxford. Crown 8vo. 1s.

ARITHMETIC FOR SCHOOLS. Based on principles of Cause
and Effect. By the Rev. Frederick Sparks, M.A., Mathematical
Master, the High School, Plymouth, and late Lecturer of Worcester
College, Oxford. Crown 8vo. cloth (416 pages), 4s. 6d. [*Just ready.*

ALGEBRAICAL QUESTIONS AND EXERCISES. For the
Use of Candidates for Matriculation, Responsions, and First Public
Examinations, and the Oxford and Cambridge Local and Certificate
Examinations. Crown 8vo. 2s.

ARITHMETICAL QUESTIONS AND EXERCISES. For
the Use of Candidates for Matriculation, Responsions, and First
Public Examinations, and the Oxford and Cambridge Local and
Certificate Examinations. Crown 8vo. 1s. 6d.

QUESTIONS AND EXERCISES IN ADVANCED LOGIC.
For the Use of Candidates for the Honour Moderation Schools.
Crown 8vo. 1s. 6d.

The RUDIMENTS OF LOGIC, with Tables and Examples. By
F. E. Weatherly, M.A. Fcp. 8vo. cloth limp, 1s 6d.

'Here is everything needful for a beginner.'—Educational Times.
'Is a clever condensation of first principles.'—School Guardian.

QUESTIONS in LOGIC, Progressive and General. By Frederic E.
Weatherley, M.A., late Scholar of Brasenose College, Oxford. Fcp.
8vo. paper covers, 1s. [*Just published.*

A FEW NOTES on the GOSPELS. By W. E. W. Collins, M.A.,
Jesus College. New Edition. Crown 8vo. paper covers, 1s. 6d.

ARITHMETICAL AIDS to RESPONSIONS; containing Concise
Rules and Examples worked out. Crown 8vo. paper cover, 1s.
[*Just published.*

CLASSICS AND TRANSLATIONS.

The **NICOMACHEAN ETHICS of ARISTOTLE.** Books I.–IV. and Book X. Chap. 6 to 9, being the portion required in the Oxford Pass School, with Notes, &c. for the use of Passmen. By E. L. HAWKINS, M.A., late Postmaster of Merton College. Demy 8vo. cloth, 8s. 6d. Interleaved with writing paper, 10s. 6d.

The **NICOMACHEAN ETHICS of ARISTOTLE.** A New Translation, with an Introduction, a Marginal Analysis, and Explanatory Notes. By Rev. D. P. CHASE, D.D., Fellow of Oriel College, and Principal of St. Mary Hall, Oxford. Fourth Edition, revised. Crown 8vo. cloth, 4s. 6d.

The **ELEMENTS of ARISTOTLE'S LOGIC,** following the order of Trendelenburg, with Introduction, English translation, and Notes. By THOMAS CASE, M.A., Tutor of Corpus Christi College, and sometime Fellow of Brasenose College. [*Preparing.*

ARISTOTLE'S ORGANON : Translations from the Organon of Aristotle, comprising those Sections of Mr. Magrath's Selections required for Honour Moderations. By W. SMITH, B.A. New College, and ALAN G. SUMNER GIBSON, M.A., late Scholar of Corpus Christi College Oxford. Crown 8vo. 2s. 6d.

The **POETICS of ARISTOTLE.** The text after Vahlen, with an Introduction, a New Translation, Explanatory and Critical Notes, and an Appendix on the Greek Drama. [*In preparation.*

DEMOSTHENES on the CROWN. The Text after BAITER. With an Introduction, a New Translation, Notes and Indices. By FRANCIS P. SIMPSON, B.A., Balliol College, Craven Scholar, 1877. Demy 8vo. cloth, 10s. 6d.

FROM THE PREFACE.—Several of the Notes—which I have tried to make as concise as possible—may appear unnecessary to a scholar; but they have been inserted for the practical reason that the obstacles they should remove have been felt by some of the many pupils with whom I have read this speech.

The main difficulty which Demosthenes presents to the student lies in the close logical connection of his arguments; and most commentaries consist largely of translation or paraphase. Paraphase is dangerous, as it may lead a novice to a belief that he quite understands a piece of Latin or Greek, when he is some way from doing so. I have, therefore, taken the bull by the horns, and have given a continuous rendering, as close as I could decently make it. Its aim is purely commentatorial—to save its weight in notes. It is intended to show what Demosthenes said, but not how well he said it. And, I may say, I believe that every lecturer and tutor in Oxford will admit that an undergraduate, or sixth-form boy, cannot get full value out of reading the De Corona without such help.

In Introduction I. will be found a sketch of Athenian history, as far as is necessary for the thorough understanding of this Oration. In Introduction II. a precis of the oration of Aeschines, as well as that of Demosthenes, is prefixed to a brief analysis of the two speeches considered as an attack and a defence.

CLASSICS AND TRANSLATIONS—*continued.*

The **PHILIPPIC ORATIONS of CICERO.** A New Translation.
By the Rev. JOHN RICHARD KING, M.A., Fellow and Tutor of Oriel
College, Oxford. Crown 8vo. cloth, 4*s.* 6*d.*

'The translation is forcible and fluent, and, so far as we have compared it with the
original, accurate.'—ATHENÆUM, *Dec.* 7, 1878.

'The translation is evidently the work of a competent scholar......who is beyond all
question master of the text.'—SPECTATOR, *July* 12, 1879.

The **FIRST** and **SECOND PHILIPPIC ORATIONS of
CICERO.** A New Translation. By the Rev. J. R. KING, M.A.
Fourth Edition. Crown 8vo. 1*s.* 6*d.*

The **FIRST FOUR PHILIPPIC ORATIONS of CICERO.**
A New Translation. By the Rev. J. R. KING, M.A. Crown 8vo.
2*s.* 6*d.*

The **SPEECH of CICERO for CLUENTIUS.** Translated into
English, with an Introduction and Notes. By W. PETERSON, M.A.,
late Scholar of Corpus Christi College, Oxford ; Principal and
Professor of Classics, University College, Dundee ; late Assistant to
the Professor of Humanity in the University of Edinburgh.
Crown 8vo. cloth, 3*s.* 6*d.*

'We have gone over the translation with some care, and we have found it of uniform
excellence. If any young scholar ever takes Niebuhr's advice about translating the
speech, he could not do better than compare his own with this version before he began
to retranslate it. The translation is not only accurate, but it abounds in neat and
scholarly renderings of awkward Latin idioms.'—GLASGOW HERALD, *September* 1, 1882.

'This is a sound and scholarly piece of work......The version is faithful without
being unduly literal......both the Introduction and the Translation will prove trustworthy guides to the young student......For the more advanced scholar the chief
interest of the book lies in the valuable notes with which Prof. Nettleship has enriched
it. These deal both with the diction and with the text, and are as suggestive as might
be expected from the reputation of the Oxford Professor of Latin.'
The ACADEMY, *Jan.* 27, 1883.

The **LETTERS of CICERO after the DEATH of CÆSAR :**
being Part V. of Mr. Watson's Selection. A New Translation by
S. H. JEYES, M.A., Lecturer in Classics at University College,
Oxford. Crown 8vo. cloth, 2*s.* 6*d.* [*Just published.*]

'There is much to praise in the translation ; nearly every letter contains some
striking and suggestive expressions which will be useful to students......Mr. Jeyes
often shows great skill in the management of words.'—OXFORD MAGAZINE, *June* 6, 1883.

'The work is intended for the use of candidates for Classical Honours in Moderations,
and supposing them to need a translation at all, they could scarcely have a better one.
Besides help in reading their Cicero, students may gain an insight into differences
between English and Latin idioms, which will be most useful to them in writing Latin
Prose . . . happy turns of this kind are to be met with in every letter. . . . We might
read page after page without discovering that the work was a translation, yet a comparison of these very pages with the original would probably fail to reveal the least
inaccuracy.'—JOURNAL OF EDUCATION, *Oct.* 1, 1883.

The **AGAMEMNON of ÆSCHYLUS.** A new Prose Translation.
Crown 8vo. cloth limp, 2*s.*

Printed in the USA
CPSIA information can be obtained
at www.ICGtesting.com
LVHW021951211223
766918LV00003B/9

9 781015 687356